The
Paper Wasp

Lauren Acampora

riverrun

First published in the United States in 2019 by Grove Atlantic
First published in Great Britain in 2019 by riverrun
This paperback edition published in Great Britain in 2020 by

riverrun

An imprint of

Quercus Editions Limited
Carmelite House
50 Victoria Embankment
London EC4Y 0DZ

An Hachette UK company

A CIP catalogue record for this book is available
from the British Library

Paperback 978 1 52940 102 8
Ebook ISBN 978 1 52940 100 4

10 9 8 7 6 5 4 3 2 1

Printed and bound in Great Britain by Clays Ltd, Elcograf S.p.A.

Papers used by Quercus Editions Ltd are from well-managed forests and other responsible sources.

For Thomas

If the dream is a translation of waking life,
waking life is also a translation of the dream.

—*René Magritte*

In each of us there is another whom we do not know.
—*C. G. Jung*

The
Paper Wasp

I.

I wore red capris on the plane. After I'd resolved to go to you, I couldn't imagine wearing anything else. The red made me feel bold, like a matador. I hadn't been able to sleep the night before, and it was still dark when I'd risen from bed and stuffed my suitcase with summer clothing. Despite my fevered state, I'd had the presence of mind to fill my backpack with old photographs, graphite and ink, and the best of my drawings.

The airplane seat beside me was unoccupied, so I was able to spread the drawings out on my lap. All at once you were there with me, resplendent on the sofa in your starry dress, the fiery wave of hair over your shoulder. Your eyes were the green of a forgotten lake, your sweet mouth quirked and curved. My own form in the drawing was a blunt shape beside you. Next to the sofa was the table lamp with its base of intertwined brass snakes. The potted orchid with its protruding tongue. The print of cardinals on the wall, and the painting of tents in the desert. And the energy, the love, coiling invisibly between us. I felt it all again. That moment was forever captive, mine.

Electricity prickled my fingertips as I looked at the drawings, and I wanted to run in the airplane aisles. Instead, I folded the papers away and emptied a bullet of bourbon into my Coke. My heart accelerated, an engine primed for action. I'd been waiting for this feeling to come, this gorgeous surge, and was proud of myself for channeling it so constructively, for boarding this plane. When this ecstatic state arrived, when I flew inside my skin like this, it was worth all the dark days, every periodic ugly lurch.

I paged through the issue of *Dwell* that I'd bought at the airport. Looking at beautiful rooms always settled me. Deeply, I breathed the recycled air of the cabin. I'd flown before, as a child, but had been cushioned by dumb trust. Now I understood that the plane could drop through the sky. I knew that every new moment contained this possibility, though it seemed remote through my exalted haze. I felt the exhilaration of a deity, with power over the future and past, capable of creating new worlds at will.

Slowly, the view outside my window transformed from a flat midwestern checkerboard to an exotic topography of pink and red mountains. This, then, was the West. The vast emptiness was startling. There were no roads. Nothing circumscribed the strata of rock. Only primeval scrub grass. Probably snakes and coyotes. Rodents in their burrows. All at once, the mountains genuflected and flattened. One last shallow range, then humankind. Roads spidered into the valley. Arteries of freeways and branching capillaries led to the cell of each house and its adjacent pool of blue. And finally—like a drop from the edge of the earth—the ocean. I'd never seen it before. I'd never been this far from my own house, from my bedroom and my box of magazine clippings. As the altitude of the aircraft decreased, I felt the thrilling intimation that I'd never enter that house again.

It had been just five weeks since I learned about the reunion. My mother had come home one evening more addled than usual. Her jacket, the same drab brown parka she'd been wearing for a decade, had missed the coat hook and dropped to the floor. She looked to me at the stove where I was frying chicken and making green bean casserole. I was the one who cooked, even though my father was home all day. After the layoffs, the men in town had become suddenly idle—machinists, inspectors, production engineers reduced to building deer stands, drinking Schlitz—and years later they were still idle.

"How was your day?" I ventured, whisking milk and eggs in a bowl.

"The usual." A long pause. There was something skittish about her eyes. "I saw Leslie Lomax in the office. She came in for a mammo."

"Oh."

"Do you remember Liz Lomax, in your class?"

"Sure."

"Well, Leslie told me that Liz is going to your ten-year high school reunion. It's on Wednesday. Did you know that? The night before Thanksgiving."

I looked at the pot on the stove in front of me. "Is that right."

"Leslie asked if you're planning to go. It sounds like a lot of people from your class are going." She paused. "Maybe Elise Van Dijk will be there."

My heart released a roll of blood.

"I hope you'll consider it, Abby," she said. "It would be good for you to get out."

I kept whisking. Finally my pigeon instinct took over, and I nodded my head. "Thanks for letting me know."

I'd planned to rewatch *Land of the Beings* after dinner, as I'd been doing all week, but instead I opened the memorabilia cabinet and took out our senior yearbook. I went straight to your page. The electric shock came before my brain even registered your face. All the years peeled back. There was nothing embarrassing or dated about your appearance: plain white scoop neck, undulating hair. You were glamorous, timeless. Beneath your photograph was a Bob Dylan lyric: "You don't need a weatherman to know which way the wind blows." I'd been disdainful of this choice at the time. Now, I was struck by its precocity, and by the girl whose worldly-wise look suggested she knew exactly which way the wind was blowing for her, and had paused for just a moment to say good-bye.

4

Inside the back cover was your inscription, painfully for-mal: *Abby, I'm sorry we're not close anymore, but I hope we will be again someday. My love always, Elise.*

I'd been having the loveseat dream more frequently. It had been coming, in some form or other, every week. In the dream, I tried to call you, but my fingers were too shaky to dial the digits of your phone number in the correct sequence. I tried several times before getting it right, before you finally answered, and I said, "I'm here, I'm coming." I rushed through narrow alleys of a foreign city, looping in circles of frustra-tion before finally finding the building—a stone structure covered with ivy, like an English manor house—and climb-ing the carpeted stairs to the room where you waited. Then, at last, the door swung open. In the dream, we sat together on a loveseat holding hands. You wore a gown of jet beads. I wore a black-and-violet sheath split by a white stripe. We talked and laughed and basked in each other. The desperation fell away; the regret of our lost years fell away. The objects around us were glazed with phosphorescence. I awoke at the apex of love.

This dream was so detailed and intentional that, each time it happened, I was certain it was really you, Elise. I believed that you sometimes came to me this way. I had no way of proving it, but I was convinced that the two of us were shar-ing this dream. I was never able to recall the actual words we exchanged, but I awoke with the imagery in my mind: the sinuous base of the table lamp beside us, the potted orchid, the print of cardinals on the wall, the framed watercolor of tents in a desert.

I sat at my vanity table and tore a long sheet from the roll of drawing paper. I closed my eyes for a moment, then opened them, and with the pencil I began to outline the scene. Your body and mine on the burgundy cushions, your river of red hair, the lamp and its lamplight.

My breathing deepened, my heart rate slowed, and I fell into a narcotic lull. It was as if the pencil were controlled by an external force, as if the scene were preordained. It meant that you were coming back for me, as I'd always known you would. We would be reunited. All these years at home in Michigan—dreaming, drawing, watching Perren films, working the register at Meijer, treading water—had been leading to this. I'd long nurtured the private suspicion that I was an outcast not because I was inferior, but because I was exceptional; that the fulfillment of my purpose awaited activation from the universe; that I just needed to wait. And now, as simple as a music box clicking open, it was time.

I never told you—not even later, in our most intimate moments—that I'd been seeking you out in the magazines for years, ever since high school. All that time, I'd hungered for proof of your existence in the world, some mention of you, some small notation in a movie review, or a thumbnail photograph. Just knowing that you were alive, that you were thriving, helped rinse the demons from my mind. I clipped the photographs and articles meticulously and stored them in a pink fabric box beneath my bed. That box was my most precious possession, the first thing I'd save in a fire.

After my register shift was over that Friday, I approached the magazine rack at the checkout aisle. The usual mass formed in my throat. This moment just before I allowed myself to look at the magazines was always excruciating. And then, all at once. The clot broke open in my throat, and I could breathe again. There you were, vamping in a backless red dress, hand on hip, hair gelled into pin curls. Sportive smile aimed over your shoulder, directly at me.

Lifting the issue of *People* from the rack, I had the urge to gather all the copies for myself. I detested the idea of their being taken by others, whose interest in you was superficial at best, spiteful at worst. I stared at you, and our eyes locked. I remembered the slumber parties—how we'd squeeze into the same sleeping bag when the other girls were asleep, so close that your hair cascaded over both our faces. Now, I stood in the checkout line with the magazine, like a regular customer, like a stranger. I wanted to tell the woman behind me, with her bald eagle T-shirt and cartful of pet food, that I knew this person in *People*.

I know her. I knew her.

Instead, I gripped the magazine and showed it to the checkout clerk, a skinny teenager with a sniffle. Rather than letting his hands soil it, I swept it over the scanner myself.

Afterward, I drove around to the back of the Meijer superstore lot where there was a Goodwill shop. The windows displayed white-stumped mannequins in formal dresses with lamps and books at their feet. I stood at the entrance for a moment, gathering the nerve to go in, then laid my mittened hand on the door handle.

Inside, the clothing racks were acutely unglamorous, full of big peasant blouses and elasticized pants. I cautiously fingered the first rack, then turned and accidentally met the gaze of the store clerk. Her cat-eye glasses were intimidating, incongruous with the merchandise. After a moment, I cleared my throat and blurted, "I need something to wear to my high school reunion."

The clerk looked coolly at me, passing her eyes up and down my body. I was sure she could read the whole story there: I was a fool to think about the reunion, a fool to consider exposing myself. True, it would be a mad aberration for me. For years, I'd been assiduous in my withdrawal. I commuted thirty minutes to work just to avoid seeing acquaintances. I'd chosen not to know about my classmates and to remain unknown by them. Let them scrabble with their social media; I didn't have or want a computer or smartphone. The crush of information was overwhelming. I did best when my orbit was small, just my drawing paper and pencils, movies and magazines. Everyone could imagine what they wanted. *Our valedictorian, what about her?* Why reduce all the brilliant possibilities, now, to one hard, unbrilliant fact? Abby Graven, plain and stout, roundly unaccomplished, emotionally imbal-anced, right there on a plate.

Then, from deep within a hidden rack, I pulled out a dress: half-black, half-violet with a white stripe down the middle. My breath caught. It was the dress from my dream, the same white bolt of lightning. The dress was magic—the purple audacious, the black forbidding, the stripe running from collar to hem. It cost four dollars and ninety-nine cents. As I carried it out of the store, I felt the deep clunk of a gear falling into place. I'd had prescient dreams before, but never as explicit as this. No one could tell me this was a coincidence. No doctor could convince me it was a symptom of delu-sion, attached to a mood cycle. Over the years, I'd come to realize that I was unlike anyone else. I knew that my visions were attached to something much larger, a giant scaffolding meant only for me, sections of which I could just glimpse, bit by bit, as I climbed.

Back home, I squirreled the dress in the rear of my closet and pulled the yearbook out again. There I was: fat-cheeked and stunned in a black turtleneck, my eyes latched to a focal point somewhere over the photographer's head. My hair hung limp, black as a carrion crow. Beneath ran the words of Emily Brontë:

I have dreamt in my life, dreams that have stayed with me ever after, and changed my ideas; they have gone through and through me, like wine through water, and altered the color of my mind. I cannot express it;

but surely you and everybody have a notion that there is or should be an existence of yours beyond you. What were the use of my creation, if I were entirely contained here?

I can still clean up when I need to. I'm not unattractive. There might even be something enticing about me if you look the right way, if you're the right kind of person. My eyes are wide and yellow-hazel like a cat's. My dark hair—jet when I dye it—is striking against my pale skin, and my patch of acne scars can be camouflaged with concealer. I've always been short and heavy, but the extra cushioning gives me curves. And so, looking at myself in the mirror on the day of the reunion, in the glass still gummy from old stickers, I wasn't displeased. I put my shoulders back and posed a little. The dress was stiffer than I remembered, a little more severe, but maybe that was all right. It would be armor.

When the nerves came to my stomach, I exhaled all the way, emptied my lungs. There was nothing to fear, I told myself. You'd be there tonight. I knew you would. You'd be waiting for me, as in the dream. I calmly went for my lipstick. If there was a time for red, this was it.

Downstairs, my mother was standing at the sink, rinsing dishes beneath the faucet.

"I'm going to the reunion," I announced.

"You're going! That's great, Abby. I'm so glad."

As I went past her to the door, her smile cracked and for a clear instant I saw that she was imprisoned in this house, deteriorating with each passing year, commuting to work in the dirt-brown parka, breathing exhaust fumes on the highway.

"Please be careful," she called after me. "And promise you'll let us know if you'll be home later than midnight. Do you have your phone?"

"Yes, of course," I said, pushing the irritation from my voice. "I'll see you later."

"Promise you'll call."

"Okay."

As she watched me go, she seemed to be begging for something beyond an assurance that I'd call, that I'd come home. I reached down to pull out the thing she needed, but not far enough. I went out the door and locked it behind me.

Usually when I drove through town, I wore sunglasses and a brimmed hat like a celebrity, though I was the antithesis of famous in my parents' dented Impala. I played soothing music—Fleetwood Mac; Cat Stevens; Crosby, Stills and Nash—suggestive of an easier era, corded phones, and handwritten letters. Still, the other cars sometimes turned vicious. When I was in a vulnerable state, in one of my dark times, even tree branches seemed to bend toward me, fanged and taloned. At those times, I distrusted my own foot on the accelerator, the neurons of my own brain prone to mutiny. I fixated on the other drivers on the road—all of us sentenced to some detailed death, driving to our graves. It would be natural to jerk the steering wheel over an embankment. As I drove, I could see it happening. I could watch a weird holo-gram of my car veering off the road and out of sight.

Tonight, mercifully, there was no hologram. I'd be in the presence of my classmates soon, so I was free to prowl down Main Street undisguised. So many storefronts were empty, brown paper hanging behind the windows. On the side streets, most houses had crossed the line from homey to unkempt. After the auto plants shuttered, the media had reported that capable young people were draining out of the state, but I knew that most of my classmates had remained right here, raising dispirited families in these weatherworn houses.

I passed Everts Elementary and the concrete bench where you and I often sat. Opening the car windows, I breathed the cold, abrasive air. There were margins of black snow at the curbs, left from the first storm of the season. I steered west, away from town and toward the dunes, in the direction of your house.

How I'd loved your house, Elise. Compared with so many hovels in town, it was a palace. I'd loved to wander your living room—what I imagined might have been called a parlor in some other era—with its beige carpet, heavy glass table, and chairs with buttoned cushions. I'd loved the ingenuity with which, by adding an upper floor and black shutters, your parents had made their basic ranch resemble a New England colonial. To me, the way the deck reached out toward Lake Michigan symbolized some intrinsic human striving. It was a launching pad. Standing on the deck overlooking the water and the lighthouse, the stirrings of the future already in me, I felt that I could be lifted by the wind and carried anywhere in the world.

We played for hours. You wore your nightgown with ruffles at the hem and sleeves, a print of hearts erupting from clouds. I remember you in this nightgown, sitting on the toilet lid in the bathroom, plastic scepter in hand, as I knelt on the bath mat in front of you, giving directions. The rubber frogs, ducks, and crabs made a circle around us. "Round and round the garden," you said at my prompting, and the animals came to life.

At night, the beam from the lighthouse would enter your bedroom, lay a stripe across your sleeping face, then lift away—and, from the trundle beside your sleigh bed, I'd count the beats until its return. It was utter safety, being in your room under a white eyelet comforter. I'd stay as long as I could after breakfast the next morning, until your mother would gently suggest that my parents would want me home soon.

The other girls blistered with jealousy. You were beautiful and I was not. I was neither witty nor mean. Still, I was the one you invited to sleep over every Saturday night. Our friendship was real and deep, our games transcendent. I knew that, as unlikely as it seemed, I brightened your life the way you brightened mine. Like the Brontë sisters, we'd created our own womb of imagination. Even then, I knew not everyone had that privilege. We were fortunate to dwell in dreams as long as we did. It's easier to linger with a partner.

I didn't let you see me when I was sad. But when I felt good, when my bright surges came, I showed off for you. I drew extravagant murals based on my stories. You held my hand and said, "You're going to be a great artist someday, Abby." I didn't argue. I let you believe the world awaited me with the same hunger it awaited you. But the truth was that, as you were born to be seen, I was born to crouch in the shadows. I was the hidden source, quietly generating the scenes you played out. I knew this, even if I didn't yet recognize mine as the superior gift.

One night at your house, toward the end of middle school, we fell upon an Auguste Perren film. It was *Eureka Valley*, one of his earliest experiments, a Swiss man's vision of California: desert basins, old mines, drugs. We were too young for it, and the story had no logical arc we could find, yet we couldn't stop watching. There were fantasias of inflatables, imaginary beings with human faces, rituals in darkened ghost towns. One unbroken shot lasted five minutes, through the lens of an acid high. Warped faces, halogen haloes, winged beasts emerging from ears. Watching it with you was like sharing an outlandish dream, being plunged into a mutual subconscious. The images cracked open a kind of elation in me. At the end of the film, we looked at each other, and I knew that you felt it, too.

I remembered that night now as I drove slowly past your house, then around the cul-de-sac where we'd ridden bicycles, and past the house again. There were lights on in the bedrooms, but no silhouettes. Still, I sensed you were there. My sense was intuitive, but also stood up to logic. Even movie stars must come home, sometimes, to visit their parents. Even movie stars must succumb to curiosity about their old classmates. And really, if anyone should attend a high school reunion, it was a movie star.

It was dark and beginning to snow by the time I reached the community center and parked toward the back of the lot. I didn't get out of the car right away. The building glowed. I could see the shapes of people inside already, each a living vessel of memory, holding a piece of my own history, whether I liked it or not. Blow this building up, and there'd be almost nothing left of me.

I crawled out of the driver's seat, and a few snowflakes stung my face. I stood for a moment in that unlit corner of the parking lot and was suddenly afraid you'd really be there. I was afraid that if I walked inside that building, I'd see you and disintegrate into a cone of powder on the floor. Slowly, I reapplied my lipstick in the sideview mirror. The effect was encouraging. The red mouth was a message of confidence, competence. I asked my feet to carry me across the parking lot. This was autonomy, I thought, for better or worse. I'd put it on like a coat.

Indoors, the community center resembled a nursing home. Pine-green carpeting, polyester curtains, flowered wallpaper. At the check-in table, I wrote my name on a sticker and put it on my dress, over my heart. The reception room was furnished with mismatched groupings of sofas and armchairs, side tables and lamps, arranged as if to facilitate multiple intimate conversations. A random assortment of framed prints and watercolors hung on the walls, clashing with the wallpaper. A round hors d'oeuvre table dominated the middle of the room, ringed by small clusters of people. No one was sitting on the sofas.

"Abby!" someone shouted, breaking away from one of the clusters.

A woman trotted toward me in a red taffeta dress with spaghetti straps, something we might have worn to a home-coming dance. I frantically cycled through my index of tall blonds with overbites, but found no matches. The woman was now directly in front of me, stooping in for an awkward hug. As she pulled back, I sought a name tag, but the red bustier was anonymous.

"Wow, how are you?" I attempted.

The woman smiled in delight. "You don't recognize me, do you?"

"Of course I do. Meg?"

The woman laughed and gave my shoulder a little shove. "No! Becky Bordo!"

This, of course, was impossible. Becky Bordo was fat and had been getting fatter since kindergarten. By high school, she'd fallen off the social wagon completely.

Becky did a little stomp dance. "I am getting the biggest kick out of this. Nobody recognizes me!"

"Well, you do look different. I mean, you look great."

"I lost *a hundred and ten pounds*."

"Amazing."

Becky stood there smiling, waiting for me to ask how she'd done it. But there were more people coming in, and the room was enlivening with squeals and laughter. My instinct was to bolt for the door.

"Wow, this is going to be such a fun night," I muttered.

Becky took my hand and led me to a group of women standing nearby. As the faces came into focus, I found that I was among girls who'd never spoken to me in school. Now, they smiled in unison. Most were still generically attractive, dulled versions of their prettier teenage selves. Cupped by this crescent of women, I felt that my dress was misshapen on my body, and I didn't know what to do with my arms.

"Wow, it's so good to see all of you," I piped.

The girls—the women—seemed to be looking at me through a gauze of pity. They blinked slowly, their smiling teeth like vise clamps. The pity was in my imagination, I told myself. It had to be. There was no way they could know about my trouble in Ann Arbor, the long years in my childhood bedroom. And yet, at that moment, I felt they could see it all on me like a rash.

I excused myself and slithered away, past men in T-shirts with hunting-club logos. I edged by without making eye contact, as if they were loiterers at a bus station. I retreated to a window and faced away from the room. As I looked out to the dark parking lot, the wave of fear approached. The tightness in my chest began. To counteract it, I focused on breathing slowly and did a quick Perrenian exercise. I attempted to turn off my labeling brain and blur my vision. I tried to witness shapes and colors simply as they presented themselves, to heed the sounds that met my ears without identifying their source. This practice was grounding for me, better than any mindfulness strategy I'd found. "Unity Gain" was the term Perren used for the state of equilibrium between the conscious and the unconscious mind—a term borrowed from audio engineering, the balance of voltage entering and exiting a device. Over the years, I'd learned to achieve this at will, the equalizing of input and output. When I attained Unity Gain, my anxiety diminished. I could retreat temporarily through an inlet to the unconscious, and invert my surroundings into benign mindscapes. Most of the time I held a light mastery over these visions. But occasionally I lost control, and the visions skidded into nightmare. Now, through the community center window, the cars in the parking lot were becoming marshaled troops. The rhythmic jabber of conversation behind me was punctuated by a woman's delighted scream, which shot through my body. Despite myself, I envisioned a montage of atrocity taking place at that moment, outside these walls. A burning village in Africa, a migrant boat capsizing, a car crash on US 31. I heard the careen, screech, and shatter of glass. I saw babies in the water, children running from the flames.

I gasped and snapped back into the room. The tightness in my chest had become a knot, solid as a ball bearing. I pushed toward the bar, a wellspring of self-serve liquor and mixers on a card table. I filled a cup with bourbon and concealed it with a splash of Coke. I wanted nothing but my bedroom, my little chair and strawberry lamp, but leaving this place seemed as impossible as staying.

Turning around, I almost walked into a woman who beamed at me from beneath a blond mushroom cloud. "Holy Hannah," she said and enveloped my body.

"Christy?" I said when she released me. I stared, under the guise of delight. Her facial features had spread out as upon an inflated balloon, and her pillowy body was draped with something like an ivory tablecloth. The nose ring was gone, and a gold cross rested in her cleavage.

"Abby, you look great. Exactly the same!"

"So do you," I inhaled.

"I can't believe it's been ten years. What have you been doing? I can't find you online at all."

"Oh, well. I'm, uh, back at U of M," I blurted. "Grad school, for film."

She shook her head. "Really? That's great. You were always so smart."

"What about you?" I asked quickly. "What are you up to these days?"

"I'm teaching kindergarten. We have a little girl and are expecting our second." She put a hand to her abdomen and smiled. "Are you having fun tonight? Who else have you talked to?"

"No one, really. Just Becky Bordo in a thin-person disguise."

"Oh, Abby." She shook my shoulder.

Together we circulated. The tightness in my chest was still there, but it was a useful distraction to watch Christy, to see how she'd sloughed her tortured girlhood like a tight sweater, revealing the plump kindergarten teacher within. I imagined her reading a storybook to her pupils, tenderly brushing her young daughter's hair, and felt a bite of envy. Watching her chatting with other women now, I was struck by her easy laugh and uncomplicated self-possession, and understood that Christy had never truly been a misfit.

I returned to the bar periodically to refill my bourbon and Coke. Slowly the knot in my chest loosened. Christy and I found other members of our old troupe: Ted Yoakim and Andrew Sweeter, sardonic theater boys. They were both office workers now, in accounting and insurance. Ted, at least, had moved to Lansing.

All at once, there was a change in the room, a dip in volume, a joint catching of breath. I turned and saw that a new group had formed and that people were heading across the room to join it, metal shavings to a magnet. Becky Bordo—somehow omnipresent in her new thinness—appeared at my side and breathed into my ear, "It's Elise Van Dijk."

Like a dog at the sound of its dinner dish being filled, I experienced a momentary response of joyful anticipation. But the next moment it was undercut by panic. As I stood there holding my plastic drink cup, it was eighth grade again, the juncture of our disunion. Our sleepovers had come to a halt while you were at a summer acting camp in Grand Rapids, auditioning for parts at the city theater. When you were cast in *Oliver!* a group of classmates went to the opening performance. You accepted our flower bouquets with an air of experience, your eyes alight against the dirt-streaked makeup. We waited, expecting you to leave the theater with us, to go to dinner at Bennigan's. After a moment, seeing us still there, you thanked us for coming and explained that you needed to get home to rest for the next day's performance.

Soon after, you began making trips to Chicago, then flew to Los Angeles with your mother. You missed the first week of ninth grade. You'd been cast in a car commercial, you breathlessly told me on the phone. When you finally appeared at school, in October, you wore a vintage lace dress, and your hair was cut in a pixie style. You were an alarming new creature, poised and long-legged, universally charitable. I hung back and observed how you mixed between classes, exchanging adult pleasantries as easily with the volleyball team as with a huddled group of Trekkies—a flowering lotus atop our pond of mediocrity.

You flew to California every few weeks. Then, with one well-placed role in a drama about drug trafficking, your destiny was sealed. You took the rest of the year off from school and studied with a tutor in L.A.

I remember watching that first film in the single-screen theater on Main Street, the same theater we'd come to as children, where we'd raised our little faces to that heroic expanse. Now, barely out of girlhood, you were magnified to god size, your freckles washed in a fusion of makeup and light. Your enormous eyes, hermetically green, stared past mine to a brilliant horizon.

For most of high school, you lived part-time in California. I rarely knew when you were there and when you were home. You finally returned for senior year, a phantom in bright tights and ankle boots. Although you were physically present, it was clear that you wouldn't be rejoining our world. It was evident to me that our friendship had ended, naturally, through no fault of our own. For your sake, it was important that I reveal no regret. To be seen as unhappy would be an unfair burden to you. And so I didn't turn to stare like the others when you passed in the hall between classes. Stealthily, I marked your movements in my peripheral vision. When I glimpsed you walking in my direction with your diplomatic new smile, I slipped around a corner into an empty classroom.

At the reunion, I didn't turn to stare either. Ted and Andrew were talking in raspy whispers, but I'd stopped paying attention. The most important thing was not to turn around, not to let you see me seeing you. It was crucial that I kept a dignified distance, maintained visible poise, while the other classmates unabashedly swarmed.

"I can't believe she actually came," Andrew stage-whispered. "I wonder if the paparazzi are outside."

"Oh, no," Ted said. "They wouldn't follow her here. I mean, she's not *that* big. Yet. I don't think."

Christy joined our group, aflush. "I just talked to Elise."

My face convulsed involuntarily. With an effort, I returned it to a neutral expression, took another drink from my cup.

"What did she say?" Andrew demanded.

"She was really nice, totally down-to-earth. She gave me a hug and everything and asked what I've been doing since graduation. Just like anyone else."

"Her hair looks really red, don't you think?" Andrew asked.

"It was always red," Christy said.

"You don't think she does anything to it?"

"Abby," Ted said suddenly, turning to me. "You used to be friends with her, didn't you?"

My voice, when it came out, was a frog croak. "If you're asking whether she dyes her hair, I highly doubt it."

Through my interior turmoil, I was thankful for Ted, Christy, and Andrew—this core of old comrades, my only friends. After your defection, I'd become socially unstable.

For a while, I was still accepted in the comfortable pocket of the advanced-track crowd, the brushed and tended girls with corduroy skirts and big backpacks. But then, one dark winter when there was nothing to do, I watched all of Perren's films. After each film ended and I was delivered back to the wood-paneled family room, the faded paisley couch, the overhead fan at a standstill above my head, it was as if the film were still rolling. Everything around me vibrated with umbrous power. Outside the window, the moonlit trees were paralyzed against the sky. I was reminded of the wild potential beauty in everything. I felt that you were with me, Elise, that I could turn to you as I had after watching *Eureka Valley* and see the wonder in your eyes mirroring mine.

When I mentioned Perren to my schoolmates, one of them wrinkled her nose and said, "Isn't he the one who made a movie about defecating?" I tried to illuminate them, but it didn't seem to matter that Perren's work was considered the pinnacle of artistry, celebrated at Cannes and in college textbooks. The more I argued, the more incensed I became and the more they pushed back. They were ignorant and provincial, and I told them so. Only you understood, Elise. I know now that it was foolish to expect more from anyone else. From then on, the other girls avoided me like a contagion.

Thus infected, I descended toward the last remaining social refuge, the mash-up of oddballs who ate lunch in the school courtyard no matter the weather—girls with pink hair and piercings, boys in army fatigues. Christy, Ted, and Andrew. As I joined them, I told myself they were expatriates rather than outcasts, self-exiled. They were judgmental of our peers, those timorous puppets being groomed by Middle America. They were impatient to throw off their pinched surroundings for a larger world that could contain them. They were members of Amnesty International and PETA. Or, prematurely nihilistic, they were members of nothing. .

I sat outside with them, bundled in my parka. I began to wear black and dyed my dark hair darker. I wore lurid eye makeup. I knew my eyes were my best feature, that they made me look adroit even when my head was muddled. And the black clothing was good, slimming. I already had oversize breasts, and I layered chain necklaces upon them. I pierced the upper cartilage of my ears and shaved the hair around them. My father grimaced. "Disgusting," he mumbled, but didn't push further. He was exhausted from my sister, who was already rolling home after midnight in ripped tights.

But now, at the reunion, the outsiders were indistinguishable from the anodyne crowd. I followed Christy, Ted, and Andrew to the other side of the room. The party was loosening up. People had taken the bottles from the self-serve bar and were passing them around. Some were sitting on the sofas now, in cozy little groups. The glow of lamplight turned each scene into an uncanny tableau, the faces of classmates softly tweaked by ten years' work. Former members of the theater group intermixed with soccer players, and I saw pairings of peers that didn't occur in nature: Nicole Oberink and Lydia Groen, Brendan Haverstraw and Greer Nolan.

There was no sign of you, Elise, no buzzing hive. I pulled away from the others and circled the reception room. Perhaps you'd slipped away somehow. Perhaps you were already on your way to the airport, boarding a flight back to California. The blood drained from my head as I searched the room with rising agitation. Finally, I refilled my drink cup with straight bourbon and dropped into an armchair upholstered in a blurry toile. Anchored there, I passively absorbed the lap and sway of the party around me. People washed past, and I caught a feverish tone in the voices of two women.

"Definitely a boob job," flat-chested Amy Cunniff was saying.

"And her face?" breathed her companion.

"Probably. I mean, they all do it."

I knew they were talking about you. I finished my bourbon and stood, which was when I realized I was drunk, or close to it. I waded to the ladies' room where, in the amber light of the vanity bulbs, I stared at my own face in the mirror until it turned foreign, until the features warped and my skull showed through the skin. *The face, what a horror. A monstrous hood.*

When I went back out to the party, something had changed. How long had I been in the ladies' room? There was music now, or I was just noticing it—country rock, the kind of thing that blasted from high-schoolers' pickup trucks. Some people were vaguely dancing. I hated them all. Brad Bunton was pouring tequila shots and making a toast to the football team. Someone handed me a shot. I drank it and dropped the plastic cup to the floor.

For what felt like hours, I cruised aimlessly. The room seemed to flatten around me like a stage set. With a shove of the shoulder, I could knock its walls down. I circled around the paper-doll people, walked right into them. None of them counted. None of them were you. Then, all at once, the overhead lighting came on, and everyone stood blinking.

"Shit, seriously?" someone said. "How'd it get to be twelve already?"

I was standing in a corner surrounded by hundreds of rosebuds that were replicating like cancerous cells on the wallpaper. There was a delay in my processing as I watched my classmates push together in a herd. The cold wattage exposed tight dresses, pinched flesh, curdled mascara. Christy appeared. "Abby, are you okay? Don't worry, I can drive you home." She led me through the room, past the ransacked crudités table. "Did you check your coat?"

As we joined the crowd that streamed toward the door, I glimpsed a shimmer of dark diamonds. It took a moment to deduce that the shimmer was you, Elise, that you were in front of me right now, a three-dimensional, physical body. I yanked free of Christy's grip and pushed ahead, close enough to see the dress, black and crusted with beads. I heard the upsurge of your laughter, and a bilious tide rose in me. The reunion was over. The impossible had flashed and vanished in an instant. Why hadn't I raced toward you the minute you'd arrived and embraced you with the force of our lost years? How could I have squandered those minutes, those hours in the same building, wasted those breaths of the same air? Now, as I came close enough to touch your bare shoulder—to make you turn to see who it was—I stopped short. As in a dream, my feet were glued to the floor, and you pulled away with each step toward the exit, escaping again, a comet dipping through the solar system on its way to distant stars.

But in the next moment, miraculously, I heard your voice. Perhaps you'd felt my presence behind you, because all at once you'd turned toward me, a monarch in the parting water of admirers. The air in the room altered, became conductive. When our eyes caught, there was an instant of raw recognition. Your mouth curved in a brilliant smile. It might have been your usual smile, practiced for the cameras, but to me it was electrically intimate.

The others stepped back in deference, and you lurched through the gap and took me into your arms. The beads of your dress pressed against me, and my cheek brushed the dangling sapphire at your ear. I breathed a honeysuckle scent at your neck that triggered an intolerably sweet memory of childhood. The others closed up the circle around us and hovered, listening.

"Oh my God, Abby! I didn't think you were here! I'm so glad I found you!"

I held your arm and laughed, surprised at the music that rang out of me, a xylophone scale.

"Abby, my best friend!"

You leaned into me, and instantly the past decade hadn't happened. What did it matter now what forces had conspired to keep us apart? We were reunited.

"Come," you commanded and pulled me by the elbow. You led me against the exiting crowd, back into the reception room, and sat me down beside you on a burgundy loveseat. The loveseat was plush and overstuffed, and you sank sideways into its cushion to face me. The embellishments of your dress were on full display: all of its folds and crenellations, the elaborate hand-sewn beads. I sat at the mercy of my loosened senses, my vision slipping and narrowing.

"Abby, Abby, I've missed you so much." Your words slurred, and you shook your head, your face turning exquisitely sad. You'd had too much to drink, I realized. "I've never had another friend like you, in all these years," you said. "Oh, Abby. Do you remember when we used to go to Angelo's for pizza? Remember how we used to get root beer and pretend it was beer?" You laughed and leaned into the couch cushions. I laughed, too, and swam in your green eyes. "Do you remember playing 'shark' in my pool?" you asked, putting your hand on my arm.

"Of course I do," I sang.

Then your voice grew quieter. You stared at me, swaying slightly. "Do you remember the stories you used to make up for me to act out?"

Your eyes seemed to open another degree as you said this, a shadow passing through them, and I knew that you were remembering the stories at that moment.

"You told such strange, incredible stories," you said in a lower voice.

I was holding my breath. "Which ones do you remember?"

"All of them, all of them. I'm sure I remember all of them."

A flame danced inside me. You reached out again, and grabbed my hand.

"I haven't forgotten anything." You closed your eyes briefly. When you reopened them, a new gleam was there. You opened your little string purse and drew out a pack of American Spirits. I stared as you inhaled the lighter's flame, and a ribbon of smoke came from your mouth. With the hand that held the cigarette, you pushed hair from your face. "But, my God, it's been such a long time. Tell me. What are you doing now? I know you went to U of M."

"Yeah, yeah. I'm back there again," I said, the lie having bitten me earlier in the night. "Just some grad work in the film department."

"Oh, that's great! That's so, so great! Are you making films, Abby? I always thought that you'd make films."

"Some," I heard myself say. "But not many, yet. Just some experimental stuff."

You smiled fully now, looking straight at me. It wasn't a mistake. It was there—an unmistakable cord of energy running between us, strong and solid as a rope. I was certain you felt it, too.

"Oh, you'll be working on real films soon, I *know* you will. I always had faith in you."

Your hand was still on mine. You squeezed it. And then, as if a sheet had been lifted, the scene was revealed. We were in my dream, positioned on the loveseat. The table lamp was beside us, with its base of brass snakes. There was the orchid. I glanced up and saw on the wall above us the cardinals, the watercolor desert tents. Your figure was starred with beads, mine sheathed in violet and black, split by the white stripe like a dagger. I blinked, and when my eyelids lifted, you were still there, watching my face as if waiting for me to say it.

And so I told you about the dream. The swirling buttons on the phone, the alleys of the city, the stone manor and the ivy. When I reached the moment when you opened the door, our rapturous dream meeting, I saw what I thought was an affirmative glint in your eye. You knew. Your hand still squeezed my hand, and your eyes shifted between my eyes. I finished my description—the loveseat, the lamp, the cardinals—and gestured to the scene around us. You blinked and nodded your head. My heart beat violently.

"That's amazing, Abby. So amazing."

I waited for you to tell me that you'd had the same dream, that we had, in fact, dreamed it together. But the intensity in your gaze was gone, and your eyes lost focus. You released my hand and touched the side table, the brass lamp. You were drifting away.

Suddenly, you turned back to me. "Listen, Abby, if you're ever in L.A. you have to call me. We have to hang out."

I breathed in. "I'd like to go there someday."

"Here, give me your phone," you said. You laughed when I handed you my old flip phone, and I watched you type a pattern of numbers, a secret code, like the one in my dream. "You just have to promise to keep the number to yourself, okay? I've already had to change it twice."

We stood, and you touched my shoulder, balanced yourself. You stared at me, and with what seemed to be intense concentration, carefully articulated, "Abby, do you remember what I wrote in your yearbook?"

I tried to speak—*Yes, I remember. I still love you*—but the words couldn't penetrate the fleece in my brain.

"I really meant it," you slurred. "I hope we can be close again someday."

For a stretched moment we stood there, boxed in with the anarchic floral wallpaper. For that moment, it became the setting of a Perren film—springing from the director's imagination and mine together, with you cast in the lead role, fully costumed and sensuously available to my slow, loving scrutiny—before the film spun and sputtered. "Abby," I heard Christy call as she came into the room. "The building's closing." She pulled me away from you, into the careening carnival night.

The day after the reunion, my family sat for Thanksgiving dinner. I slumped in my chair as the tide of alcohol receded in my blood and a tiny metronome clicked in the pith of my brain. The wonderland of the previous night been abruptly demolished, and rather than ensconced with you on the love-seat, I was wedged between my parents at the old Formica table with grime beneath the metal lip. In lieu of a turkey, a rotisserie chicken squatted on a Corelle plate. My father mumbled a blessing. At the end, my mother spoke up, as if to an audience.

"And, Lord, thank you for watching over our daughter for us. We're thankful that Abby is safe."

"Amen," my father muttered and began to dismember the chicken. "You said you'd call if you'd be home after midnight. I'm sure you can understand your mother's concern, given the history."

"Abby," my mother said. "We'd like you to consider going back to Dr. Miller."

I coughed. "What about Shelby?"

"What about her?"

"Why aren't you worried about *her*? Why don't you thank God for keeping *her* safe?"

"Let's not ruin the dinner, please."

I looked at her. "Thank you, God, for keeping my sister alive and out of jail."

"Amen," my mother murmured.

The metronome in my skull grew louder, painful, striking a tender panel of tissue. I sat still in my chair. If I didn't move or speak, if I didn't feed it, it would die out. I stared at my chicken. My father's icy eyes watched me as he ate, but finally he excused himself from the table and put his dish in the sink for somebody else to wash.

Shelby had looked in on me the night she left home. It was something she used to do when I was small, opening the door a crack and smiling at me in my bed where I lay in the light from my strawberry lamp. "Good night, sugarplum," she used to say, and I'd always loved that her heart-shaped face was the last thing I saw before sleep. She stopped doing it at some point. Whatever affection she'd had toward me cooled as I'd morphed from child to adolescent. Eventually, I stopped caring. But that last night at home, she'd opened the door and peered in. "What are you doing?" I asked. She'd grinned and said, "Good night, sugarplum," and I knew what she was doing. Her voice still sounded in my ear sometimes, lilting and sarcastic, the sound of failure.

We'd never been close the way sisters are supposed to be close. With just eighteen months between us, we looked so much alike that strangers asked if we were twins, which annoyed us both. We were axiomatically incompatible. She'd come out hard and blustery with a love of the physical. I was a morose thing who agreeably lost at running races, stood stiffly in the jewelry she draped on me, didn't scream when she stole my things. When she raged, I shut down, retreated to my room, and closed the door. This just made her angrier—until she finally stopped bothering with me and found her dramas outside the house.

I never forgave my sister for her choices, but maybe they weren't her fault. She lacked discipline and imagination. She was destined to follow the code written in her genes—bad men, drugs, vagrancy. When she left our worn neighborhood with its chain-link fences and barking dogs, it was for a place called Hesperia just a couple of hours north. I couldn't imagine this new town was much better, though I'd never visited her and didn't plan to. There was a different story in my blood.

After Shelby's departure, there was a noxious silence in the house. As difficult as she'd been, at least my parents had understood her. They operated on the same histrionic level. They knew how to fight with her, and had cared enough to do it. The flames in the backyard had looked like a midsummer bonfire on the night Shelby tried to go out in hot pants and a sheer halter top. The neighbors wouldn't have noticed my father coming outside with armfuls of my sister's clothing, then going to the garage for a gas can.

In contrast, I was introverted, dully inscrutable. There was no need for bonfires. Whatever happened inside me stayed inside. My parents may have believed my opacity was something I'd created for myself, and that it shielded me somehow. They assumed I would be all right.

I had money, but not enough for a plane ticket. I'd been paying for my own groceries those past years, as well as for my art supplies and film collection. It would take weeks, months, to save enough. Logically, of course, I could have packed my things the day after the reunion and flown to you on my parents' credit card. But I wasn't in the right state of mind. I had to wait for the surge to come, to lift me off the ground. And so I exhausted the next stupid, agonizing weeks in my bedroom turret. As time passed, the thought of simply calling the number you'd given me—of actually speaking to you again—became an impossible abstraction. I began to doubt that I'd even seen you at all. Maybe our encounter had been a vivid, alcoholic dream.

It was possible. The walls around my dream life leaked. My night visions were three-dimensional, lavishly detailed scenes, feature-length films. I went through at least three cycles each night that I could remember, and sometimes four or five, one bleeding to the next like orchestral movements. Many of them recurred, again and again, with slight variations. They'd been the engine of my imagination since childhood, and consumed me still. I'd wake with the sharp sense of having experienced them, of having been yanked from a real place. For years, I'd been drawing these dreams from memory. I'd long ago run out of room in the art port-folios beneath my bed and had begun rolling the drawings into poster tubes in the closet.

Recently, I'd been having the satyr dream with more fre-quency. In it, you were a professional dancer in a midnight-blue leotard and gossamer skirt, pointe shoes, and a headdress with artificial horn bulbs. You took the stage for an outdoor performance in a wooded clearing. There was a rustic amphi-theater with log benches, filled with admirers. You danced with lightness and grace, and the audience stirred. They became more impassioned as the dance continued, standing and jos-tling to get closer, until finally they stormed the stage. They surrounded you and became satyrs—naked beneath goatskins, with hairy masks and horns, erect phalluses attached. I tried to run, to intercept them, but my legs wouldn't obey. I watched helplessly from afar as they engulfed you.

In the daytime, when I wasn't at Meijer, I was in my bed-room watching Perren films and rereading passages of his book *The Rhizome and the Spring*. I was intrigued by his references to the Rhizome, his academy in Los Angeles, tucked in the Santa Monica Mountains. It catered mostly to Hollywood types—actors, screenwriters, directors, costume designers—who aspired to enhance their creative abilities and deepen their craft. "We're all part of the universal Rhizome," the book said, "which is an infinite, horizontal root that dwells within the Spring, the greater waters of the unconscious, the source of communal imagination. We depend upon the creative nourishment of the Spring the way rhizomatic plants depend upon nutrients from the water. Whenever we sleep, or wakefully turn off our clamoring consciousness, we rejoin the Rhizome, renew contact with the Spring, and open ourselves to powerful images and messages." There were no photographs of the physical Rhizome campus, but I pictured a Gaudí-like building, florid and organic, embedded in a tropical mountain studded with palm trees.

Whenever I looked at the author's photograph on the back of the book, a bolt would shoot through me, just as it did when I saw a photograph of you. It was a formal portrait, lit in a dramatic way that highlighted the curtains of Perren's blue-white hair, shadowed the hollows of the cheeks, and turned the light eyes spectral. Those eyes seemed to stare straight into me. Although remote, I was Perren's best student. I'd all but memorized the chapter on active imagination; it was a playbook written especially for me. Now, I not only could project my nighttime dreams onto paper, but could do the same with my waking visions, dark or light. Thanks to Perren, I was no longer at the mercy of my mood swings, but could channel them productively. There were twenty-three poster tubes in my closet already, each containing at least a dozen rolled-up drawings—the makings of a hundred films. All I needed was someone to help transmogrify them, translate them to celluloid, aerate and distribute them. And Perren, I felt, was the only one who could do this. He would understand at once, if I ever met him. The minute he saw the pictures, he'd recognize our partnership.

In the meantime, it was difficult to wait. Dreams saturated my days. The waking world seemed thin and false in comparison, in danger of crumbling away. I drove over the ashen tundra to Meijer. I endured the assault of fluorescence, metallic music, plastic packaging shells. I stood blinking at the register in my navy polo shirt, sliding products over the scanner: marshmallows, condoms, Frisbees. The customers manifested one by one and disappeared as quickly as they came. There was always some face in front of me, blinking or glaring or gabbing. There was always the strident squeak of shopping cart wheels and the odor of the grocery section. The rest of the store swirled to infinity, a Charybdis of pillows and patio sets.

In the news: a massacre at a school in Pakistan. An airliner, vanished into the sea. I often practiced my Perrenian techniques at the register, but sometimes I wasn't able to hold off the tide of terror, and it broke over me. A crash of toppling cans in the grocery section might became the automatic fire of a weapon, smashed fruit and spilled milk mingling with blood on the floor. My heart would race and my ears would thunder. I'd have to stop what I was doing and grip the register shelf, to keep from running out the door. But after the reunion I stood at my register and simply replayed our communion on the loveseat. I closed my eyes from time to time and remembered the scent of your hair at my cheek, the benediction of your smile. Again, I heard your invitation to visit, clear as a church bell. It had happened. You had been here. You remembered.

When my shift ended, I bought all the magazines, in hope of finding you. Sitting in the little armchair in my bedroom, I opened *Vanity Fair* and hunted through the pages. I didn't really expect to see you—you'd never been in *Vanity Fair*—but all at once I felt the sharp report in my chest followed by the wave of warm bathwater. You were there: your viridian blouse iridescent as a leaf beetle, your hair like a sweeping foxtail. It took effort to look away from the twin crescents of light in your irises and read the article:

> *She eats her quinoa salad in small, deliberate forkfuls and brushes a lock of bright auburn hair—she's a natural redhead—away from her face as she speaks. At the mention of her upcoming film, Vespers, in which she plays opposite costar Rafael Solar, she puts down her fork and comes alive. "I play a satyr-type creature," she says with clear delight, "with, like, cloven hooves and little horn bulbs on my head." She wiggles a finger at each temple. "Beautiful and deformed."*

I put down the magazine and closed my eyes for a moment. I sat, watching the flittering spores behind my eyelids. The dancing satyrs. They all settled into place like pieces in a kaleidoscope: preordained. I took my pair of heavy sewing scissors that cut the finest line. The sound of paper separating from magazine was a whistle through a grass blade. I dropped to the floor like an animal, pulled the old pink box out from under the bed—the box where I'd once laid my dolls down to sleep—and set the new magazine pages atop the others. I took a last look at you. Your eyes stared up at me, my old friend, and I saw something pleading in them, imploring me. My dreams hadn't been wrong. They were never wrong; they were truer than life. As I held your gaze, I understood that our bond had never truly been broken. You needed me as much as ever.

On the last day of the year, the dream of the house on the hill came back to me. It was the rarest of my recurring dreams, and the one I'd been waiting for, the one that would spring open the gates. In the dream, I found myself in an alpine landscape near a lake so pristine it made me cry. *This*, I thought in the dream, *is the place I've been looking for, and I'll never leave.* As the dream unfurled, I recognized the place. I knew what would happen next. The appearance of the white house on the hill, a glimpse of the mad genius inside.

I awoke in a surge of euphoria. I shoved my blankets off and sprang from bed to my vanity table. I drew without pause, dismissed my mother when she came to check on me, and worked through the afternoon. I had no appetite or need beyond capturing this dreamscape—the details of the house, its baroque furniture, its icing-sugar trim. The tall windows overlooking the lake, the coruscating chandelier over my head. *This is the place.*

Outside my window, fresh snow blew from the ground in sparkling sheets. The light was nearly painful, the crackle of subzero temperatures. It was a new year, I remembered. 2015. The number seemed false, futuristic. Dazzlingly blank. I sat all day and drew. In front of me stretched a fully detailed panorama of the white house on the hill and its furnished interior, each of the rooms, and all the children contained in them. Every chair and sofa, every crystal in the chandelier. Outside my window, twilight painted the sky a blue so deep it edged beyond human perception. I was charged with energy and exaltation, as if I might meld with God, as if my body were a machine for divine creation. This was the feeling I'd been waiting for. Now, I could go to you. I could do and be everything I wanted. I could create masterpieces at will. I laughed to myself as I finished inking the front hall, the staircase and its banister, each of the delicately carved spindles, the volute like a nautilus shell.

I walked a circle around the room. Here was the rabbit wallpaper I'd chosen as a child. Here were the ruffled dolls from my dead grandmother, the ceramic animals from tea boxes, the snow globes with dolphins and dancers. Everything carefully positioned on little shelves, powdered with dust and dead skin. I circled the room, and it shrank with every rotation until I felt dizzy. Then I stopped and stood, listing sideways, the walls still turning around me, and I felt myself grow. I grew, with my feet planted on the mottled old carpet, until I could reach out and touch each wall with my fingers, sweep the shelves bare with one stroke, topple the dresser and cabinet and spill their contents to the floor. I could punch through the ceiling and through the roof. I could elbow out through the drywall and step into the yard and keep growing and growing.

I stood tottering on the carpet, and laughed at my room.

II.

THE LOS Angeles airport was bright and open, with feather-light people coasting over a pastel carpet. I became one of them, floating beneath the signs for ground transportation, trailing my little suitcase behind me. I had to use the restroom but didn't dare stop. Finally, near a clot of reuniting lovers and returning soldiers, among cabbies and chauffeurs, I pulled out my phone and found your number, where you'd typed it for me. As in a dream, I pressed the Call button and held the phone against my ear.

There was a click, and a recording told me to leave a message. I watched a little girl in a yellow dress run to her grandparents, and felt my heart skip. "Hi, Elise," I squeaked, still watching the girl. "It's Abby Graven. Guess what: I'm in L.A.! I can't wait to see you. I'm at the airport. Call me back."

I hung up and gripped the phone at my side, breathing rapidly. The little girl's family trundled toward the sliding doors and disappeared. I became aware of the taxi drivers surrounding me, the commingled smell of cologne and body odor. I fastened my gaze to the sign over the baggage carousel and waited. At last the phone vibrated in my hand, and your voice was in my ear, that long-lost music. I smiled out into the terminal, meeting the eyes of strangers who quickly looked away.

"Abby?" you said. "Uh, wow. I didn't know you were coming."

"Surprise," I breathed.

"It *is* a surprise," you said, and I heard other voices in the background. "How long are you here?"

"I don't know yet."

You were quiet for a minute. "Where are you staying?"

"I don't know," I said. "I'm at the airport now."

"You're at the airport," you repeated.

"Yes. I'm standing in the baggage area."

"You don't have a hotel?"

I laughed lightly. "No, no hotel yet. Just me and my bag. What should I do?"

There was a long, muffled pause. Maybe you'd put your hand over the phone. Maybe you were with someone and needed to excuse yourself. The pause was excruciating. I wanted your voice back.

Finally, I spoke into the void. "It's okay that I came, isn't it?"

Your voice returned then, with a thin metallic note. "Yeah, yeah, of course it's okay. Why don't you find a taxi and come here. Do you have a pen? Write down the address."

*   *   *

The taxi gave off the nauseating smell of hot leather and microfiber. There was no music on the radio, no news commentary. It drove in silence along avenues and wide freeways until at last it turned onto a narrow, winding road through scrubby hills. All evidence of urbanity had, at some undefined point, been rubbed away. This was a Los Angeles I hadn't expected: a barren, undulating terrain that appeared more suited to wildcats than movie stars. I had no precise notion of where you lived, but I'd assumed it would be near the water.

I cleared my throat and asked the driver, "What's this area called?"

"Malibu," he said with a musical lilt.

Perhaps he had an odd sense of humor. I didn't know much, but I knew this was not Malibu. Just then, the car began to slow, stopping in front of a wrought-iron gate.

"Here, okay? One hundred dollars."

I blinked at the driver, handed him my mother's credit card.

A moment later, the cab was gone and I was alone outside the gate, shielding my eyes in the white light. Through the glare I saw there was a call box, a button I needed to push. I looked at it for a long moment and felt myself come slowly awake. My frenzy had been so absorbing, it was almost as if my body had been hijacked. I distantly remembered scrawling the note to my parents at dawn that morning—*Going to see Elise in California, will be in touch*—and pulling the Impala out of the driveway, its engine sputtering in the cold. I remembered parking in the long-term airport garage, as if it had happened to someone else, and shivering in my red capris at the airline desk as I put the one-way flight on my mother's Mastercard. What had I done, coming here? Belatedly, I heard the perturbation in your voice on the phone. Was it possible you didn't want me? I stood trembling outside your gate. You were so close now. Tears gathered behind my eyelids, and I tried not to think as I pressed the button. I might have made an epic mistake, but you'd appear in front of me soon, and that was all that mattered.

I peered through the gate, waiting. Your house was surprisingly modest, snug to the ground. I'd pictured something grander. It was warm stucco, with a red-tiled roof, verdigris shutters, a rustic wooden door. The ground sank beneath my feet as I watched the door open inward. You appeared, moving through the sunlight in a loose dress and sandals, not smiling as widely as I would have liked.

"This really is a surprise," you said.

"I'm sorry I didn't give more notice."

You leveled a look at me, and my body buzzed with pleasure despite itself. Your face was so familiar, so much sweeter than in the magazines. I smiled, and your lips curled up. It was still a reflex for you to smile back at me.

"It's fine," you said. "Come in, I'll show you around."

I followed you over the cobblestone driveway edged with violet flowers. You were somehow smaller than I remembered, compact like a cat. And yet I could take in only one part at a time: your hair falling in its natural waves, a few strands tucked behind an ear; the exposed pink backs of your heels; the long ikat-patterned dress made of some rough cotton or hemp, clinging as you walked. This was a style I'd never anticipated, this California earth girl.

"I bought the house a few months ago," you said, shielding your eyes from the sun. "I really love it. It's not huge, but it has tons of character. I just had these cobblestones put in."

I left my suitcase and backpack on the front step, and we circled around the house to the pool and bluestone patio. It was straight out of *Dwell.* Beneath a pergola was an arrangement of upholstered furniture with throw pillows, as if an entire living room had moved outdoors. The back of the house was a wall of glass that looked over the canyon. In the distance, a dark strip of ocean. I'd never seen anything so magnificent. This was the sweeping scenery you saw each day. This was where you slept, and where you woke. Of course it was. The vista might have been a mural painted for you: nature in its ease and ravishment, equal to your own splendor.

I was hungry and still had to use the bathroom but couldn't bring myself to interrupt you. You'd become more animated, caught up in your tour like a child displaying her toys. I followed along a path that wound through a grove of gnarled lemon and orange trees until nothing else was visible. It was a shaded bower of our own. You took a ripe lemon from the ground and offered it to me. I put my nose to its waxy skin and, catching its covert scent, felt a swell of joy.

"I love the ocean," you were saying, "but I don't like so many people around. Everyone jockeys for their own little cove on the beach, but the houses are so packed together down there. I like it better up here. It's so secluded I can forget I'm even in L.A."

It occurred to me that this was how you'd speak to a journalist. The intimacy of our reunion on the loveseat was absent. But it would return, I knew. You just needed time to adjust to me. I clutched the lemon in my hand like a blood-pressure pump as I followed you into the house. In the foyer, my own ghostly face looked back at me from a pressed-tin Mexican mirror, and for a moment my black-ringed eyes were the eyes of a stranger. You ushered me around the rooms, which were sunny and cluttered. The floors were layered with faded Turkish rugs, upon which sat pieces of fashionably weathered furniture. There was a deconstructed divan and a hanging wicker pod chair. From the ceiling hung a light fixture of elk antlers. Art covered the walls, salon style, in mismatched frames. I couldn't take it all in at once.

"Where's your bathroom, if you don't mind?"

I closed myself into the downstairs powder room lined with wallpaper, a repeating motif of pagodas on a black background. It was the most dramatic bathroom I'd ever seen, and I tallied every painstaking choice: the porcelain faucet handles, the smoky mirror with chipped gold paint, the green-glass soap dish shaped like a sleeping cat. My face was mercifully fogged in the mirror, and I had a flashback to the ladies' room at the reunion, my drunken swirl and plunge, just before you rescued me.

When I emerged, you were waiting in the hallway. You smiled spontaneously, and I smiled in return. We looked at each other. This was the beginning. Right here. I knew it, and I felt that you did, too. It was the beginning of our new story together.

You led me up a staircase with painted Talavera tiles on each riser, the walls hung with photographs, drawings, paintings.

"I love how you decorated," I said to your back. "It must have taken a lot of work."

"Not really. I hired a designer. I chose most of the art myself, though."

We reached the top of the stairs and went into a room lined with books.

"Obviously I haven't read them all. In fact I haven't really read any of them. I chose them mostly for how the spines looked." You stood in the middle of the room and looked at me, your arms at your sides in the slack sundress, suddenly vulnerable, "You know I've never been a reader."

I looked back at you and smiled. "I know."

Above your head was a pink pendant lamp in the shape of an octopus, and as you saw my eyes go to it, you said, "It's from Anthropologie, but it's designed by a real artist in Philadelphia. And, here, look at this." You gestured toward a pedestal in the corner of the room, with a glass dome upon it. Inside the dome was a diorama: a miniature house overhanging a sinkhole. One of the house's exterior walls was blasted away, exposing the furnished rooms inside and the miniature people going about their business. There was a woman running a tiny vacuum cleaner, a man watching television—either unaware of the disaster, or indifferent. The house was a generic ranch style, with shutters and drainpipes, a small sedan in the driveway, a metal swing set. The property was brown, and the trees were bare.

"It's by an artist in New York," you told me in a quiet voice, as if the little people might hear. "It kind of reminds me of home."

"I didn't know you were into art," I ventured.

"I like to go to the galleries out here. They show artists from all over the world. I've kind of gotten addicted to collecting."

I stood for another moment, looking at the diorama. Ringing the bleak backyard was a wall, and I saw a child crouching at its base, looking out through a hole where a stone had fallen away. Beyond the wall and around the perimeter of the piece was a verdant grove, golden orbs clustered in the foliage as in a mythical garden.

"Oh, here's one I've actually looked at," you said, pulling an enormous book down from a shelf. "It kind of doesn't count, because it's mostly pictures and the writing's in German." You laughed. "But it's so cool, isn't it?"

The book was heavy, bound in red leather. The name on the spine was C. G. Jung.

"Did you read Jung in college?" you asked.

"No." I hesitated, unsure of how to explain academia's snobbish ranking of thinkers, and why Jung was near the bottom.

"Well, this was recommended to me by my guide at the Rhizome. It's this place where I go, kind of for professional therapy. My guide thinks it's important for me to know about Jung's work, to understand the idea of the collective unconscious."

My heart pitched. You were quietly turning the pages, each of which was illustrated with elaborate, colorful mandalas. There were snakes, trees, and eyes woven into the designs.

"You go to the Rhizome?"

You glanced at me. "Have you heard of it? I wasn't sure you would have." There was a questioning upturn in your voice.

My face went cold, then hot. "Of course. It's Perren's place."

You blinked. "Ah, you're still into Perren, then?"

I nodded mutely.

"Remember the time we saw *Eureka Valley* together?" you said, smiling. "It was life changing for me." You glanced up, at a point over my head. "Anyway, I started going to the Rhizome a couple of months ago, and it's been completely transformative. It's really taught me to think like an artist."

You put the huge Jung book back on the shelf and led me out of the room, through the hall, moving a rope of hair over your shoulder as you walked. I felt a disturbance in a hidden well inside me, a rumble from some dark geyser. You'd pronounced Perren's name too casually. You'd used the word "artist" in reference to yourself, and it hit my ear like a flat note. I watched your body move beneath the loose dress. There was your child's back, now stretched to its full length, the same back I'd once gently, rhythmically pummeled with my fists. I remembered the chant we'd learned at slumber parties when we were nine or ten: "People are dying, babies are crying. Concentrate. Concentrate." Now I looked at the place on the back of your head where I'd once rapped my knuckles, "Crack an egg on your head and feel the yolk drip down"; and the spine where I'd glided my fingers, "Stab a knife in your back, feel the blood drip down." I closed my eyes for a moment as I followed you down the hall.

You stopped and opened a door. Stepping aside, you gestured for me to enter first. The room was painted entirely black. After a moment of disorientation, my eyes adjusted to the darkness and I saw a collection of colored glass spheres hanging from the ceiling, at least a hundred of them, faceted like the compound eyes of insects and refracting brilliant light.

"Go in," you said.

I entered the room, navigating around the orbs, which hung at staggered heights. Some held a luminous glow, as if lit from within; others flashed gaudily. It was like being in outer space.

"This is incredible," I muttered, just as I brushed against an orb, which began to sway and twirl, sending convulsions of light onto the walls.

"I commissioned it from a Japanese artist," you said. "It was my first manifest dreamscape, from one of my first sessions. You know those round shapes you see when you close your eyes, that kind of float around behind your eyelids?"

I watched the rise and fall of your eyelids as you spoke, weighted by the heavy, lush lashes beloved by so many. You were like a child, standing before me now, awaiting my praise. To you, it was something novel, miraculous, your discovery of your own eyelids, the geometric dance that was identical to mine and everyone else's.

"Yes, I know exactly what you mean," I said.

"The Rhizome encourages bringing your dream visions to life in whatever way feels constructive. So I thought I'd try to physically bring my dreams into the waking world. I have my own house now, so why not?"

You looked at me and waited. I understood that you wanted my validation. You wanted me to effuse, to offer admiration and encouragement, as I'd done when we were children, to tell you that you were special, incomparable. My throat felt dry, and for a moment I couldn't speak. The sense of interior rupture persisted, the threat of the dark geyser.

Finally I managed to croak, "It's beautiful."

"Thanks," you said. "It felt a little indulgent at first, but I love it."

You showed me the master bedroom next. The decor was minimal compared with the rest of the house. The platform bed was high and wide, resting on a hairy sisal rug, and the walls were plain beige. This unfinished quality was the opposite of your frilled childhood room. Still, there was clutter: designer shopping bags huddled in a corner, shoes capsized on their sides, beaded jewelry tangled on the dresser top.

"My designer kept it spare on purpose," you explained. "My Rhizome guide says a simple bedroom is better for dreaming. Anyway, it's the bathroom I want you to see."

You opened the bathroom door onto a glowing cube of ultramarine. It took a moment to understand that I was looking at an immense aquarium tank. The tank arched up and over, composing the walls and the ceiling. Flat gray creatures slid through the blue water, passing overhead, tails trailing behind. Only the muted gurgle of a tank filter was audible.

"This is from a dream, too," you said. "I never used to think of stingrays as beautiful, but in the dream they were magical, and now I'm fascinated by them. They're so graceful and prehistoric. Doing this was a lot more expensive than I thought it would be, and the maintenance is insane, but it's my favorite place in the house now. I just lie in the tub sometimes and watch them."

The presence of a sink, bathtub, and toilet seemed sacrilegious here, and yet I would have liked to lie down in the tub myself and watch the water ballet, these captive creatures endlessly searching for a way out. Or perhaps they were unaware of their confinement, swimming from mindless instinct, back and forth, over and over again.

"It's gorgeous, Elise. Beyond belief."

"Thank you. I haven't shown it to many people. Obviously. I'm glad you don't think it's stupid."

"That would be impossible," I told you. "Nothing you do could ever be stupid."

You looked at me in the blue wash of light, and I thought I saw love in your eyes. Then you said, "Where did you say you're staying tonight?"

I blinked. Clearly, I'd misread your look. You were waiting for me to go. Now that you'd shown off your house, you were finished with me. "I, I haven't looked into it yet," I stammered.

"Would you like to stay here?"

"No, no," I said, renewed warmth spreading through me. "That's not necessary."

"I know it's not, but I'd like it if you did. Come on, I'll take you out tonight." You looked at me for another beat, your smile widening. "You're crazy, you know. I can't believe you just showed up like this."

You took me to the guest room. It was a muted space furnished in black lacquer. The bed frame was inlaid with mother-of-pearl, and there was a Chinese panel screen painted with cherry blossoms. An enlarged color photograph dominated the wall opposite the bed.

"It's by someone we were just talking about," you said. "Can you guess?"

It was a photograph of a woman, her spine exposed in a backless navy gown. The fabric was fluid, as in a painting by Whistler or Sargent, and her skin was flawless ivory. But, as the woman turned to look at the camera, the skin of her face peeled away, revealing something mangled and cartilaginous beneath.

"Perren," I breathed.

You stood there, smiling pensively in the doorway, rubbing a hand over the jamb. "Well, I'll let you get settled and rest. Take a nap if you like."

After you'd gone, I sat on the edge of the bed and felt the room spin. This must be jet lag, something I hadn't considered. It wasn't natural for the human body to traverse a continent in a day. I couldn't stop staring at the Perren picture. His films were full of sinister images, but they flicked past as quickly as they appeared. This one was fixed in my field of vision.

When I awoke in your guest room, there was a dark patch where I'd drooled on the satin bedspread. Standing, I saw that my capris were horribly wrinkled, deep pleats fanning out at the crotch. In the bathroom mirror I confronted the fact that nothing could be done with my lank hair. I rubbed concealer on the purple moons under my eyes and put on my drugstore blush.

You hadn't told me what to do when I was finished resting. I crept downstairs and found you on the phone in the
entrance hall. When you caught sight of me, you hung up
and pushed your hair behind your shoulder.

"Are you hungry? Let's go get dinner. There's a little Italian
place nearby, if that's okay with you." You stood and stretched
your arms out and back, as if you'd take flight. As if going to
a restaurant were easy and obvious. As if my presence wouldn't
be a humiliation for you. I wanted to ask if we could stay in,
but instead I said, "What should I wear?"

"Anything. What you have on is fine."

"Just give me a minute," I said and hurried back upstairs.
I rummaged through my suitcase, frantically trying on and
casting off clothing before finally surrendering to the safest
option: a black wrap dress made of cheap jersey material.
The neckline was too low, exposing the fabric of my bra,
but with a safety pin I was able to secure the two panels
together. I hadn't brought dress shoes. The best I could do
were open-toed wedges, which were awful with the dress
but could maybe be seen as Californian. You waited for me
at the bottom of the stairs, and as I descended I was keenly
aware of the safety pin, the glint of metal I was sure you
could see.

And then we were in your car, a blue convertible Mustang with the top up, winding through the canyon. The
setting sun brushed rouge over the scrubland. For a while
I saw no sign of human life at all and wondered if we were

passing over the same empty expanse I'd seen from the plane. Then the ocean appeared. I felt a little jump inside me, the excitement of a child. I didn't tell you that I'd never seen the ocean in person before. People liked to brag that Lake Michigan was an ocean unto itself, that it was larger than some saltwater seas, but I saw right away that this water was different. Its color was deeper, a sick jade tint, and it moved in a way the lake didn't, drawing into itself with a singular force.

We turned onto a road that paralleled the coast, passing clam shacks and empty tracts of land with real estate signs. I was surprised by what appeared to be a dry, provincial place, with none of the luster I associated with Los Angeles. As we parked in front of the restaurant, you said, "It's nothing special, but they have good pizza, and no one will bother us here."

The pretty young hostess looked right at you without blinking and asked if we wanted to eat on the patio. It was a mild evening, but you told her: "No, inside is fine." When she led us to a table in the middle of the room, you put a hand to her shoulder and said, "Actually, could we sit somewhere else? That booth over there?"

The hostess pivoted us to the booth in the far corner. You took the banquette that faced the wall, and I was struck by your consideration in giving me the seat looking outward. Only after we were sitting, when your face hit me like a floodlight, did I understand the logic behind your choice. You didn't want to be seen.

I watched you study the menu. There was a quiet between us at the table that made me uncomfortable. I felt compelled to say something to you, something kind that would make you look at me the way you did the night of the reunion.

"I was so glad you came to the reunion," I finally said.

You looked up from the menu. "I was glad you came, too." You smiled then, and I saw the ghost of my childhood friend beneath the famous features, a pencil sketch beneath an oil painting.

Our waitress approached with a pursed, impatient look that turned to delight the instant she recognized you. "Well, *hello!*" She smiled broadly at you, then at me. "What can I get you ladies to drink?"

You looked at me. "A bottle of cabernet is fine."

A few customers at nearby tables glanced slyly toward us and away. I wondered if they were murmuring to each other about you, preparing observations for their friends—or if the people here were immune to fame. Your green eyes were trained on me, exotic and familiar at once. When our wine arrived you took a deep drink and watched me over your glass.

"So," I began, a nagging tremor in my voice. "I meant to tell you that I saw you in *Vanity Fair.* The new movie seems like a really big deal." My hand went instinctively to my hair. I didn't need a mirror to know it had fallen limp again.

Your eyes brightened. "I was really lucky to get that role. It's opening up new possibilities for me. I'm already getting to read scripts I never would've gotten before."

Delightful rosy patches appeared on your cheeks. You'd never talked to me about your acting when we were younger. You were still holding back now, I could tell—still speaking like the subject of an interview—but I sensed that you'd tell me more if I waited.

"I just hope I don't blow it," you continued after a moment, in a lower voice. "It's such a crucial moment in my career, and I have to be careful what parts I audition for right now."

"But isn't it too late for you to blow it? You're on fire. I'm sure people are begging you to be in their movies."

"Yeah, well, kind of. But that's why it's important for me to nurture an image that sets me apart from other actresses. Now that I have some leverage, I need to take control of my career. It's a lot of pressure. So many people make false steps when they're young and never get back on track."

"That does sound like a lot of pressure."

You sighed. "What I really need now is more artistic credibility. It's important that my next film is a serious one. I need to distance myself from the sugar-pop girls, you know? But it's hard to convince the studios to send me the heavyweight scripts. Already I'm sort of being pigeonholed."

"Already? That's not fair."

You rolled your eyes. "No, of course it's not fair. I mean, this is the least fair business on the planet. Especially for women. But I have a mission. What I really want is to be in a Perren film."

I drank from my water glass, swallowed an ice cube whole. It inched down my throat, a sharp pain.

"Of course, I'm not the only one. Everyone wants to work with him, or at least everyone with big ambitions. It would be an incredible boost for me. It would stamp me as a real artist to do a Perren film, to have that *imprimatur*, as they say." You gave me an unblinking gaze. "But he's notoriously selective. He doesn't even hold auditions."

"How does he cast people, then?"

"It's kind of a mystery, but it's sort of understood that he gives preference to people who go to the Rhizome. He visits sometimes to do his own sessions, and I guess he sizes people up while he's there. He comes every few months, I've heard. It's all under the radar, but it's generally agreed that going to the Rhizome is a prerequisite for being cast. He really believes that it brings actors to a higher level, so in his mind, going there shows that you're committed."

The pizza had arrived and was now steaming between us on a metal stand. There was a long pause in which I tried to process what you were telling me. Auguste Perren lived in Switzerland and was famously reclusive. I'd been under the impression that he'd founded the Rhizome for the benefit of others, not for his own use. I never thought he'd visit there himself, or even touch the shores of this country.

You lifted a piece of pizza onto your plate, and the silence extended. You glanced up at me, gauging something as you put fork and knife to your slice. You leaned forward and whispered, "And, on another topic, I don't remember if I told you at the reunion, but I've started seeing someone."

I felt a torque at the base of my diaphragm. "No, you didn't."

You glanced to either side of you. "Rafael Solar." You slid back into your preteen face as you said this, and all at once I felt the sympathetic burst of excitement that once came with our old sharing of crushes. He was from Argentina, you told me, a couple of years younger but in your opinion the most gorgeous man in Hollywood. He'd cracked into the scene a few years ago in a role as one of Genghis Khan's marauders and had been rising steadily since.

I widened my eyes and put my wineglass down carefully, even as my excitement subsided. "Wow, that's fantastic."

You nodded, your mouth curling up into the devilish little smile I remembered. "And it happened so fast. The first day on the *Vespers* set, I swear something just clicked. It was like we could read each other's thoughts."

The torque at my diaphragm tightened. As I attempted to transfer a slice of pizza to my plate, strings of cheese trailed onto the table.

"He's from an aristocratic family in Argentina, and he's the most elegant person I've ever known. And much more traditional than you'd think. It's his Latin background, I guess, but it's important for him to be a gentleman. He's always gallant, which is so refreshing compared with other men in the business. He's unlike anyone I've ever been with."

I knew all about the other men you'd been with, of course. The magazines reported everything. Your boyfriends had seemed disposable to me, elfin and overgroomed, slightly older versions of your eighth-grade crush, Topher. I remembered how we'd snuggled our sleeping bags together at slumber parties and aimed a flashlight onto a pad of paper to play MASH. We'd listed the names of movie stars as possible future husbands, along with the cutest boys in school—Topher among them— and the most repellent. Had you ever landed on a movie star's name? Had you ever landed on "Mansion"?

"He said he wants to take me to Argentina one day. His parents breed polo ponies. They have a whole stable. And Raf's an amazing polo player. He's, like, the best in L.A." You refilled your wineglass and took another drink. "It's so nice to be able to share all this with you, Abby. It really is. I know I was a little tipsy at the reunion, but it was true what I said. I've missed having friends who really know me. Old friends like you, who've known me since I was a kid." It was clear you were drinking too much again, your words begin-ning to blur into each other. "I mean, I do have friends here, but it's different."

My face was so hot it must have been purple. My neck itched from sweat, and my armpits were wet beneath the jersey dress.

"There was a friend, well not a friend, but this woman I *thought* was my friend, this actress. You'd know who she is, but I won't say her name." You rolled your eyes again, holding your wineglass. I drank from my own glass, to encourage you. "Before Rafael, I was dating this other actor, and the minute she found out, she started moving in on him. Like, total seduction, movie style. It was totally uncalled-for. I mean, I wasn't even that into him. Anyway, it was an eye-opener, how competitive and catty people in Hollywood can be." You gestured to the waitress and pointed to the wine bottle. "Ever since then, I've been having a hard time trusting anyone here."

I already knew this story from the tabloids, of course, but hearing it from you was heavenly. Looking at your flowering cheeks, your fingers twirling your red hair, I orchestrated a fantasy in which I created a film and cast you as the star. I mentally ran through my drawings, picturing you in each world, animating it. I costumed you as a garden nymph, gathering golden apples. The waitress arrived with another bottle of cabernet and refilled your glass without asking.

"It can be really lonely, to be honest," you said quietly as the waitress withdrew. You leaned forward, jostling your wineglass. "Abby, I'm sorry if I seemed strange when you arrived. I just wasn't expecting you. But I'm so glad you're here now. I feel like myself with you. I haven't felt like myself in a long time."

Your hand was on the table, and I reached for it. A tear had formed in your left eye, and I watched as it gathered into a quivering drop on your bottom lashes.

"Would it be weird if I asked you to stay here a while?"

I kept my right hand on yours and held the base of my wineglass down with the other.

"Really, I hope you'll think about it. It would be great to have a real friend again. Someone who's not competing with me, you know? And whose kindness isn't conditional. The truth is, I've been getting really down on myself lately. It's weird, but the more attention I get, the harder it is to feel good about it. You were always such a cheerleader, Abby. You always made me feel special, like I deserved everything that happened to me."

I took in your words, then said solemnly, "You were my cheerleader, too." I stared into your eyes. "No one else was."

"And of course it would be good for you, too, to stay here. You can get to know L.A., the way the movie business works. Maybe I can even show you around and get you some introductions. I'd love to see you get a foot in the door. You were always so talented."

"No, no," I said mechanically, as my heart soared. "I can't intrude at your house. I'll find a hotel."

"It's not intruding. I *want* you to stay. I really do remember those stories you made up, Abby, that I used to try to act out. After we talked at the reunion, I've been thinking about them a lot. Like the one about the little girl who gets lost in the supermarket, who goes up to a stranger and convinces her to take her home. Because she doesn't want to go home to her own house. Remember? It was so twisted and great. And I remember how you had the woman's house all detailed

67

in your mind, what it looked like inside and what the yard was like, the rose trellis and the maze of hedges in the back and everything. I still remember it so clearly, like it actually happened."

I tried to respond, but nothing could get past the joy ballooning in me.

"You helped me when we were kids. You may not realize how much. Now maybe I can help you a little."

There was a sound of shattering glass. The restaurant fell silent as our waitress ran to a table where an apologetic young woman stood up and backed away from the shards of a water tumbler. The waitress crouched to sweep, and the sounds of the restaurant burbled back to life. I kept watching the scene after everyone else had looked away. Then I looked at you.

"Is the Rhizome nearby?" I asked.

"The Rhizome? It's just up the road, actually." You stared at me strangely, your cheeks pink, your elbows on the table. I nodded.

"Stay, Abby," you said, and the look in your eyes was the one I'd seen in *Vanity Fair*. The pleading, the imploring. You did need me. It was true.

The waitress appeared at our table. "I'm sorry to bother you," she said quietly. "But do you think I might have your autograph, Elise?"

I glared at the waitress, indignant on your behalf. But you flashed your public smile and accepted the pad and pen. The waitress watched coolly as you signed your name in slow, looping letters. When you handed the pad back to her and she slipped it into her apron pouch, I felt an illogical jealousy. Clearly, I was the privileged one. I was the one whose shoulder you leaned on as we went toward the door. I was the one who helped you descend the stairs without falling. I was the one who unlocked the Mustang after you dropped the keys on the ground, laughing, "Oh, Abby. Look at us!" And, as you melted into the passenger seat, I was the one who drove you home.

III.

IN YOUR guest bedroom, I tilted the blinds open to the craggy landscape, the ballistic blue sky, and felt instantly unburdened. The light was simple and abrading. How silly of me, for so many years, to have subjected myself to the stale Midwest. How silly to have never come to California. Already Michigan was a figment, a prolonged, dank dream from which I'd finally awoken. I'd left my winter coat behind, and I found myself thinking of it now, trying to recall the weight and feel of the boiled wool, the hide that I'd sloughed and abandoned. I thought of my parents coming down to the kitchen to find my note, the Impala missing from the driveway. On my phone there was already a message, which I had no desire to play back. If they hadn't yet discovered the credit card charges, they would soon. It didn't matter. I sat up in your bed, thrilled. My escape had been simple, ingenious. Even Shelby would have been proud.

I slipped downstairs to the kitchen. The room was banded with sunlight, and it took a moment to see the man standing at the far counter, facing away. Dark hair curled at the back of his neck. He wore a black T-shirt with green jogging pants, and his feet were bare. I froze, like a mouse coming upon a predator. I instinctively began to back away, but the man turned and our eyes met. His face—the heavy mandible and Cupid's bow lips—had a beauty so exaggerated it felt menacing.

"Hello," the deep voice said, with an accented lilt, and I made myself look up. "I'm Rafael."

He held his hand out, and I forced my own hand forward. He clasped it for only a second, not even really shaking it, and yet I felt the scorch on my palm. He explored my face with an amused spark in his black eyes.

"I'm Abby."

"I know. Elise told me. Would you like some kombucha?" He held up a bottle of yellow liquid.

"Uh, sure."

I stood stupidly as he tipped the substance from the bottle to a glass. "I make my own," he said. "Let me know what you think."

I sipped, choked on the sour liquid.

"You're not a regular kombucha drinker?" he asked.

"No."

"Oh, you've got to get into it. A glass every day. It will change your life."

He held out his glass for a toast. He kept his eyes on mine, and as our glasses touched, I had the irrational sense of performing an illicit act. When I heard your voice behind me, it was with a mix of chagrin and relief.

"Oh, honey, I feel awful." You glided to Rafael and pressed yourself against him. "Will you pour me some of that?"

You were in gym shorts and a tank top. No bra. Your hair fell in twisted cables over your shoulders. You rose on your toes with the guilelessness of a child and kissed Rafael's neck. He slid a hand candidly down the side of your body, and I felt a shower of sparks along my own skin, as if I were the one he'd touched.

"Aw, you already met Abby." You pouted. "I wanted to introduce you."

Rafael moved his hands to your shoulders and turned you away from me. "Come, let's go outside and get you some fresh air," he said. "I'll make you all better."

I hesitantly followed the two of you out to the patio, and was grateful when Rafael pulled three lounge chairs into the shade of the pergola. As we settled into them, I thought of our classmates back in Michigan, driving through the snow to their jobs, children, and mortgages. I thought of Christy Peters and the crucifix at her breast. She'd be in her kindergarten classroom, dispensing crayons and Kleenex. Ted and Andrew would be at their office desks, staring at Excel documents. None of them would be seeing anything like what I was seeing right now.

You lay back in your chair with an arm over your eyes as Rafael gave a monologue. His voice was mesmerizing in its melodic lifts and inflections as he spoke, loading praise on you, his *gorgeous gift*, his *guiding angel*. He recounted the story, ostensibly for my benefit, of the day he'd first seen you in your horn prostheses on the *Vespers* set, how he'd been briefly mystified, as if he'd stumbled upon a magical new being.

"I'll stay as long as she'll have me," Rafael was saying in my direction. "Like a loyal pet."

At this, you took your arm down from your face, hoisted yourself up in the chair, and leaned forward to kiss him. I turned my face away. The kiss was loud and long, unbearably sensual, and I wondered if I was expected to excuse myself or sit and endure it.

At last the suction was broken, and you both stood up. Your lips were swollen red.

"Abby," you said brightly. "We're going to the polo club today. Raf's going to give me a riding lesson. But I'll be back soon."

Looking up from the lounge chair, I felt like your daughter. "All right."

"Will you be okay here, by yourself? I won't be long, I promise. Make yourself at home."

You lingered, a questioning look in your eyes. "I'll be fine," I assured you. "Have fun."

While you were gone, I slunk downstairs with bare feet. Softly, I opened drawers and cabinets, found them all empty. There was a price tag still affixed to a sideboard in the dining room, and my eyelid spasmed at the number printed there: $4,950. Back upstairs, I went into your bedroom. The same shopping bags were still on the floor, the new clothes wrapped in tissue paper. Jeans and shirts were strewn on the unmade bed. I ran a hand over the bottom sheet, leaned down, and put my nose to the pillow, hoping for the honeysuckle scent of your hair. I peeked into the walk-in closet and saw the mess of shoes, the clothing dripping from hangers. A red dress pooled on the floor. I smiled to myself. You'd never been a neat person. This closet could have belonged to a spoiled teenager.

In the library, I took the Jung books off the shelves, one at a time. *Man and His Symbols, The Archetypes and the Collective Unconscious, The Undiscovered Self.* I went to the window and pretended I was you, gazing out at the thin lip of ocean on the horizon, trying to feel the quickening you might feel in your blood, the promise of the planet spread before you, every island and continent beyond that great curve.

After that, I settled into my own quarters. I sat at the glossy black desk and pulled out my art material. The familiar feel of the pencil between my fingers, the act of drawing and coloring, eased my brain to a slower wave. I watched my hand from a remove as it outlined the garden I'd seen in a dream, with torches planted in the ground. I drew fallen torches, and flames latticing the flowers and trees. Against the background of the lustrous desk, my drawing hand was brutish, the fingernails ragged, cuticles split and overgrown.

In this sleek room, I felt like a matted beast just emerged from hibernation.

When I finished, I slid the drawing beneath the bed and climbed under the blanket. I closed my eyes and followed the shapes behind my lids until they resolved into a face and a body. Rafael. My blood thickened, pulsed through its revolution, pooled at the base of my pelvis. It was the opposite of rest, this gathering of carnal energy. I tossed over onto my stomach, breathed into the pillow.

I didn't know I'd slept until I was woken by your return, startled by the sound of your movements downstairs. I felt a dip of fear that you'd somehow notice my fingerprints on the furniture I'd touched in your absence. I clambered out of the bed and neatened the covers, then pulled a brush through my hair and went downstairs.

Your face lit into a smile as I descended the tiled steps.

"Hi," you said. "It's so strange to have you here, Abby. There you are, coming down the stairs like a ghost from my past."

"Thanks for letting me stay the night," I said, stopping on the bottom step. "It was nice to meet Rafael."

"Isn't he amazing?"

"He surprised me. I mean, when I came downstairs this morning."

"Oh, yeah, he does that to me, too. I don't expect him, and I jump out of my skin. Sometimes I forget he has a key to the house."

"Oh," I said, trying to keep my voice light. "How long did you say you've been dating?"

You thought for a moment. "Three months? But it feels like three years. It's like we're on fast-forward."

I nodded dumbly, holding the banister. "How was the riding lesson?"

"Terrible. I guess it's not the best idea to get on a horse when you're hungover. But I love the polo club. It's beautiful, and all the men are gorgeous. You should come sometime. Raf told me that he might start to breed ponies, to expand the family business. Who knew that polo was such a big deal? He told me that when they breed a champion mare, they actually transplant the embryo to another mare so that the champion can keep playing polo."

"That's crazy," I said.

"They also *clone* ponies. They take the ovaries from a mare in the slaughterhouse and scrape her eggs out. Then they replace the nucleus of one of the eggs with a nucleus from the champion pony and get a surrogate mare to give birth to a new champion pony."

"Wow."

You looked unblinkingly at me for a long moment. "Have you thought about my invitation? To stay?"

I tried to appear serious, as if I were considering the wisdom of the arrangement, but the smile broke through my effort. "Of course I'll stay."

You gave me your smile, wide and bright as a beach blanket, and seized me in an embrace. "Oh, I'm so glad. Thank you, Abby."

"No, thank *you*."

"We're going to have so much fun," you said, pulling away. You brushed a piece of hair from my forehead. "Tomorrow I'll show you around the city."

"That would be great." A knot came to my throat, a mix of terror and joy. "And, please, Elise. You don't ever have to worry about me."

Behind the wheel, you wore big black sunglasses. Alien vegetation blurred past the windows—clumped grasses and loose sprays of flowers—until you finally steered us onto a freeway ramp. All at once we were among thousands. I didn't dare speak to you, for fear of being a distraction, but you drove expertly. You'd learned to navigate this place, your home.

Exiting the freeway, we proceeded down a long straight thoroughfare past buildings that pulsed with reckless color and information. I'd expected a mild plasticity to the city, had thought that the legendary California light would kiss every surface with equalizing ardor, assuring those caught in its rays that they were loved and capable of seizing happiness. Instead, the sunlight lacquered a junky streetscape, a clog of cars in front of us, a clog of people on the sidewalk. Among the pedestrians I glimpsed costumed characters: a blond Batgirl, a dirty SpongeBob.

"Here we are," you announced. "Hollywood Boulevard. I'd stop, but it's impossible to park. Some other time we'll come back and see the Walk of Fame."

We drove through the rest of Hollywood, which was scrappy and hard, a parade of liquor stores, car washes, fast food. The people were dour faced in the flat light, holding grocery bags and waiting at bus stops. We continued along the infinite boulevard, cars linked one to the next like caterpillar segments.

"Here we go," you said, pointing to a green lawn with the words BEVERLY HILLS arching over it.

"This is Beverly Hills?"

"Well, you can't see much of it from the street."

Still, the place was unimpressive. Rodeo Drive was laughably short and antiseptic, a hastily constructed movie set. A few tourists stood on the sidewalk, stunned by the bright blankness. I wondered if we might stop at Gucci or Prada, but as if reading my mind, you said, "I don't shop here."

Instead, we traveled along one of the interminable arteries through the city and rejoined the freeway. We surfaced in a place you called Venice. Here, there were human-scaled houses, bright flowers, bicyclists. We parked at the curb on a sleepy street, outside a stranger's bungalow, and walked to the main boulevard. "Abbot Kinney's my favorite place to wander around," you said as we went into one of the trendy design shops. I suppose I'd expected you to hunch in public, to avoid notice, but you walked tall, flaunting your fame like a neon cloak. As you studiously browsed, the other shoppers glanced away, their awareness palpable. What a sustained effort it must have been for you to remain focused on the activity you were engaged in: looking at lamps, thumbing through area rugs. I was sure I'd collapse under the weight of the cloak, had it been mine to wear.

In a vintage clothing store, you carefully sorted through the racks, holding dresses against yourself.

"What do you think?" you asked about a blousy dress with a tiny flower print.

"It would be beautiful on you," I said truthfully.

You slung it over your arm and continued through the rack. "I've been trying to soften my look," you said. "So many people are trying to be edgy and hard right now. I want to be soft." The hangers clattered as you thrust things to the side. "What about this? For you." You held up a diaphanous black shawl with silver threading. Without speaking, you arranged it across my shoulders, and led me to the full-length mirror, where I saw myself as you must have seen me.

"You think so?" I murmured.

"Mm, yeah. It's good on you." Your eyes flashed. "You do black really well, and the silver gives it a little kick. You look badass."

I stared at myself.

"You do," you affirmed. "You look like a rebel filmmaker."

My face heated. I wasn't sure if you were making fun of me. "I think I look like a witch," I mumbled.

"Yeah. Well, honestly a haircut might help with that."

Back outside on the sidewalk, you took my hand. Once the initial voltage had subsided, I was consumed with something like embarrassment. My hand went limp in yours. Being seen in my company would have an immediate and negative impact on your image, I was certain. At your side, I was portly and short, even in the unfortunate wedge sandals. But you led me along the sidewalk like a rescue dog and drew me into a hair salon, where you sat me in the chair and told the stylist what to do. I came out with a hard bob that cut at my jawline. Framing my round, primitive face, the haircut looked like an expensive wig. But if I wasn't beautiful, the haircut implied, at least I was worthy of note.

As we were walking back to the car, two men ahead of us on the sidewalk abruptly turned around. I froze. It took a full moment to understand that the objects they aimed weren't weapons but cameras. You didn't falter. Instead you continued straight toward the men, forcing them to walk backward while shooting. You didn't smile or pose but strode forward in a natural fashion—a lady out shopping with her friend. I felt my own face tense into a shrewish pucker. I had a pair of sunglasses, but they were in my purse, and as I trotted next to you, I dug down to find them. The camera shutters fired unremittingly.

"Elise," one of the photographers called.

You kept walking at the same pace, though I sensed an almost imperceptible pause in your gait, as if you were considering whether to respond.

"Elise," the other photographer parroted.

You smiled stiffly and increased your speed. "Excuse me," you said, not unpleasantly. I hurried to keep by your side. "Excuse me," you repeated and, taking my hand, turned into the street. Cars were rushing past, but you edged into traffic and seized the first moment to dart across.

IV.

OVER THE next few days, you fluttered off to appointments and auditions, and I paced the house like a watchdog. Rafael sometimes let himself in during the day, but most often he came at night. Once, I heard him jiggling his key in the door after dark and ascending the steps to your bedroom. After that I couldn't hear anything, but I soundlessly turned the knob of my door and edged down the hall. I stood outside your bedroom and listened. In my mind, I saw you and Rafael together, your softness and his hardness, and my own body throbbed. The sounds you made were glorious, a song of pleasure so pure that it brought me near orgasm without a touch.

On Tuesday, the eve of our seventh day together, we ordered Thai food and stayed up late on the patio, a swollen gold moon above. Rafael was out of town for the weekend, and you were all mine. You chain-smoked American Spirits while rambling about the clothes your stylist wanted you to wear. You were cultivating a different kind of persona, you'd told her many times.

"She should know this by now," you kept saying. "I want vintage, I want bohemian, I want *real*. I don't want to be a sex symbol or the cutesy girl next door. She *knows* that. If she can't be on my team, I'm going to have to find someone else."

After each pronouncement, you spilled sauvignon blanc down your throat. When the bottle was finished, you asked me to open another, and I obliged. I sat and listened, nodding and making encouraging or disapproving noises. My opinion, unsolicited and ungiven, was that you were anything but bohemian. You weren't tough or iconoclastic or earthy. You were delicate, finely crafted, a light and vitreous thing.

"I'm too tired to get up," you moaned, lighting another cigarette. "Ugh, and I have to have lunch with Mireille Sauvage tomorrow."

At the sound of this name, an image came to mind of a sinuous blond with an antelope face. "I think I've heard of her."

"I'm sure you have. She's been in a lot of things lately. But honestly I don't even want to see her," you sighed. "There's a rumor that she's being considered for the new Perren movie and I'm sick about it."

My heart skipped. "There's a new Perren movie?"

You glanced away, mouth twitching. "Yeah, it's pretty far off though. I'm still hoping I might catch his eye. My agent's trying to put my name forward, but he doesn't really care about agents. I probably won't have a chance."

"Of course you will," I said robotically. "You have just as much of a chance as anyone."

"No, I'm a mess."

I didn't respond.

Your eyes met mine at a feline angle as you took another pull from your wineglass. "Anyway, it's good for me to keep building a friendship with Mireille, in case she does end up getting the part. So much of this business is about connections, and I have to take the long view."

It occurred to me at this moment, for the first time, that I now occupied a space—as remote as it might be—in "this business." In this web of connections, I was only two degrees from Auguste Perren. Excruciatingly, exhilaratingly near. For a moment, my breath left me.

"Oh, and I found out I didn't get the *Shadow Wolves* role. The callbacks came in, and I was cut from the first round. I don't understand why. It's true I'm a little young for the lead, but since when does that matter?" You flicked your cigarette indignantly. "They said I didn't have the weight to be an ICE agent, that they wanted someone with—what did they call it?—*sangfroid*. I don't even know what that means."

"It means cold blood. In French."

"I mean, I know pretty much what it means, but I don't understand why I don't have it."

"Maybe they just think you look too nice," I said, but it sounded cruel on my tongue, and I wanted to snatch the words back.

You glowered. "It's embarrassing. They gave the part to an actress who I swear is even younger than me."

At this moment, you didn't look like a federal agent so much as a petulant girl, but I said, "It's their loss," putting conviction into my voice. "The movie will probably tank."

You looked at me for a moment, bruised, and I saw a spark of hope flash and fade in your eyes. "Thanks, Abby. I know you're just saying that to make me feel better, but I appreciate it. And maybe you're right. Anyway, I have a session at the Rhizome tomorrow afternoon. I heard someone say that Perren was coming this month, so maybe I'll get lucky and he'll be there. He only visits a few times a year. And it's usually a surprise. He likes to just show up randomly and do a session with his own guide, like a regular person. Then he walks around the property and has lunch in the restaurant. Everybody pretends like it's no big deal, but really they're killing themselves to get near him."

I'd finished with wine hours before, and now I took a long drink of water as I absorbed this information.

"I didn't know there was a restaurant there," I said.

"Oh, yeah, it's great. It's organic, macrobiotic, five-star chef. Everybody eats together at these long farmhouse tables. It's a really interesting group. Screenwriters, directors, and some of the more complex actors, the unusual ones who want to challenge themselves and aren't content to just look good. The kind of people I want to be associated with."

You stopped talking. I was looking at you, but I was imagining sitting at a table beside Auguste Perren. I imagined him turning toward me to ask my name. Our eyes locking.

"Sounds incredible," I said.

"It is. And the place is so beautiful, Abby. It's this whole campus, with a spa and gardens and a natural pool. Like a retreat center. It's so serene and relaxing. I swear, sometimes it's the only thing that keeps me sane."

You stopped talking then, and looked into your glass. Studiously you swirled the wine, then drank it down. I didn't say anything. I let you have this moment of solipsistic contemplation, which was what I imagined all actresses needed.

It was after midnight when I helped you into the house and followed you up the Talavera stairs, in case you missed a step and fell. After you were tucked into bed, breathing loudly through your mouth, I stood in the room for a few moments, watching you. I remembered those everlasting slumber parties, those torturous nights when I'd stare at your face in the dark—your profile like that of an illustrated girl in an English children's book, the fine articulations of an Alice or a Wendy, the curl at the nostril, the vermilion of the upper lip—before you turned away, in slumber, and the hair fell across your face, screening me out.

✳   ✳   ✳

You slept until noon the next day, took your kombucha in a thermos, and left me alone in the house. I sat in the brown velvet chair by the window and tried to read, but I could only think of the Rhizome. A bitter substance threaded through my veins. I resented you for going, for leaving me behind. You might be sitting limply at a table beside Perren at that very moment, gazing at him through dull, hungover eyes. I saw the other hollow sycophants at the same table and fantasized about inserting myself among them, lifting the table and tilting its contents to the floor. I gripped the book in my hands and glared through the plate glass window at the bolt of land rolling into the Pacific.

For years, I'd imagined the moment of meeting Perren, the instant understanding that would pass between us. Although the circumstances surrounding this encounter remained opaque, I knew it would someday happen. Of this I was certain, just as I'd been certain of seeing you again, Elise. It was fated, as all great artist alliances seemed to be fated: Van Gogh and Gauguin, Emerson and Thoreau, Pound and Eliot. Sometimes it was the younger one who approached the elder, whose supreme confidence drove him to write adulatory letters to his idol and introduce himself. This boldness was often, astonishingly, rewarded. The legend replied to the admirer, in warm letters full of encouragement and validation, and a lasting correspondence began. Mentorships were established. Later, when the neophyte flowered into his own abilities and matured into an artist the equal of his senior, the mentorship became friendship, and both legacies were imprinted on history.

Weren't such couplings inevitable? The senior artist must suspect this. On some unconscious level, he must await the arrival of the letter, the knock on the studio door. It wasn't merely out of egoism that he might respond, but also an element of fear. Trembling, he must sense the encroaching tide of youth just outside the gate: he must foresee his own usurpation. Wiser than resistance was appeasement, ingratiation. The artists who responded to their brazen admirers, and invited them in, were aligning themselves with the brute force of the future. In crouching to lift the next generation, they ensured their own continued relevance.

I'd begun letters to Perren but had never gotten past the first line. There was too much to say, and nothing to say. It was impossible. Someday, though, it would not be. I'd write the letter, knock on the door. He'd recognize my purpose, respect my power, and bend to welcome me.

It was dark by the time you came home, and you were with Rafael. I could hear your voice in the driveway, shouting, "And how is that supposed to make me feel?" Rafael's response was indecipherable. The front door burst open, and neither of you spoke as you went toward the stairs. You gave me a faraway look as you passed by the living room. I could tell you'd been drinking. Rafael didn't look my way but followed you up the stairs in a boorish hunch. Once your bedroom door was closed, the voices returned, low and toxic, followed by thuds—perhaps a shoe thrown to the floor, a slammed dresser drawer. The ceiling above me tremored, and I wondered whether stingrays had a sense of hearing. Were they frightened by the noise? Or were they oblivious, numbly adrift in another dimension?

I curled on the sofa, making myself small. At last, a door banged upstairs and I heard you screech some pejorative, your voice hoarse and quavering, as Rafael glided down the steps and out the door.

A moment later, you were downstairs, crumpled in the chair in front of me. You wore the same white romper that had been pristine when you left the house that morning but now was stained with wine and mascara. With your hair curled in wispy tendrils at your temples, you resembled a giant infant.

"I hate him, Abby," you hiccupped. "He's vain and shallow and doesn't care about me at all."

"What happened?"

"God, I don't even remember what started it. We were out at Cecconi's, and he said something insulting. I don't remember the exact words now, but it was something about women not needing to develop a craft, because they either look the part or they don't. And before I could even argue with him, I saw him checking out this other girl. It turned into a whole scene. It was horrible. And when I went in the bathroom, Jessica Starck came in to ask if I was all right. What nerve! She's the one I was telling you about before, the one who tried to steal Chris Coonan away from me. She's a snake. And she knows that I know that. So I'm there crying in the bathroom, and she comes in and says she heard the whole thing and that she's *so sorry*. It was humiliating."

It did sound humiliating, I said. You told the story again, your face reddening as the tears returned. When you went back to the beginning, again, I came to you and helped you stand and brought you up to bed. I wanted to interrupt, to ask whether you'd seen Perren at the Rhizome, but instead I soothed you. *Everything will be better in the morning*, I said. *Don't worry. I'm here with you.*

For each of your fights, you and Rafael had a passionate reconciliation. Whatever he'd done wrong had been a misunderstanding, you'd tell me. He'd apologized for everything, and you didn't remember half of what had happened anyway. You'd probably overreacted; you sometimes got that way when you drank. You became stupid and suspicious. He was your soul mate, you said, and you'd marry him someday.

In the midst of one such apologia, you handed me the keys to your second car—a silver Tesla, sleek as a bullet—and encouraged me to explore. The car was fun to drive, and I loved traveling down the coastline, discovering the beach towns—Redondo, Manhattan, Hermosa—with their In-N-Out Burgers, Hawaiian food huts, and indolent houses worshipping the water. Venice captivated me most of all. There was a romance, a sun-bleached purity, to its grit. As I traveled the boardwalk, I thought of Michigan's scuttling crustaceans hunched in their parkas and cars and houses. Here, nothing was cloaked. Everything was laid bare in the sun's great photographic flash.

One afternoon, I went to the water's edge and sat cross-legged on the sand. The clatter and whir of distant skateboarders washed into the ferment of the waves. With a lip of ocean foam flirting a yard from my knees, I quieted my conscious mind and let my sense of identity blur. Like that, I entered the Spring, established Unity Gain. The waters of my unconscious seeped through, and I let them pool into a waking dream. Perhaps the ocean suggested diving imagery, because in my subsequent reverie I enjoyed a kinship with cetaceans, rode on their backs through tropical depths. Afterward, I walked back over the beach in a state of calm. As I coasted past the skate park, a boy arched up in front of me, the wheels of his board inches from my face—and I caught a glimpse of an open eye on the bottom of the slab. Back on the boardwalk, I passed henna tables and tattoo shops and briefly strode alongside a rollerblading, dreadlocked guitarist before he pulled ahead of me, singing to himself, deep within his own waking Spring.

I parked the Tesla in the driveway and breezed into the house. You were in the living room, cross-legged in the hanging wicker pod chair. A bright yellow sundress draped over your knees and, paired with the vivid flame of your hair, made it hard to look straight at you.

"Hi, Abby," you said lightly, though I sensed something new in your voice, wavering.

"Sit down for a second. I want to tell you something."

I sat on the Navajo couch, resting my bag at my side.

"Listen," you said. "I should probably just say it right away. I found out I got the Joan Didion biopic."

"You did? That's fantastic!" Even as I uttered these words, my heart sank.

"It really is, I know." Your smile was tight. "I'm happy but also kind of terrified. But, yeah, it's a great thing for me. A total game-changer." Your pod chair swung gently. "Of course it means things are going to get hectic. Like, I don't even know if I'm going to have time for Raf."

I was silent. Sitting on the couch, I felt like a small child about to learn of a divorce.

"I mean, I won't be able to spend time with you the way we've been doing." You seemed to be gathering your words carefully, and I felt a crimp at my throat. "But I've loved having you here, Abby. I really want you to stay."

The crimp intensified and moved through my body, like the wringing of a wet rope. "Of course," I interrupted, speaking through the pain. "I completely understand. I'll figure something out. It's been an absolute pleasure staying here. I'm so grateful that you hosted me for so long and showed me so much."

After the effort of speaking, I took a long breath. I couldn't process, yet, the sudden annihilation of my grandest hopes. All I could think of at that moment was how accustomed I'd become to seeing your face every day. Simply looking at you, I was certain, made me a better artist, a better person. You couldn't have known this, of course. You could never have known the effect your physical presence had on me or what it would mean to thrust me back into the darkness. You could never have been that cruel. All at once, the prospect of returning to Michigan reared up, and I was overcome with vertigo. I realized that I was gripping the arm of the couch.

"No, no," you said. You shifted on the pod chair, uncrossed your legs. You looked hard at me, your eyes glittering. "I wanted to ask if you'd consider staying here and being my assistant. I mean, my personal assistant."

I still gripped the arm of the couch, as if it might capsize. The meaning of your words penetrated slowly.

"A lot of actors have friends as their assistants," you continued. "People who already know them and live with them and anticipate what they need. People they trust. I was thinking maybe you'd consider that. I'm at the point where I need help. It would just be day-to-day things. Keeping track of my appointments, answering the phone, maybe organizing some household stuff. My agent keeps telling me I need an assistant, but I've been putting it off. I thought it might be awkward, too rigid or something. But if it was *you*, it would be different. It would be fun. And I trust you completely." You blinked, and rode the swaying pod chair. "I'd pay you, of course. And you could stay here for free."

I concentrated on keeping my grip on the couch, so as not to dive at your feet. Finally, I spoke. "You want me to be your personal assistant?"

You nodded.

"And keep staying here?"

You shifted forward and put your feet onto the floor, halting the chair's swinging. "Please, Abby. I hope you'll say yes."

I inhaled. "Are you sure it wouldn't be weird for you?"

"No, no." You shook your head. "It would be a relief." You blinked again, rapidly. "But take some time to think about it. No pressure. If it's uncomfortable for you, I totally understand."

You looked deeply at me for a long moment. You fluffed the dress over your legs, and a fluttering warmth spread through my body.

"It would be wonderful," I said solemnly.

Your lips curled into a smile, and you pushed yourself up from the chair and came toward me. "Oh Abby, I'm so glad. I really love having you here. You're such a great support to me. There's no one else I can trust like I trust you, who I know will always be loyal." You embraced me and kissed my cheek. "How crazy is this? Who would have thought we'd end up here, from when we were kids? It's so crazy."

"Yes, crazy," I echoed.

Suddenly, amazingly, I was your closest confidante. I'd slipped back into your life as if I'd never left, as if we'd somehow awoken from a slumber party as grown women.

At first, being an assistant simply meant keeping you company when you wanted it and leaving you alone when you didn't, as I'd already been doing. You were sweetly hesitant about asking me for things at first, afraid of demeaning me with a load of dry cleaning. "No, this is my job," I said firmly and took the clothes into my arms. Dry cleaning would happen every week, we decided. You'd put it in a bin in the laundry room. As for regular laundry, you wanted to give it to your maid service, but I insisted on doing it myself. I emptied your bedroom hamper on Mondays and Thursdays, poured a dab of clear liquid detergent directly upon the fabric of your underwear, and fastened the hooks of your bras before putting them in zippered mesh bags. The fabric of your garments was splendid, tinseled with copper strands of your hair.

You gave me your credit card and checkbook so I could pay for everything. You sent me to a natural food store where, instead of gum and breath mints, there was organic chocolate bark and artisanal spring water in the checkout lane. I bought some of your wine there, too, a few bottles of pinot noir and rosé, sustainably grown from the local vineyards you publicly favored. The rest of the wine supply, and the hard liquor, I purchased from a roadside place where the paparazzi wouldn't track me.

You got a new phone and gave your old one to me to serve as your administrative line. Only Rafael and I had your updated number. The old phone rang incessantly, and I turned down lunch appointments on your behalf and took messages from your agent.

"Oh, you're her assistant! Good, I'm so glad she took the leap. Please have her call me when she can."

At your insistence, I set up my own email account. I adopted a friendly, professional tone in answering messages and texts from the acquaintances who hadn't rated access to your new phone number. I felt a frisson each time I rejected a request for a social appointment. You were swamped with your big role coming up, I'd tell them, but you'd be in touch as soon as you came up for air.

It was wonderful, you said, to have this new peace. You shut yourself in the bedroom, or in the dream room with the glass orbs, to go through the script. You walked outside the house, wending around the citrus trees, talking to yourself, becoming Joan. For the next few weeks, I knew to avoid you, to give you space. If I came across you accidentally, I bustled away like a housekeeper—unless you stopped me, as you did a few times, and asked me to listen to your delivery. Then, I stood stiffly in front of you as you spoke in an affected warble, gesturing with a limp hand.

When you finally came out of your trance, you sought me out, knocking on my door as I hunched with my drawings. I shoved them under the bed, out of sight, before answering. Your eyes were alight when I opened the door, as if you'd been loosed from a chain.

"Let's go shopping," you commanded.

I'd become accustomed to being "papped" and had even begun to recognize some of the photographers, although I never understood how they found you and why they sometimes didn't. It never stopped being a shock when they materialized outside your car, a disorderly squadron aiming their cameras like stubby cannons. I sensed a submarine current of excitement beneath their workmanlike demeanor. Some had an alcoholic blear in their eyes as they barked your name, or a twitch at the mouth that suggested a cyclical dependence on adrenaline. And as much as you, like every star, professed to dislike it, I wondered if there might have been a corresponding shade of addiction on your part, too. There must have been something energizing—life affirming—in hunting and being hunted that kept you and the whole city going.

I was an observer, a tagalong, a pet. It didn't bother me to be left in waiting rooms during dress fittings, to sit in the parking lot during script workshops. I didn't mind not being introduced when you ran into an acquaintance at Nobu. I was admittedly lost by the politics of the film industry, useless as a strategic adviser. I was simply there to listen, to groan in sympathy and glow with pride. And listening was what I did best, what I was grateful to the heavens to be able to do. I loved the sound of your voice. Whatever its petty grievances or vacuous prattle, I would have been happy to hear it forever.

V.

FOR THE *Vespers* premiere, the stylist worked on you for hours, and when you emerged from your room, the bohemian girl had been replaced with the archetype of *woman*. Your dress was bridal white, long and demure but for metal hooks at the sides, stapling the front and back together like pieces of paper, hitting a precise note of aesthetic risk. Your hair swept over one shoulder in a wave, secured by invisible combs. In your hand was a silver clamshell just big enough for car keys and a tube of lipstick. The stylist helped me, too, laying out an assortment of dresses for me to try. She decided on a black satin dress with a sweetheart neckline and swing skirt, and handed me gold-cluster earrings.

"Just some red lipstick and you're set," she said. "You'll look like Diablo Cody."

Later, I asked you who that was.

"Oh, that's a big compliment from Bianca." You jostled my shoulder. "Diablo Cody was, like, the hippest thing in Hollywood a few years ago."

Rafael, I supposed, was with his own stylist. The plan was that you and he would arrive in a limo to appear together for photos, and I'd be dropped off in a taxi. I was to stay near but not beside you on the red carpet. No one told me anything else. The stylist was in a fluster. She popped into my room to check in with me, nodding her approval at the black dress and red pumps, the cherry-bomb lipstick. As I teetered out in the heels, I had a momentary flashback to our high school reunion and wished that our classmates might somehow know about this—that they might see me here in this black minx dress, this parallel universe.

The premiere was at Grauman's Chinese Theatre. I'd been told the theater was iconic, but it looked like a tacky shopping center to me. Traffic cones and cattle barriers lined the sidewalk where the stars would appear. There was an actual red carpet. Cars and taxis passed the spectacle without slowing, a constant stream down Hollywood Boulevard. A herd of fans huddled across the street, holding up camera phones and screaming out names.

I was ushered onto the red carpet, and abandoned there. The nerves swarmed in my stomach as I withdrew against a metal barrier. Around me, a group of unfazed industry people loitered. The glare of the klieg lights gave the scene an eerie surreality. Only the actors were brushed and glitzed; only they strode and posed within this bright bubble. Everyone else was businesslike, focused on moving the evening forward minute by minute. Time seemed rushed and clipped: the cursory interviews in front of massive TV cameras, the quick struts and pivots you and Rafael performed as if ballroom dancing, the artillery of flash photography. I bent down and touched the red carpet. To my surprise, it was made of rough industrial fabric, not the velvet I'd imagined. The name of the movie was printed on it. It occurred to me that a new carpet must be manufactured for every premiere.

Then, policemen stopped traffic, parting the waters long enough for you and Rafael to cross toward the pen of jostling fans. I watched as the two of you moved along the metal barrier, pausing to sign autographs, tilting your heads to pose for photos. You were completely exposed, at the mercy of the mob. Whose idea was this? What member of your public relations team had decided that touching heads with strangers on Hollywood Boulevard was good for your image? To my consternation, the photographers followed you across the street. Rafael threw an arm around you and squeezed, planted a photogenic kiss on your forehead. You were so airy in your sheath of white, just a trace of a person. I saw the labor it took just to inhabit your name. Watching you and Rafael posing together, I understood that you were no different from the red carpets—thrilling, but ultimately disposable, interchangeable. The only real sovereignty belonged to the producers, the jowly, deep-pocketed men in black suits. The only real freedom belonged to the writers and directors.

By the time we filed into the theater, I was exhausted. I sank into my seat at the rear with the other minions. The movie itself was generic sci-fi, visually luscious but formulaic. Your role consisted mainly of searching gazes held in camera close-ups, whereas Rafael was the galaxy explorer, discoverer of your planet, barking commands to his crew and clenching his jaw.

At the after-party, I stood alone near the food table while you held court in a banquette with Rafael. There was an ice sculpture, and a jazz quartet on a revolving stage. I recognized the narrow-faced actress who came up to your table—the French starlet, Mireille Sauvage, leaning in to kiss Rafael on both cheeks. She wore a sheer layered gown that showed the outline of her breasts and buttocks, and I saw Rafael's hands travel down her back as she pushed into him. It was clear, as if I were watching a scene in a movie, what would happen between them, if it hadn't already. I could see the dress dropped candidly to the floor, the languor with which he'd pull her astride him on the bed.

I watched as Mireille Sauvage slid into your banquette, as Rafael poured champagne into her glass. I reached nervously toward a garnished platter and pinched a crab roll between my fingers. I watched you crane past Rafael in your white envelope dress, a piece of your hair escaping from its clip as you smiled and said something pleasant to Mireille.

The table was weighted with food, but no one else seemed to be eating. I finished the crab roll, and as I took another, a man came up to the table. I glimpsed dark hair, unevenly cut, shaggy over the ears. He slouched in a way that suggested he was not an actor in the film. He put an empanada on his plate and shot a sideways glance at me.

"I really don't like these things," he said.

I swallowed. "Empanadas?"

"No, these parties."

"Oh," I said and took an empanada for myself. He stood, waiting for me to continue, and I thought of something to say. "Why are you here, then? I mean, what's your connection to the film?"

"I'm a camera guy, but I finagled a plus-one from the DP." I detected an accent in his voice, though I couldn't place it. He faced me and stared. "You?"

"I'm, uh, a friend of one of the actors." My face heated, and I wished I had a drink in my hand.

He kept staring. "Which one?"

"Elise Van Dijk," I breathed. I thought of adding, *I live in her house,* but stopped myself. I glanced at the banquette where you sat pressed against Rafael, your hair still artfully arranged over your shoulder.

The man didn't respond but put a whole empanada in his mouth. A long moment passed as I waited for him to finish chewing. Very likely, he had nothing else to say to me. He'd just walk away, and I'd stay shuffling at the table until it was time to leave. A kind of nervous plaque had been building in me all evening, and I realized it would actually be a tremendous luxury to have a meaningless conversation right now, just to sit down with a drink and talk about anything.

There was something about this man, or his low status, that put me at ease.

As if attuned to my thoughts, he finished swallowing the food and said, "I'm going to the bar, do you want to come?"

"Sure."

"I'm Paul," he said, loping beside me. "I was watching you before and wondering if you came with the Solar crew."

"The Solar crew? Uh, so to speak, I guess."

"How do you know Elise?" Again, the sideways look. I entertained the suspicion that he might be in love with you, might be angling to get closer. That was how it happened in Hollywood, I imagined. Even camera guys hoped to swivel into the orbits of stars, hoped that one serendipitous contact might lead to a promotion to director of photography and to an affair with Elise Van Dijk.

"I've known her since we were kids," I said.

"Really? Well, she seems nice," he said. "Still untainted, you know? What would you like to drink?"

"Gin and tonic, please."

I watched him as he talked to the bartender. His suit was the right size but didn't seem to fit. There was a looseness to his movements, as if his joints were slightly misaligned, and the shine in his hair didn't seem to be from styling gel, but from natural oils. The skin at his chin and neck was irritated pink.

"I was hoping you'd talk to me," he said as he handed me the drink.

"Well it doesn't take much." I put my lips to the straw and channeled the first jeweled string of quinine and juniper. I took another, longer sip and felt the cold bloom at my chest.

"Let's sit, if you don't mind sitting," Paul said.

He led me past the stage, away from the music, to a lounge area. The men were young and dart-eyed in colorful shirts and skinny belts. There were only a few women among them, dramatically leaning. They all seemed to be doing more looking than talking. By the time I sat on an ottoman, I'd nearly finished my drink.

"So, friend of Elise Van Dijk's, what brings you to this place? I'm guessing you're from Michigan, too, if you knew her back when. But you're not in the industry, are you."

I was momentarily stunned to hear the word "Michigan," but I reminded myself that this was common knowledge about you. The humble midwestern girl making it big. The rough gem, refreshingly real.

"No," I conceded. "I'm not in the industry."

"So just here for moral support? Or on vacation?"

"A little of both." My drink was now drained, even the juice sucked from the lime carcass. I didn't know what else to say. I wasn't used to talking to new people. You'd mediated nearly all of my introductions in L.A. and, excluding my cash register interactions at Meijer, I'd hardly spoken to a stranger independently since college. Now I remembered the suffocating sensation that sometimes came over me, the feeling of being trapped inside hard layers, like a Russian nesting doll.

But Paul didn't push. We just sat, angled away from each other on ottomans. He didn't cross his legs the way most of the men here did: ankle to knee. Instead, he leaned forward, forearms on thighs, like someone waiting for a bus. He seemed to be concentrating, listening critically to the music.

When he looked back toward me, I asked, "So what's your camera job?"

He straightened up, pushed a strip of hair off his forehead. "I load the film."

"Oh."

"It's more complicated than it sounds."

"I believe you."

He explained the importance of loading film correctly. One mistake could lead to hours of wasted shooting. On digital films, he took care of all the data. He'd been working cameras for years now and enjoyed the cooperation and camaraderie of the crew. There was a rigid hierarchy that he'd learned to appreciate, each worker adding his stealth contribution to the apparatus, subordinating himself to the whole. Working on *Vespers* had been particularly enjoyable, he told me; the stars had been interesting to watch. He was a bit of an anthropologist, he explained, observing the behavior of industry people from the inside.

"And I'm a filmmaker, too," he added softly. "I do my own stuff."

This, I imagined, was true of every man in L.A. But there was a smolder in his look as he glanced away from me and took a drink.

"Tell me," I said.

"I'm making a documentary about Central American refugees. At least I'm planning to, when I get the funding."

He looked across the room as he said this, toward your banquette. Perhaps it was nothing to blame him for. It was hard for me not to look, too.

"By the way, we have something in common," he said. "I'm also from Michigan."

I was instantly suspicious. He didn't look or speak like anyone I'd known in Michigan. If anything, his accent sounded European.

"No, you're not," I said.

He smiled, and there was real pleasure in his face. "I really am. You don't believe me?" He held up a hand, palm out, fingers together, in the mitten shape every Michigander knows. He pointed to a spot halfway up the western shore, the base of the pinkie finger. "Right here."

My own town was on the western shore, too, at the spring of the lifeline. My surprise must have been visible, because he said, "We can talk more about it next time."

After I gave him my number, he stood from his ottoman and put out a hand. I shook it, still sitting, and watched him go across the room, past the jazz band, to the exit.

VI.

WHEN I thought of Michigan now, the kitchen linoleum and freezing rain, I shuddered. I looked out your guest room window to the vibrant, replenishing vista and felt as if I were balanced on a threshold, in danger of falling back into the past. In Michigan, the sun had been permanently blocked by clouds, the trees bare by November. The low-wattage bulbs put an anemic cast on everything inside the house. Stains on the paisley couch. Scuffed baseboards. The artificial Christmas tree and its yellow tinsel.

I'd called home only a few times in these past weeks—on Sunday mornings, when I knew my parents wouldn't be there. I'd left the requisite messages on the answering machine, putting a casual tune into my voice. "Sorry I missed you! Everything's great out here. California is beautiful. I'll try you again soon. Hope all's well."

I hadn't answered my mother's quavering rings on my phone. As her messages played back in my ear, her voice had a wheedling, sucking quality that returned me to my earlier self. I remembered the bad days in Michigan, the bad years, wilting in unwashed bedsheets. I feared that speaking to her would somehow yank me back there, that it would pop the balloon that encased me. As long as I remained disconnected, I could float on the breeze of this daydream, extend it indefinitely.

"I'm working now," I chirped into my parents' answering machine. "I'm doing some administrative stuff for Elise, getting to know the movie industry. I'll try you again later."

My mother's response, on my voicemail: "Thanks for calling. We're glad everything's okay. Call back, please, when you can. We want to talk to you."

As concerned as they purported to be, at heart they must have been relieved. At last, I'd pulled out from the dark undertow they'd assumed to be permanent. They didn't care that I'd stolen the money to get here. I'd done them a favor by leaving. Their disappointment in me had long surpassed their atrophied frustration with Shelby. The one who'd exploded, the one who'd imploded. The one who'd bolted, the one who'd sunk.

Here, I was a new person. Just as you'd left Michigan far behind, Elise, so had I. The sunshine of California made everything easier. My moods were generally lighter, less abruptly volatile. For weeks now, I'd avoided the trapdoor of anxiety. Even my artwork was different. I was using brighter colors, expanding beyond dream visions to create imaginative scenes. I drew the hedge maze from my old story, the one you loved, about the abducted girl. I drew the two of us as children, dressed as animals: you as a zebra, me as a goat.

Perhaps inevitably, you found my drawings. I thought I'd put them away, but it's possible I'd left them out that day. Subconsciously, I may have done it on purpose. I was angry—having been abandoned again while you went to the Rhizome—and had gone to Venice for my own self-guided Perrenian session. You were in my room when I came back, standing at the glossy black desk. The drawing on top of the pile, the one you were looking at, depicted a red-haired woman adrift at sea, clinging to a plank of wood. For a moment, I held my breath. When you turned your head toward me, there was a startled look in your eye, as if I were the intruder.

"Holy shit, Abby," you said.

I moved reflexively toward the drawings. "I'm sorry. I thought I put those away."

You shook your head, staring. "No. Don't put them away. These are incredible. Why haven't you shown them to me?"

"I don't know," I mumbled. "You've been busy."

"You're unbelievable, Abby. Really. You're so freaking talented. You always were, from the beginning." You gave me a look somewhere between fear and pity. "How long have you been doing these?"

"I don't know. Years."

Your head tilted, and before I could think, I was telling you the truth. "Actually, I dropped out of U of M," I said. "I never went to graduate school. I made that up so you wouldn't know I was at home all that time. I was at home, doing this," I gestured to the drawings. "And I've been following Perren's program, independently. I have his book."

I felt the shame of a child admitting a lie, and waited for the consequence. Irrationally, I felt that I'd invaded your space by admitting my involvement with Perren, when really it was you who'd invaded mine.

You came toward me and put your arms around my neck as if to slow dance. "Why are you hiding your gifts, Abby?" you said quietly. "All these years, you've been hiding, haven't you? But now you're here. Now you have to come out. Do you understand me?"

I nodded. You tilted your head, your face so close to mine, as if you would kiss me. I smelled smoke and the sweetness of alcohol on your breath.

"These ideas, these pictures, they can't just stay in this room. You have to get them out into the world."

I shrugged. "Yeah. Well, that's not so easy to do."

You held my shoulders and blinked at me. "Maybe I can help you."

My face reddened, and I pulled away. My earlier feeling of animosity toward you had dissolved, or I'd lost my grasp on it. "How was your time at the Rhizome?" I asked, moving toward the desk, blocking the drawings with my body.

"Great," you said. "I'm totally spent, but in a good way." You sat on the bed in your burlap dress with embroidered feathers, your hair in two loose braids. "I'm supposed to keep practicing at home, but I can never find the time. Or maybe it's not really that I don't have time. It's more that I feel self-conscious doing it by myself. I like it better at the Rhizome, with my guide telling me what to do."

You looked so young and helpless, there on the bed in your silly ensemble, that I almost felt sorry for you. The Rhizome was far above your level, and Perren was in a different orbit. You weren't creative in the slightest, and you were wasting your time. It seemed unfair to allow actors to join the Rhizome at all, when they were inherently unequipped for the work.

You'd stopped talking and were looking intently at me. "Seriously, Abby, think about how I might help you. I'm willing to make introductions. I'm sure I could arrange an internship somewhere. I might be able to talk to someone in the costume department at Paramount or the camera people, if you want to go that route." You paused, then said, "Or, you could always try to be a PA, but that's so competitive. So many people come here to try to break into the business."

I looked back at you in disbelief. It seemed impossible that you were unaware of the insult you were giving me. Having just seen my drawings, having recognized their value, you had the temerity—or ignorance—to suggest an internship in the costume department. I blinked rapidly, as if to clear the implications from my mind. If I considered the injustice, the outrageous condescension, it would be too great to swallow.

You stood from the bed. "Hey. Your birthday's coming up, isn't it?"

"Next week."

"I always remember it," you said.

My anger softened a bit. "I always remember yours, too."

On the morning of my twenty-eighth birthday, I found myself in your blue Mustang, winding inland on Malibu Canyon Road. You hadn't told me where we were going. I pictured some secret restaurant in the woods, where you could order a bottle of champagne in honor of my birthday and drink it yourself without being seen. We pulled off onto an unmarked, unpaved driveway that stretched through the trees. At the end of the driveway stood a tall, ivy-covered stone building, crenellated like a manor house. I recognized it at once. I blinked and shook my head. It was the stone building from my loveseat dream—the place where I'd finally found you. A chill spread through me, and goose bumps came to my arms.

"What is this place?" I asked softly as I climbed out of the car.

"Any guesses?"

You parked between a Mercedes sedan and a Mercedes SUV. We walked wordlessly to the entrance, a massive arched door, and you pressed the buzzer. The door magically unlatched, and we stepped into a marble lobby. A grand staircase swept upward. You took my hand and led me to the reception desk, where a willowy young woman flashed a smile at us.

"I brought a special guest today," you said. "It's her birthday, and I'd like to give her a day pass to the grounds and spa and an introductory guided session."

"Oh!" exclaimed the receptionist, looking at me. "What a wonderful birthday gift!"

The goose bumps were still on my skin as pleasure and fear rushed through my body. I opened my mouth, but nothing emerged.

"Okay, sweetie," the receptionist said to me. "Just sign in here."

I glanced at you, and you nodded, smiling at me like a mother as I wrote my name in the Rhizome ledger.

"I'll get her set up with Tello," the receptionist told you. "He's got an open slot at twelve, same time as your session, Elise. Room seven."

"Come on." You put a hand on my shoulder. "Let's get manicures and massages first."

We went through the foyer, our footsteps echoing off the marble walls, and came outside into a landscaped courtyard with a triple-tiered fountain. The sound of splashing water lent the garden an enchanted quality. I could picture nymphs emerging from the foliage, holding immortal fruit.

"Oh, I want to show you something," you said. "This way." You led me to a wall of boxwood and took me into a slot in the hedge. Before us were more hedges, intersecting paths. "What do you think? Left, right, or forward?" You still held my hand, and pulled me to the path on the left. When we finally came to a dead end, you laughed and spun me around. "It's like your story about the woman with the hedge maze," you said. "Remember? And the little girl who wants to stay with her."

A breeze of joy passed through me. I gripped your hand and didn't feel the ground under my feet as we went through the maze, losing direction. At last we came out on the other side, into a tropical copse. Agave plants splayed their limbs among purple verbena. A wave of honeysuckle overtook me, and from far off, I heard the sound of children.

"Are there kids here?"

"Oh, yeah. There are always kids around. There's a camp in the summer and after-school sessions and a daycare. It's all free for members. People even bring their babies here."

You led me over a winding path to the spa, a separate stone structure that contained a nail salon, massage rooms, and a sauna. We visited each of these in order. I didn't tell you that it was my first manicure. You sat beside me with your ivory hand extended like a duchess's. After my own nails had been scrubbed and clipped and the polish applied—a seafoam green that you chose for me—I kept my fingers motionless for five minutes beneath a heat lamp and tried to lose myself in the ocean sounds pulsing from the speakers.

"It's almost time for our sessions," you said afterward. "They take about an hour, but I'll probably stop in the actors' lounge afterward. Maybe you can have someone give you a tour in the meantime? You can ask the receptionist."

Back inside the main building, we climbed the grand staircase carpeted in a pattern of black and violet knots. At the top, we paused at a tall doorway.

"This is the actors' lounge," you whispered. The room had sheer curtains and low velvet daybeds. Handsome men and women sprawled, some of them recognizably famous. They barely seemed to register our presence.

As we withdrew, I spoke softly. "Are they here for Perren? I mean, are they hoping to catch his eye and get cast in a movie?"

"No, I don't think so. I found out that it's actually the guides who make that happen. Somebody was telling me that the guides are his talent scouts, in a way—that they recommend the artists they think have the most creative depth and scope, or whatever. They're Perren's gatekeepers, I guess you could say."

I was quiet as we went down the long corridor, following the dizzying carpet pattern, knots interlocking with knots. "Well, what does your guide think of you?" I ventured.

You glanced at me. "I'm a work in progress, let's put it that way," you said and stopped at one of the doors. "This is my room. I'll see you back downstairs later?"

"I'll wait in the garden by the pool," I offered, to show my equanimity.

I continued down the hall until I found a door with the number 7. I knocked softly and turned the handle. Suddenly, all the questions I hadn't asked you shot to the surface like panicked fish. The room was small and narrow with a window at its far end. There were two wooden spindle chairs, facing each other. A man sat on one of these chairs and stood as I entered.

"Abigail?"

I felt weightless, my heart speeding uselessly like a rabbit caught in the open. "You can call me Abby."

"I'm Tello." He was middle-aged, with close-shaven hair and an ovoid face. When he smiled, there was warmth in his eyes, which were small and dark with no visible sclera. This small detail lent him a puppet-like, oracular look. "Have a seat, please," he said, gesturing to the chair across from his.

I positioned myself on the uncushioned chair and felt its hard spindles against my back.

"Today we'll keep it simple," Tello said. "I'll take you through your first active imagination session."

I strained to keep my back straight. As I sat, I struggled with a mix of excitement and shame. It felt oddly public to be sitting this way in front of another person, rather than by myself in my childhood bedroom. And yet it was electrifying to pursue Unity Gain right here, in the very building where Perren had his own sessions, his own visions.

"As we go through the session, you'll witness your inner self, and as your guide, I'll witness your outer self." Tello lifted a panel in the wall and pressed an invisible button, filling the room with a wash of harmonious sound—an intimation of ocean and wind, with the low bassoon notes of a foghorn. "Please close your eyes," he directed, "and witness as light and shape take form in front of you."

I closed my eyes and stared at the dark sheet behind my lids. The dim molecules that skimmed past at first were always vague and fleeting.

"Do you see?"

I nodded.

"Rub your eyes. Are the shapes stronger now? Do you see the checkerboard patterns, the black-and-white geometry?" He paused. "Now, watch it all dissolve and turn colored . . ."

It always happened that way, just as he described it. As I took my hands away from my eyes, the op-art canvas erupted before me, an elaborate grid taking rapid form and pulling apart.

"Now, watch the pieces of the checkerboard slide out of sight. Choose a piece and follow it. See where it leads you."

This was the hardest part. I waited for one of the fragments to draw my attention. The shapes traded places, assumed stronger contours, until the amphitheater of my eyelids showcased a fox-trot of orange crescents and white bars, all bubbling from some inner turbine. I snapped to the awareness that this was how dreaming began, and at the same instant my awareness became a searchlight that bleached the images out. It was paradoxical to be both performer and audience at once. But then a yellow sphere appeared, rising from a black sea. As I watched, the sea became a river, and the sphere was the setting sun. I was on the sidewalk in Ann Arbor, going toward the bridge, the traffic intersection, the medical center looming ahead. I saw the falling snow. I saw the cars approaching with their headlights.

Tello interjected, "Don't force the imagery. Just sit back and be the audience. Watch what's presented to you."

I reversed course, walked backward away from the bridge, erased the scene. I drew down a dark curtain, aware of myself sitting on the chair, rigidly inert. My back ached as I watched the roulette of microbes on the black background. After a few moments, one of them abruptly grew in size, turned fishlike, and swam out of the frame. Instantly, the scene changed.

"Stay open," Tello said. "Witness."

There was a bush with red leaves. It looked familiar, like the burning bush in my childhood Bible. And now a snake, banded black and yellow, gliding under the bush. *Archetypal*, my labeling brain intruded. The snake and bush trembled and then hurtled away as if the film had been yanked off the reel. My eyes opened. Tello sat in the spindle chair with a little grin on his face.

"Excellent start," he said, as if he presumed to know the content of my visualization. My face heated. "Try again."

I closed my eyes.

"Same thing," he said. "Rub your eyes, then choose a compelling fragment and go with it."

This time, white nodules like snowfall—afterglow from the recessed ceiling lights—organized themselves into rows. They became fish, swimming in a choreographed school. It was warm in the water, and I found a whiskered bottom-dwelling creature that was large enough to ride. I rested on its scales as it took me through shadowed pockets. It rose to the water's lambent surface, then dove again into the murk. Finally, a last burst to the surface, and my eyes opened to the powerful beam of the sun atop a hill. The sun became the white house from my dreams, and I was in the blue lake below.

"You may be experiencing water imagery," Tello chimed in. "That's very common."

I ignored him and climbed the hill to the house. The door was blue, with a bronze knocker in the shape of a head. On either side of the head, where the ears should be, were wings. The children were there in the parlor, perched on the gilded couch and pink damask wing chairs. They smiled at me in recognition, and my heart swelled.

"Go into the water, if you see it," Tello prompted.

A tiny girl with black curls gestured to a chair and nodded. The children watched me as I came into the room and sat. The little girl opened her hands and flashed light into my eyes. I blinked and found Tello beaming in the chair, saw his black-marble irises.

"That was an excellent session. You have a lot of potential, Abby."

"How do you know?"

"I've been doing this for a while. I can always tell."

Despite myself, I blushed. I thought of telling him that it wasn't technically my first session, that I'd been following Perren's program for years. But it was nicer to be seen as a prodigy, to feel the old valedictorian's pride.

"I hope to see you again for another session." He presented me with a handsome leather journal with an embossed eye on the cover. "In the meantime, use this journal to capture rushes from the Spring: creative bursts, notable synchronicities and serendipities, or imagery from dreams."

I thanked him. I didn't mention that he'd just described what I'd been doing my entire life.

Back downstairs at the reception desk, I asked timidly for a tour, and within minutes a young ponytailed woman named Tasha was leading me back up the staircase. She launched without preamble into a description of the children's camp and the daycare center.

"I don't know if you have kids yet, but even if you don't, you should know about these programs. I'm a daycare provider here, so I'm partial." She smiled with her strong white California teeth. "I can't wait to have my own babies someday. I'm even more excited about it, knowing that there's such wonderful child care here."

Tasha opened the door to a room arrayed with miniature tables and art supplies. "This is the art room for the day camp," Tasha said. A woman was in the process of collecting watercolor paintings from a drying rack. The woman smiled at Tasha and held up one of the paintings, a blue-and-black swirl like a whirlpool with a vaguely human form in the center. "The kids have access to all kinds of materials, and they're encouraged to draw and paint their dream imagery."

Tasha took the stack of paintings from the woman and handed them to me. They were flamboyant and crude: herds of red antelopes, plumes of confetti, jewel-toned anemones. Oddly marvelous, they yanked at my heart.

"Aren't they fabulous?" Tasha said. "Those are by the preschoolers. Wouldn't it be great if we could all be like that? The kids who spend time here have a better chance of strengthening their connection to the Spring for the long term and becoming lifelong creators. Usually the older they get, the more they restrict and censor themselves, and the less interesting their creations become. That doesn't really happen here."

Tasha took me down the hall to the daycare center.

"Of course, with babies the connection to the Spring is still primal. Nothing has interfered with it yet." She lowered her voice to a whisper as she opened the door to a room with rows of cribs. The walls were painted beige, and there were no decorations, no musical mobiles. "Their surroundings are kept simple on purpose, to cut down on distractions. This is where I work."

Together, we wound through the rows of cribs, each with a sleeping or quietly wiggling occupant. I said nothing, but felt an unexpected shift inside me, a kind of raw unfurling.

"I wish my parents had brought me here when I was a baby. I'd be a totally different person," Tasha sighed. "I'm an actress, but I feel like I've gotten a late start. So many of us adults are here because we're trying to reaccess our childhood creativity. How much better if we'd never lost it to begin with? Anyway, the Rhizome is letting me work here in exchange for guided sessions. It's a great arrangement, and I'm humbled to be part of such a high-quality operation. They evaluate everyone for creative talent. People have to include portfolios and screen tests with their applications, so everyone who works here is top-notch, and really, really cares. The full-timers are phenomenal. Some even work overnight shifts, so that people can leave their children for longer periods when they need to. I can't imagine a better place to bring a child."

We'd stopped in front of a crib where a small infant lay splayed in a starfish shape. The name LINCOLN was engraved on the brass nameplate on the crib. Tasha gazed adoringly at the little figure. "Oh, I just love these babies so much," she said. "I get so attached to them, and then when one of them stops coming, it breaks my heart."

She pushed back a tendril of blond hair, and in her mirrored eyes I saw a pinprick of maternal need, deep and consuming.

Tasha led me through the corridor of private guide rooms and showed me the restaurant. Everywhere we went, I looked for Perren. It was possible that he was, at that moment, under this same roof. You'd told me that he visited every few months. It was possible.

After the tour, I was free to explore the grounds on my own. I roamed the courtyard and over the paths of the garden, stocked with flowering trees and junipers. I passed the spa and found a little stone building that appeared to be a boutique. I scouted all the way to the periphery of the property, or what I guessed was the periphery. There were no fences delineating the border, just an erosion into the surrounding terrain. Once I'd seen everything, I spent some time in the hedge maze. I walked all of its circuits, doubling back, until I lost my sense of direction. After several attempts, like a lab mouse, I learned the correct route.

At last, I lowered myself to a teak bench near the fountain and remained there in a kind of sublime oblivion as the minutes folded into each other. I closed my eyes and listened to the babble of the fountain, the crescendos of insects. I tried to picture Perren here. He could appear at any moment. He could come ambling down any of these paths, right toward me. I blurred my vision and waited for him to arrive. In my mind, I heard the rustle of leaves and the thud of steps approaching, saw the pale specter shimmering before me.

Instead, it was you who appeared, your hand raised to visor your eyes in the sunlight. For a moment I was worried for you, unguarded in public, but your gait was relaxed. Fame wasn't a liability in this place.

I stood from the bench. "How was your session?"

"Great. My guide thinks it was my best session yet. He said my dreams are deepening and I should pay special attention to their messages. He always tells me that dreams can be truer than life."

I pictured you with your guide, attempting to engage in active imagination, sitting quietly with your eyes closed. The idea struck me as preposterous. Even now, as you looked at me, your irises resembled gemstones, hard and impenetrable. They were meant not to mine but to be mined.

"What about you?" you asked after a moment. "What did you think of your session?"

"Oh, it was even better than I imagined."

You smiled broadly. "I'm so glad, Abby." I waited for you to ask for more details, but you just lifted your hair off your neck and said, "God, why am I always so *hot* in this place. Let's go swimming."

"I don't have a bathing suit," I said.

"That's all right. You can get one here."

"No, no," I said. "You can swim. I'll just watch."

"You're going to make me swim alone?"

You grasped my hand and took me over a path to the little stone boutique. Within moments you'd found a navy two-piece with sailor buttons and held it out to me. "This would be *perfect* on you. You'll look like Bettie Page."

"I think a one-piece would be more my speed."

"No, no. You have to at least try it on." You thrust the suit at me and parted the curtains to the dressing room. Helpless, I went in. I struggled out of my shirt, adhesive with sweat, and dropped my elasticized skirt to my feet. My breasts sprang out of their engineered bra, and I folded my underwear carefully to conceal the chalky smudge in the crotch. As I fought my way into the suit, I glanced at the price tag: $375. Perhaps there was a reason for the price, perhaps the designer was a magician, and this suit would do something for me that a cheaper suit couldn't.

I pulled back the velvet curtain and peeked out tentatively. "There's no mirror in here."

"Come out," you said. "I'll be your mirror."

I had no choice. I drew the curtain the whole way across and stood in front of you, with my pasty skin and dimpled thighs. I was thankful that at least I'd thought to shave my bikini line that morning. But until your eyes went to my midriff, I'd forgotten about my scar. I rarely even saw it anymore; it had become a familiar part of my body, stretching like an earthworm from sternum to pubic bone.

You hesitated, then said with forced exuberance, "That's adorable on you."

"Too bad about this hideous thing," I muttered quickly, waving a hand in front of my belly.

Your eyes struck mine, questioning. This would have been a chance to tell you about Ann Arbor, but I couldn't bear to ruin the moment, the day. And there would be no benefit in your knowing the truth, I decided. It would only shock you. You lacked the sophistication to understand it as an incident within the context of a deeper, more complex story. You wouldn't have been able to reconcile that kind of darkness with any person who was present in your life. Instead, I turned and went back behind the dressing room curtain. A throbbing had begun in my head, as if my heart had displaced my brain. I shivered in the air-conditioning, and my hands trembled at the buttons of the bathing suit.

"Don't change," you called to me. "Let's go straight into the water."

I came out still shivering, holding the bundle of clothes in front of me to cover the scar. If you asked, I decided I'd tell you the scar was from an appendectomy. Someday, maybe later, I'd tell you the real story, a gentle version of what happened, and I'd assure you that I felt much better now, thanks to you.

You went into the dressing room next and emerged in a crocheted bikini. I stopped shivering when I saw you. With your flawless skin and warm hair feathering your shoulder blades, you were thoroughly, outrageously a movie star. I could understand, looking back on your girlhood, how you'd attracted all of us like iron filings. I was weak just looking at you.

"Come," you said and waved to the salesclerk as we left the store.

"Don't we have to pay?"

"They'll put it on my tab. Happy birthday."

We walked in our suits over a narrow path that led to a hidden garden. I'd found it earlier and had assumed it was a frog pond. Dragonflies darted over the water's surface, a dark unchlorinated green. "It's a natural swimming pool," you explained as you dipped a toe in the water. "It blends with the environment and lets the plants do the filtering and cleaning, instead of chemicals."

The pool appeared deep enough to contain sea creatures. I imagined eels curled in a submerged forest, dusky fish with lidless eyes and needle teeth. You slipped a foot in, allowing your ankle to be swallowed, then your calf—and, with a shudder, you swung the other leg around and slid in completely. For a terrifying moment, your body plunged out of view, and I couldn't breathe as I imagined an omnivorous tendril circling your ankle and pulling you down. I forgot about my bundle of clothing and let it drop from my stomach to the ground. But then your satin head bobbed back up, followed by gleaming white shoulders, and you smiled at me.

VII.

I'D ALWAYS been the one with promise. Top of my class, ticket to anywhere. Or that's what they'd all assumed. It's easy to predict a straight path for others, a flat run for those with conspicuous abilities. It's easy to dismiss them that way. And it's more telling of the class of people I come from than anything else—this notion that just by unlocking the door to a real college I'd forever be handed key after key.

I shared this faith at first. I felt a burst of freedom as I left town, sailing east toward Ann Arbor in my loaded car. But in a clog of traffic around Lansing, the cars in front of me split and doubled. My lungs seemed to malfunction, the bottom halves suddenly defunct. I couldn't catch my breath, and it felt as if my head would balloon away. This kind of panic had sometimes awoken me at night but had never come in the daytime before. I pulled off the highway to a Sunoco, locked myself in the restroom, sat on the toilet, and gripped the handicap bar. The blood rushed so violently in my ears that I barely heard the knocking on the door. "Just a minute," I wheezed. I cranked paper towels from the dispenser, wiped the sweat from my face, splashed myself all over with water. I was red and blotched in the mirror, pupils dilated like a cornered animal's. I slunk out, shouldering past the old woman waiting outside, and with a dollar in my wet hand bought beef jerky. I sat in the car, chewing, until I could finally drive again.

The town dangled a welcome when I arrived that first day: the restaurants and shops gaily tailored to students, the giant football stadium so much like a womb. I would be all right, I told myself. I would let myself be hoisted by the collective pride of state and school, this institution's blind faith in my ability. But as the days progressed, the other students struck me as smugly contemptuous. Few seemed to be from Michigan. They were from places foreign to me—Chicago, Indianapolis, Boston. They were the children of psychiatrists and businessmen, and possessed of a team spirit that I couldn't understand, that seemed to be drawn from the ether.

When the leaves flipped their colors that first September, it was a personal betrayal, sleight of hand. Rather than slowly fading into gold and umber, the trees burned red. They surrounded the quad in a satanic circle. I sat on the grass and tried to quietly read the newspaper. A terrorist siege in Russia, children taken hostage with their parents. I turned the page. The Janjaweed, burning up villages. Students threw Frisbees around me and laughed on their way to the dining hall. I splayed on the ground, holding this collection of pages, this story of doom. The wet grass soaked my jeans.

I didn't take any film production or art classes that first semester, but tried to fulfill requirements. There was no time for drawing. Courses whose descriptions had seemed alluringly dense turned out to be simply incomprehensible. *Introduction to Critical Theory: We will examine core concepts of representation, aesthetics and identity, mimesis and the hegemony of political superstructures.* There were printouts of Heidegger, Lyotard, Derrida. My first essay was on the concept of the rhizome, of "multiplicity without unity," as put forth by Deleuze and Guattari. The authors insisted that the universe was to be understood in terms of dimensions without beginning or end, as growth and spillage from a kind of infinite *milieu.* They were hung up on the relationship between a certain type of orchid flower and wasp. This orchid grew a dark protuberance that mimicked the appearance of a wasp, luring other wasps into attempts at copulation, thus pollinating the orchid itself. This wasn't trickery, the authors insisted, but an "aparallel evolution of two beings" that represented something much larger, more universal, rhizomatic. "A veritable becoming, a becoming-wasp of the orchid and a becoming-orchid of the wasp."

This behavior was in direct contradiction to what I'd learned in my biology class about the cooperative behavior of insects: worker wasps devoting themselves to the colony, slowly building the nest from wood pulp, collectively raising the brood. Only in rare instances did a worker revolt or a subservient female usurp a queen's nest. For the most part, hierarchy equaled harmony, productivity. Still, I was transfixed by the image of a solitary wasp courting its orchid. I could envision the strange collision of the species; I could appreciate its sinister elegance. And, despite the dense theoretical text, the idea of the rhizome resonated with me. When I dreamed, I felt the truth of it. I knew, as I slipped away from consciousness, that I was abandoning finitude. In dreaming, I tapped into a perpetual multiplicity. Perhaps the unconscious mind was orchidlike, folded inward, multiform—and consciousness was the vulgar protuberance that jutted from it, intent on dissemination.

I was excited by the thought, but awake at my desk I found it nearly impossible to express. I banged words together, but they slipped from me, and nothing I wrote made sense. I feared that it was futile to wrangle language into such profundity, and I'd lose my sanity if I kept trying. Gilles Deleuze, I knew, had ultimately leaped from his apartment window in Paris. I turned the essay in, unfinished.

When I met with my adviser in December, I was clammy with sweat. I'd chosen a brown cabled sweater, serious and modest, as if that would help. I sat in the visitor's chair and delivered the preface I'd prepared. I'd carefully chosen words that would obscure the fact that I was a fraud who never should have been admitted to the university.

"Lacan, Deleuze, the films of Perren, the dual nature of consciousness . . ."

"But, Abigail, you haven't completed a single paper in any of your classes."

I stammered to explain what was wrong.

He interrupted. "You intend to major in screen arts and cultures?" I nodded, and he looked at me for a heavy beat. "You may consider taking time off. In fact, I insist you do. Reconsider your goals." He leaned back in his chair ostentatiously, flaunting his leisure, his job security, and dismissed me with a Jedi koan: "Let the work find you."

My stomach plummeted, a feeling that persisted through my afternoon seminar, Cult Films of the 1960s and '70s, where my classmates sustained a slack discussion of *Beyond the Valley of the Dolls*. I couldn't listen. I could only gird myself against the sensation of falling through a trapdoor, my stomach dropping again and again.

The darkness was coming; I could feel it. I scurried across campus, and in my dorm cell I attempted one more essay, on the topic of Lacan's mirror stage: the tragic moment in a child's life when she becomes aware of herself as a thing in the world. I wrote a five-page paragraph with no breaks, about self-consciousness as a cruel splitting, the end of animalistic innocence. *Is the infant mortal before the mirror stage, or is the mirror stage fatal in itself?* I was in tears by the end of it and didn't print it out.

There was a liquor store known for selling to minors, and that's where I went in my parka to buy Jim Beam. While my roommate sat on the other side of the dorm room, face awash in the dead blue light of her laptop, I drank bourbon from my travel coffee mug in bed until I slumped into sleep, dreaming of fingers growing from the ground, trees with razor-blade leaves.

In the daytime, the darkness in me deepened. I was repelled by the riot of sound in the campus mailroom, the pinched faces of my peers, milling at their mailboxes in aggressively puffy jackets. They all pushed into me. My head thundered, and my chest knotted. I felt my head drift up above the crowd. I tried to believe I'd become truly absent, that I was in the mailroom spectrally, a disembodied mind.

A professor needed me to do research over the Christmas holiday, I told my parents, and because they didn't know what questions to ask, they had to believe me. The dorms closed, and leftover students—those without families, those too poor to buy plane tickets—moved into discounted rooms at the Red Roof Inn. It might have been a cozy arrangement, an orphanage of sorts, but I couldn't pay even the discounted rate, so I swapped cat sitting for shelter in a grad-student complex off campus. I brought my clip-on lamp, my backrest, my blanket and bourbon, and closed the drapes. The sun didn't try to penetrate the cloud cover, which was a shroud of white felt. The felt turned to gray in the afternoon, then to charcoal, then black. Overhead, a fluorescent light rattled like a pit viper.

Christmas came, a weak faraway jingle. The new year slid in. One of Perren's older films was playing at the art house cinema. I went by myself, one of five people in the audience. I'd never seen Perren in a theater, on such a grand scale, and I was in such a fragile state that it pulled me deeper into the darkness. The film soundtrack was a dissonant roar, a haunting melody trickling beneath—and that melody, that incessant *drip-drop*, wouldn't leave me for days. The Perrenian spell, the black magic I'd always welcomed, had this time been cast at a lethal angle.

In the morning, the newspaper. An earthquake had shaken the other half of the world, followed by a tsunami, removing 200,000 human lives from the planet. An "undersea megathrust" in the circum-Pacific belt, the Ring of Fire. Tectonic plates shifting to get comfortable. I stared at the word EARTHQUAKE in the enlarged headline font, the letter Q with its fanciful tail. I stared at the number—200,000—and at the photographs. A mound of waterlogged bodies. A child's hand thrust out from under the rubble.

The last cord holding me together snapped. All I remember after that was the underside of my synthetic down comforter, the clip-on lamp craning to leer at me in bed, the padded backrest like a headless torso. And then, the cold. The sky, yawning open. The stars' sharp crystals. The buildings across the bridge, paper cutouts. And me, a roving shadow with no birth, death, or knowledge, following the sidewalk onto the bridge. My feet, bare in the snow, the Huron River half-frozen beneath. Then, the leap into the *milieu*. Like Deleuze, I felt the grip of gravity, that authority. The plunge. The crack of the ice, the multiple entryways, the frigid water. Spirituality, physicality. Life, death.

Then, all at once, I was home.

I'd dreamed of the bridge ever since. The dream was always the same. Again and again, I walked barefoot in the snow. I looked down at myself and recognized my pajama top from Ann Arbor, the falling snowflakes layering the flannel. I saw the Christmas decorations. I heard the roar in my head, like radio interference, and the scrape of my breath. I felt the numbness in my feet, more hot than cold. I watched my hands unbutton my pajama top, exposing the valley between my breasts to the street. Again and again, I stepped onto the bridge and saw the headlights approach. Again and again, I leaped, and awoke with thunder in my ears.

Now, in your library in Malibu, I put my face to the pages of a book about mythology, and inhaled. I was alive, not dead in the river. I was holding a book. I'd survived. You were reading, too, on the patio. You'd showed me your paperback copy of *Slouching Towards Bethlehem*. It was about the desert, you said, all the weirdness that happens out there. You wore a sun hat, a crocheted top that bared your shoulders, and a pair of cropped cigarette pants—and as you pulled on your big black sunglasses in a dismissive motion, you were the simulacrum of a young Joan Didion.

For hours, I read by the window. I learned that the Egyptians thought the spirit—a bird with a human head—left the body during sleep and received revelatory messages. They believed that dreams were the siblings of death, and yet their term for "dream" was synonymous with "waking," represented by a hieroglyphic of an open eye. Some dreams were deceptive and some were true, depending on whether they came through a gate of ivory or horn. A full moon was a sign of forgiveness; a large cat meant a good harvest. There was an oddly common dream of eating feces. And my heart caught when I came to this: "Immersion into cold water is considered a sign of absolution for all ills."

In the section on the Greeks, I found a reference to Hesperia, the ancient land of the west, at the farthest edge of the world. I read about the river nymph Hesperia, dead from a snakebite while fleeing Aesacus, who loved her. In grief, Aesacus threw himself from a cliff into the sea, but was transformed into a bird before hitting water. His suicidal wish has been perpetuated forever after by seabirds diving into the water again and again.

Together, we drove out to the Mojave so that you could absorb some essence of Joan. On the way there, you told me about her life, how she'd spent much of it in Malibu with her husband and daughter. Both were tragically gone now. But the time they'd spent together had been so beautiful, you said. She and her husband had written their books independently but collaborated on screenplays. You handed me your phone, showing a photograph of the family on their deck overlooking the ocean. I couldn't stop looking at it. The cigarette between two fingers, the drink balanced on the weathered wooden railing. The sideways glance—the ephemerality and permanence of a moment caught on film—this delicate triumvirate perched between land and sea. I wanted a photograph of us like that someday. I hoped that you and I would be collaborating, too, before long, and I'd be looking at the camera head-on, asserting myself as your partner.

"It's hard to imagine ever being like that," you said quietly. "So much at home, with Rafael, or anyone."

"Just because you can't imagine it doesn't mean it can't happen," I said, ever the supportive friend. What I didn't say was that if you failed to imagine it, this was only because your imagination was chronically lacking. I had enough imagination for both of us.

We stopped at a café near Joshua Tree, where an old California flag hung on the wall over the counter—the lumbering brown bear forever in search of sustenance. We sat together at a little table by the window and drank coffee, the way you thought Joan might do. You quietly watched the passing cars in a way that was probably meant to be ruminative. I sat there until you were done with whatever you were doing. After that, we kept driving west, into blank space, past hopping gnatcatchers and creosote, jumbles of ancient rock.

As we drove, I remembered the dream I'd had the previous night, about a woman who goes for a swim in her backyard pool and stays there. Her husband tries to lure her out, but she won't leave the water. She spends the night and the rest of the week submerged. I'd drawn it out on paper before we left that morning. Already, I could see it as a film, with you in the starring role.

"I have a story for you," I began, in the passenger seat.

You glanced at me from behind your sunglasses and said, "Sorry. I'm trying to be in character right now. If you don't mind, it would be great to just be quiet for a while."

I sat silent after that, peering over the dashboard. I didn't want to look at you, for fear of betraying my irritation or, worse, appearing to need attention. I also didn't want to see your face right now, as you pretended to be in character. It would only repel me.

Somewhere along Route 62, we got out of the car and walked into the desert, in different directions. The sun was ruthless, impressing a sense of danger with each step I took away from the road. The heat was primordial, baking through my skin, drying my muscle and bones, desiccating everything but my darkest, wettest core. A tawny lizard darted past, feeling the air with its tongue, then froze and faded into the surrounding rubble until it was only a blinking eyelid. I'd seen this same lizard in a dream, I believed. It had darted and frozen before me, in just the same way. I'd walked over this same ground before. My eye traveled ahead and lit upon the dark spot on the ground, just where I sensed it would be. I lifted the stone, which was elaborately notched and almost too hot to touch. I knew this rock, and knew it was a meteorite placed here for me. I put it in my pocket and went back to the car.

"God, I am so ready to start filming," you said as we headed back on Route 10, toward Palm Springs. You were, apparently, no longer in character. "Don't get me wrong. The prep's been great, but it's intense. This film's so different from the others I've done. It demands a lot more. I've never been so immersed in a script." You took your hands off the steering wheel and stretched your arms. "It's hard to get back into my own skin. It feels like I'm in character all the time. Especially since practically all my Rhizome sessions have been in service of it. But it's really cool, too, kind of like living through an era I never got to experience." You glanced at me. "The sixties seem like ancient history now, know what I mean?"

I nodded.

"And the best part is that it's helped my relationship with Raf." Your voice dropped. "Seriously, the sex is so amazing right now. I mean, it always was. That's one of the things I'm addicted to, to be honest." You laughed. "But it's gone to a whole other level. Ever since I got this job, it's been different. Partly because I'm more confident, I think. And I feel like the Rhizome sessions have put me in better tune with my body and cycles. We've been using the rhythm method, old-school style, and it's so much better that way. It's natural and kind of risky, and just *hot*."

As you spoke, I felt a spiking sensation under my skin. I didn't want to hear any of it. I tried to tune out your words while I studied the black stone in my hand. I marveled at its weight and warmth. It was solid and eternal, not of this world, burning with the patience of the ages. It would outlast your folly and my pain. It would outlast everything.

When filming finally began, you spent full days on the set. I loved watching you act. It was a revelation each time you began speaking, your body inhabited by some pliable force, your face alive with someone else's thoughts. You seemed to physically shrink in size, to become tiny Joan. You were, in fact, gifted. You possessed the uncanny ability to empty yourself at will, to serve as a receptacle for others to fill. Your tools of emulation were built into you, just as the tools of creation were built into people like Perren and me. Yours was the lesser role, but a crucial one, and one for which you were perfectly made.

I loitered behind the ranks of fatigued production assistants, and from time to time our eyes would meet, as if across a galaxy. After a few days of this, you told me to go home. If you needed me, you'd call. There was enough to do at the house, you said in your Didion voice.

In truth, there wasn't enough to do at the house. After food shopping and laundry, I had time to spare. I adopted the role of household chef, creating the midwestern dishes I thought you'd crave, slow-cooker stews and pot pies. I took landscape maintenance upon myself, hydrating the rosebushes and citrus trees within the water-use guidelines for drought. I discovered the names of the plants that you'd never learned. I removed the defunct wasp nest from the downspout, admiring the drab beauty of the fibrous gray swirls, the dark hole that led to hidden pavilions. Of the two of us, I was the observer of the natural world. I was the one who noticed the growth and decay always in flux around us, who perceived so many small noises at night. We were part of it, too, although we liked to consider ourselves superior—evolved and orderly. We liked to believe our consciousness gave us supremacy, but the truth was that we were animals, mysterious to ourselves.

VIII.

P AUL, FROM the *Vespers* after-party, called to ask if I'd
been to Topanga. The word struck me as invented, a
reference to some science-fiction universe. "I don't
know" seemed like a safe response.

"Topanga Canyon, just up the coast from where you are.
You haven't heard of it? It's where I live."

We made a plan for him to show me Topanga the next
day, when your schedule was clear and you wouldn't miss me.
We met at a coffee shop in Malibu. Paul stood just inside
the door in a white polyester shirt with vertical stripes like
prison bars. His jeans were a lighter shade than was fashion-
able, fastened by a silver oval belt buckle. I saw now that he
was several years older than I'd thought. He held out a hand
to me—unusual in this city of huggers—and I shook it.

"Do you want to get anything here," he said. "Or should
we just go?" This directness was also unusual, almost rude
in contrast with the cosmetic niceties that surrounded most
meetings.

He drove a red Chevy Cavalier with a ribbon of rust along its underside. He told me he'd bought it when he was ready to leave Michigan and that it was the first car he'd learned to drive.

"When did you leave?" I asked as we wound along Pacific Coast Highway.

"Ten years ago, when I was twenty-two."

"Is your family still in Michigan?"

He laughed. "Yes."

"What's funny?"

"I grew up in a funny place." He looked at me sideways as he drove.

"Didn't we all."

"No, really. Do you know Fremont?"

"I know where it is. My sister lives up near there."

"So maybe you know it has a big Amish community. That's me." He smiled at the windshield. "Or, I should say, that *was* me."

"You're Amish?"

"I was raised Amish, but I never officially joined the church. You have to choose to be baptized as an adult. I ran away to Hollywood instead."

I glanced at his profile. The nose was a little too flat, the chin too gibbous. His mouth curled into a grin, either from amusement at his unlikely admission or at the blatant lie he'd just told. "I don't know whether to believe you."

"Why not? We all come from someplace, and not all people decide to stay there. You didn't. For me, once I decided to leave, I wanted to really leave."

"I'm just having a hard time absorbing what you're telling me," I said. "I didn't think the Amish were fond of movies."

There was a silence, and I feared I'd offended him. "That's why I usually don't tell anyone. People start acting weird. I thought you might be different."

"If you tell me it's true, then I'll believe you. I just don't know you very well, and I don't know if you're the kind of person who makes things up."

"I'm not."

"Okay."

"I don't tell most people, because they have strange preconceptions. There are so many TV shows now, a whole Amish fetish that's totally off the mark."

"What TV shows?"

"I'm surprised you haven't heard of them. *Breaking Amish, Return to Amish, Amish Mafia*. You don't watch TV?"

"Not really."

"There. I knew you were different."

"What made you think that?"

"I don't know. I just get a feeling sometimes."

I stared at the glove compartment and then at the side-view mirror. It had been an uncharacteristic risk for me to enter this person's car, knowing nothing but his first name. But maybe

I had a sense for people, too. We drove in a silence that was dense but not awkward. I closed my eyes and waited for the shapes to slide in behind my lids.

"When did *you* come here?" Paul asked.

I opened my eyes. We'd turned off PCH and were winding inland. There were tall trees here on either side of the road.

"About two months ago."

"Are you here for good?"

"No. I mean, I don't know."

"Why did you come?"

I wasn't sure how to answer and was silent.

"I'm sorry, was that too direct? Sometimes people think I'm too blunt."

"Well, English isn't your first language, right?" I turned to look at him.

"No, technically it isn't."

I was quiet for another moment, then said, "I just came to help Elise, mainly."

"How are you helping her?"

"Keeping her company, helping her stay organized. I go with her to appointments and things. She's the lead in the new Joan Didion movie."

Paul nodded. "You're her assistant?"

"Yes. But Elise is my friend."

A long pause extended.

"Here we are." Paul swiveled the Chevy off the road into a parking lot. "It's a nice hike up here. You get a terrific view."

Out of the car, I followed him to the trailhead in my espadrilles. He wasn't dressed for hiking either, in stiff loafers.

"So." He turned back to me as we walked. "What do you think of L.A.?"

"I like it so far, I guess."

"I don't really like it here, honestly. But it's where I need to be to make films. I've learned everything on the job." He turned to smile at me, and I saw darkened patches at the underarms of his shirt.

We continued onward at a slight but steady incline through a muddy stretch of trail. I might have been more careful with my shoes a few weeks prior, but you loved to shop for me, and now any new pair could be mine. My wardrobe had multiplied since I'd arrived with my little suitcase, and the original items had slid to the back of the closet.

Paul and I didn't talk for a while, until eventually we reached the peak. Here was a jutting boulder with an arched cave beneath. He stepped out onto the boulder, and I followed. Having never strayed from the flatlands of the Midwest, I wasn't accustomed to God's-eye views higher than lake dunes. Now, lording over the miles that stretched to the horizon, I felt I could drag a finger over California's rough carpet. Paul lowered himself to the rock and crossed his legs. I arranged myself into a side-splayed position beside him on the warm stone as he told me about his documentary.

"It's our generation's humanitarian crisis, happening right in front of our eyes. These children are running from death.

It's exponential each year. They're trying to escape from the most dangerous places in the world. There are twenty murders a day, just in Honduras. Parents are sending their kids here by themselves, knowing they may never see them again. It's like the kindertransport all over again, except this time no one wants them. They're being put into detention centers."

"I've heard about it," I said, with a crackle in my throat.

"And most of the children are actually sent back. They're actually sent *back* to the gangs that want to kill them. It's happening every day. And people are letting it happen. No one even wants to know about it."

I didn't answer. One of my legs had fallen asleep and was numb. I took a deep breath and closed my eyes. "I'm sorry," I said. "It's just that it's horrible, what you're telling me."

"But you said you already knew about it."

I nodded and said nothing.

"I'm going to bring it to light, make people see the disgrace of what's happening. I'm going to highlight the stories of these kids, really humanize the problem, make it impossible to turn away. That's the only way things will change. People need to be confronted, they need to be outraged. It won't be easy, though. I've been visiting children's shelters, trying to get permission to talk to the kids, but I'm getting a lot of pushback. If they're skittish about just talking, how are they going to let me shoot film?"

The question lingered in the air. I looked out over the terrain, the gnarled and stubby growth, all the dry trees bending back into themselves. "I don't know," I said. "But it's brave, what you're doing."

He didn't answer, and the silence grew between us. I drew my legs up and brought myself slowly to standing. He rose to his feet, too, and we took in the panorama.

I didn't know what I was going to say until I'd said it. "I'm not brave," I began. "I don't do anything that's helpful to anyone. All I know how to do is draw. I have these dreams that are like movies, and I draw them."

Paul was quiet for a moment, then said, "So, you want to make movies, too."

"Yes, but I don't know how."

Paul exhaled sharply through his nose.

"What?"

"Nothing. It's just that you aren't born knowing how to make films. You have to learn, just like everyone else learns. Like I learned. The best way is to work on one."

"But I'd need to know someone."

"Maybe you do know someone," he said.

As we descended the trail, Paul told me that this was a city of serendipity, that people found each other when the time was right. He told the story of how he'd alighted in Los Angeles with no job and only one connection, an Amish cousin working fruit orchards in the Valley. For the first few weeks, Paul stayed with his cousin, eating ramen noodles and watching movies. He'd gone methodically down a list of the best films of all time: *The Godfather, Annie Hall, Taxi Driver.* He must have seen more movies in those few weeks than some people do in a lifetime, he said. He had no regular civilian clothes yet, so when he finally went out, he wore his barn-door pants and galluses and wandered around in awe. He thought of all the trees and earth that must have been ground up to make room for the city. He'd always pictured Los Angeles as something softer and greener, more arcadian: palm trees and surfboards and gardens. He'd never expected so much pavement, so many cars.

One day he'd sat at an outdoor café in Santa Monica and ordered a beer for himself. It was the first alcoholic drink he'd ever had, and he found it bitter, like machine oil. The couple at the adjacent table glanced over at him. He'd given himself a haircut, remedying the Amish bowl style to the best of his ability, but knew his clothing advertised him as alien. The couple glanced again and smiled, and the man asked where he was from. Paul told them the truth. The girl had a messy bun on the top of her head, a novel variation on the Amish girls' buns, and a dress that was smaller and thinner than a bathroom towel. The man wore thick black eyeglasses. He invited Paul to join their table.

The man, as it happened, was a camera operator. They talked for a long time, and Paul's second beer wasn't as bitter. He was struck by how often and loudly his companions laughed at even the smallest thing. They asked him questions, fascinated by his upbringing and defection. "I'm so glad we met you," the woman gushed. "We can help you get settled here." Paul confessed that he had no work or prospects. He asked about the film industry. The man offered to recommend him for a job on a movie set, driving the camera truck.

"We usually work in teams, so it's nice to recruit new guys we like."

"A job would be good," Paul said. "So I can buy some normal clothes."

"No! Your clothes are awesome," the woman said. "It's such a different style. Amish chic." She and her companion laughed.

"Anyway, that's how I got started," Paul told me. "I wore my old clothes until I got my first paycheck, which meant I wore them on the film set. I think they helped, actually, in getting people to accept me. I was unthreatening to the other camera guys. I was like a mascot. So they were nice to me."

"Are they your friends now?"

Paul shrugged. "I get along with them, and we go out sometimes after shoots, but there's still a kind of barrier. Some have families; the others never sleep. There's a lot of drinking and drugs. I'm not like that. I need a solid schedule. Thirty years of waking at dawn is a hard habit to break."

Back in the car, Paul sat for a moment with the key in the ignition. In this enclosed space I could smell the iron of his sweat. Finally he turned the ignition and looked at me. His hair was damp at the temples, and his eyelashes were wet, too, dark and defined. The eyes themselves were a warm uniform brown without variegation. "Do you want to see where I live?"

I waited a moment, then said, "Yes."

When we were deep into the hills, he pulled into a hidden driveway that led to a sprawling Craftsman-style house. I turned to him, my mouth open. "Yeah, I wish," he said pre-emptively. "No, my place is in the back. I rent the guesthouse."

We drove until we came upon a small cabin tucked among the trees. The door was low for an adult. Paul opened the lock with a skeleton key, stepped aside to let me in first, then bent to enter behind me. The cabin consisted of a single room with a refrigerator and stove, a card table covered with oilcloth, and two folding chairs. A futon mattress lay on the floor. Draped over the walls were overlapping panels of colorful fabric. It took a moment to recognize that they were kites, dozens of them, of different shapes and patterns. I approached the wall, ran a finger over an arrow-shaped panel.

"I make them myself," Paul said. "Kites are popular back home, and I've always loved them."

"They're beautiful."

"That one's a delta," he said. "And this is a sled." He pointed to other shapes: diamonds, boxes, dragons.

"Where do you fly them?"

"Anywhere there's space and wind."

"I've never done it," I admitted.

"Really? Next time, let's do it."

Paul pulled out one of the folding chairs for me, then put the tea kettle on and sat in the other one. The red-checkered oilcloth was sticky on the surface.

"It's nice here," I offered.

"I really like it. Living a little bit away from the city keeps me sane. Most people who leave Amish places end up staying close by, whether they mean to or not. But I'm so far away now that I have to make a little nest for myself."

The kettle began to wheeze and rattle on the stove, and Paul rose from his chair.

"How long did it take to get used to electricity?" I asked.

"Not long. But I still give myself some restrictions, just to stay grounded. I don't use more electricity than I absolutely need." He gestured toward the overhead light, a ceiling fan with low-wattage candle bulbs. "And no internet."

"Not even on your phone?"

He reached into his pocket and pulled out a flip phone, similar to my own. "I've gotten a little protective of my privacy, actually, since coming here. It's funny. When I left the farm, it was like I morphed into a different animal. Like I changed from a chicken to a wolf or something." Standing in front of me, he took a sip of tea. "Maybe it doesn't make sense," he said, putting the mug down. "But I don't know how else to describe it. I don't feel like a domestic animal who escaped its pen. I feel like a whole other creature who uses its instincts to find shelter and get fed. It's hard. But I don't ever want to change back. I want to be a wolf forever."

He was imposing in the small cabin. I studied the dark crash of hair. His neck seemed to be in a perpetual bend, as if he were trying to see beneath something. It was easy to think of him as a wolf. In his presence, I felt a mix of fear and envy. He was stronger than the elements, directed by his own compass, utterly free. I liked to think we were similar in this way, but it was only a wish.

IX.

ONE NIGHT, when you were free of Rafael, we shared a bottle of wine on the patio. You finished it quickly, as expected, and opened another. I was loose and more loquacious than usual. "I'm so grateful to you for bringing me to the Rhizome," I said. "I don't think I've thanked you enough."

"Oh, Abby, you're so sweet." You were aglow from the fairy lights on the trellis above us. "I was happy to share it with you."

I was stunned anew by my fortune, to be here alone with you, where so many strangers would want to be. I reflected on the hours I'd spent in my musty bedroom in Michigan gazing at your image in the pages of magazines as if I were a stranger myself. As absurd as that separation now seemed, I knew that it had been correct to be apart all that time. We'd both needed those years to seek out our respective purposes—yours in the spotlight, mine in the dark. Now, we were ready to join together again with unbreakable unity.

Connected, we'd form an elegant, symbiotic mechanism of invention and distribution.

"Maybe someday I'll join the Rhizome," I blurted. "Wouldn't it be funny if I did, and my guide recommended me to Perren?"

You gave me a questioning look, as if waiting for me to finish the joke.

"I mean for art direction or something. Not acting, of course."

"Oh, yeah, that would be incredible," you said distractedly.

"I have so many new ideas now, stories and drawings. And I was thinking," I said, blood flushing my skin, "What if we did a movie together? Me and you? I could write it and do the art direction, and you could star in it. Maybe you could find a director and producer. Who knows, maybe Perren would want to get involved."

You lifted your wineglass to your mouth, and I saw the edges of your lips crook in pleasure, or amusement. You took a long drink. When you put the glass down, you smiled blandly and said, "Yeah, it would be cool to do that someday."

I felt as if you'd shoved me. I'd expected you to see it right away, the way I did: the natural partnership we could reclaim. The Eden we'd inhabited as children was now spread before us again. You loved my art—or said you did—and now you could set foot in it.

"Did I tell you about Raf's next project?" you said, lighting a cigarette. "It's a comedy. How do you like that? He never ceases to amaze me."

I didn't respond. You poured yourself more wine, although your glass was still half-full. When you tried to set the bottle back on the table, it slipped and toppled to the ground.

You wouldn't take me to the Rhizome again. I knew that now. If I wanted any chance of advancing my art, of putting myself in front of Perren, I'd have to do it alone. Not everyone was led by the hand the way Paul had been. It hurt to think that those strangers had done more for him than you were willing to do for me. Your admiration of my work may have been genuine, but it was superficial. I could see now that you'd become one of those people who effuse promiscuously and promise breathlessly, then continue on their way.

Paying the Rhizome's extortionate membership fee was out of the question, but I remembered what my tour guide had said about her work-study program. While you were busy on the set one morning, I took the Tesla into the mountains and picked up the application. I returned the same afternoon to drop it off along with my portfolio, a rolled cylinder of a dozen drawings. I'd been prepared to wait, but the phone call came the next day, offering me a working membership. "Congratulations," the director said. "I spoke to Tello, who gave you a strong recommendation. Welcome to the Rhizome."

A strange terror came over me as I listened to the director itemize the work positions that were available. I could help in the restaurant kitchen or the spa. I could do maintenance work or help the counselors in the children's camp. I stared at the Perren photograph on the wall, and the woman with the shredded face stared back. "What about daycare?" I asked quietly, even though you weren't in the house.

"Yes, of course, that's a possibility too. Do you have experience with small children?"

I searched for a moment, then said, "Not yet."

"Well, that's all right. If that's where you'd like to be, you can sign on as a helper there. When would you like to begin?"

"Isn't there an interview or something?"

"No, not for helpers. We have a rigorous vetting process for the full-timers, of course, and you'd be under their direct supervision. But we want to offer a wide range of opportunities for our ambitious work-study members, like you. It's part of what everybody loves about this place. It's accessible to anyone with talent, regardless of financial means or background."

The phone vibrated in my hand. When I glanced at the screen and saw your name, I felt a stab of adrenaline. I declined the call and put the phone back to my ear.

"I'd like to start today," I said.

I'd never changed a diaper before or bathed a baby. There were fourteen infants in the Rhizome nursery and ten daycare providers, but still the pace was frantic. When I walked in, I immediately recognized Tasha, the young woman who'd given me the tour.

"Welcome," she sang, smiling broadly and bouncing a swaddled child. The other women in white uniforms circulated around the rows of cribs, attending to mewling bundles.

"Most of them belong to industry people," a soft-faced woman named Marlene told me. "Some are big celebrities, but we try not to focus on which ones are which. We try our best to provide equal, unbiased attention."

A walk-in storage closet contained stacks of diapers in every size, a refrigerator, a dishwasher, and dressers full of organic cotton clothing. Tasha and the others were always at the ready with formula and burp pads. They told me what to retrieve and when, and sometimes gave me a baby to hold. When the time came to put it down, I returned it to its proper place, searching for its nameplate on the spindled crib, and rested it on the mattress where it curled up like a pill bug.

After my first shift in the nursery, I met with Tello again. Everything came more naturally this time: taking my place in the wooden chair, closing my eyes, letting the ocean soundtrack wash over me. I felt a spur of defiance as the shapes weaved and merged behind my eyelids. I belonged here now. I'd earned my scholarship on merit alone; I was more deserving than you or any other paying member. When my session was finished, I floated back down the grand staircase, which seemed warmer now, the grandeur of the building more uplifting than forbidding. Soon it would become ordinary. Soon my footsteps would become familiar to these floors.

I was allowed one session for each working shift at the Rhizome, twice a week. It was easy to go while you were filming all day. As I drove your car into the mountains without your knowledge, I jittered with nervous invigoration. I did a four-hour shift at the daycare, then went to see Tello. In the nursery, I came to know all of the babies well, their innate personalities and habits. Some were born to howl and others to mildly accept their lot. It was difficult, as the others had suggested, to sand down my awareness of which child belonged to whom, which infants were of divine stock, descended from the heights of Olympus. It was difficult not to remember, not to read entitlement in their eyes.

But in the evenings it was the same as before. Sometimes you wanted me—we ate dinner together, shared a bottle of wine—sometimes you didn't. I tried to maintain my bland composure in your presence, tamping down the little detonations that occurred inside me in the wake of each Rhizome visit, the pinballing sensations of exaltation and fear. I can't imagine I was entirely successful, but you must not have been paying attention because you never seemed to suspect a thing, never once smelled it on me. I was careful with the logistics, of course. I avoided the Rhizome on Wednesdays, when I knew you had your own sessions. Only once did I find the temerity to break this rule, coming in to work a shift on a Wednesday afternoon, and leaving my post at the daycare.

Only once did I take the risk of being discovered as I hovered near the door to your guide's room and listened. I could just make out your voice on the other side, presumably talking about a dream you'd had. I heard you say something about sinking and drowning. I heard the deep sound of your guide's voice, responding, and then I heard you sobbing. It was difficult not to open the door and go to you. It was difficult to pull away and stop listening.

After I began at the Rhizome, my dreams bloomed in saturated colors, as if they'd been dropped into a chemical bath. Alternating with the wondrous dreams were the troubling ones. Screaming fistfights with my sister. My father snarling, *You're a forgery. That's the academic truth, the academic truth.* A demon took a burning log from a fire and thrust it at me. I was visited by Rafael, too, holding a whip atop a frothy, pregnant mare. In the dream, he invited me to mount the mare along with him, to ride bareback pressed in front of him, and I woke in a sweat of arousal. In another dream, he brought me to a slaughterhouse and opened the door to show me the piles of dead horses.

And the satyr dream came back. Now, on waking, I was able to draw the characters in detail, in full costume. I drew the shoes that gave the satyrs their cloven hooves, and the belts that strapped their phalluses in place. I drew the crystal beads at the hem of your ballet skirt, one nacreous bead at a time. I drew myself among the satyrs, wearing the goatskin.

The way to improve dream recall, Tello advised, was to wake six hours into the sleep cycle, then slip back into dreams from there. They were fresher, easier to export to consciousness that way. I used my alarm clock to stir me with a piano sonata at dawn, then I returned to the Spring for the next few hours of morning before I had to awake for the day and face the barrage of your emails and appointments. The impervious guest bedroom permitted no sound but the hum of the central air system. The first thing I saw when I opened my eyes was the small ebony sculpture of a plump woman on my nightstand, her bare breasts softly gleaming. I'd grown to love this sculpture. Each morning, as I woke disoriented from another world, it was a totem that brought me gently back, reminded me that I was still in Malibu—that my dreams were the false and *this* the fantastically real.

X.

As the filming wore on, April became May, and you came home depleted. You were having difficulties with the role. The director gave confusing cues and was frustrated by your choices. "It's not my fault. It's the script," you complained. "The timing is awkward, and I'm doing my best to fix it. But Lorenzo's some kind of purist."

"He should trust your instincts," I said, pulling the words from the air.

"I don't know," you huffed. "Maybe my instincts aren't that good. Maybe I'm in over my head with this."

"Of course you're not." I thought of what else a loyal friend, a good assistant, would say. "You're challenging yourself, and that's when your best work will come out."

"I just don't know, Abby. I don't think I like how this is going to end up. I'm already afraid about the reception I'm going to get. And I'm nervous about Joan's reaction, too. I'm afraid she'll hate the movie." You inhaled. "She came to the set today."

"Joan Didion?"

"Yes." You covered your eyes with your hands. "It was so strange meeting her. I didn't even know what to say. Oh, God, I felt like such a jerk." You kept your hands over your face for a long moment. "I felt like the dumbest thing who ever lived, standing there. I felt like she could take me apart with one word." You took your hands away. "But it was also weirdly like looking in a mirror. She has these green eyes. In pictures from the sixties, I really do look like her, you know. Seeing her today, it was like seeing into my own future."

This, of course, was ridiculous. You were nothing like her, and never would be.

You had an annual checkup with the gynecologist that you told me to postpone until filming was done. You needed a whitening by the dentist and an acupuncture session. I held them all off, punted the appointments to July and then August. A shipment of the Edison lightbulbs you wanted came in at Restoration Hardware, and I picked them up for you.

I had new drawings to show you, but there never seemed to be a good time. "I really think you'll like these," I said. "They're all new concepts that I've never mentioned before."

"Oh, Abby, I'm sure they're great. I know they are. I just can't pay attention right now. I don't want to lose focus. I know you understand that."

"Of course I do," I said, despite the bruise.

Occasionally Rafael came and stayed. One day, he arrived in an unfamiliar car, a flagrant yellow Jaguar, which dropped him off and rumbled noisily away over the cobblestone driveway, kicking up dust at the gate. He came in with his smirking smile and went upstairs without a word. He stayed upstairs even after you came home. You poured yourself a glass of wine and gave me the report of the day, and I sat and listened stoically, waiting for Rafael to come downstairs and interpose himself, to wrest ownership of you. When he finally appeared in the kitchen doorway, your automatic expression of surprise melted into delight, and you rambled into his arms. I stared while you kissed him. He met my eyes over your shoulder and winked slowly.

That night, I dreamed I was in bed with Rafael. The dream had the same immediacy as the loveseat dream I shared with you, Elise. The charge between us was that alive, that intense. I knew he was really there, that we were dreaming mutually. We'd just had sex, and semen was puddled on my belly. As we lay together, I watched the semen travel down my pelvis, through the hair on my pubic bone, and sink into my vulva. I felt the liquid, hot and thick, as distinctly as I've felt anything in waking life.

I woke in a swirl of arousal and shame, my blood throbbing. It was barely dawn, but I abandoned my bed and went down to the kitchen, the sweat drying on my skin. Before I'd filled my coffee cup, I heard the sticking steps of bare feet and Rafael's voice. "Good morning, sunshine."

There was a jab of ice in my chest. Turning halfway, I tried to relax my face.

"How'd you sleep?" he asked, and I heard the unctuousness in his voice.

"Great," I mumbled.

He pulled a bottle of kombucha from the refrigerator. "Did you have good dreams?"

He poured the yellow liquid and looked at me as he took the first sip. His hair was a black jag, wet from the shower, and his face was shaved close. He leaned against the counter and considered me for another moment. I was wearing the expensive pajama set you'd bought for me, and I arranged an arm over my chest to cover the nipples that jutted beneath the silk.

"I had a dream about *you* last night," he said.

My heart lurched and jammed. I had the sense of standing on a ship deck without a railing, and braced a hand on the kitchen counter. If Rafael were to take even a small step closer, the ship would dip beneath me. I stood frozen, my fingers gripping the countertop, feeling the granite edge. My eyes dropped to the middle of his black T-shirt, an interstellar void. The house was silent except for the hum of the air conditioner. I could smell the cut grass of his deodorant or aftershave. I willed him to come nearer, and I willed him to move away. The room felt airtight. He stood with a questioning grin, waiting for me to ask for the details of his dream. With just a word, I could verify that it matched mine. I could confirm that he'd been the one who initiated the tryst, that the treachery was his. But I couldn't bring myself to say the words, and finally he took a drink and turned from me. Left alone in the kitchen, I gazed at the place where he'd stood but saw only the bright puddle on my belly, the slow creep of fluid.

At the next break in filming, you announced that you and Rafael would be going to La Jolla for the weekend. "If you need the Tesla, take it," you told me. "You deserve a break, too."

After the Mustang disappeared, a deep quiet settled into the house. I don't know why, but I couldn't bring myself to go to the Rhizome. I felt somehow constricted by the freedom you'd given me. Instead, I called in sick, closed the blinds, and pulled the duvet over myself in bed.

"Dress for the beach," Paul said, when I called on Sunday. I felt like a truant as I climbed into his Cavalier with ancient cigarette smoke in the upholstery. But as we jounced over the rocks and ruts of Topanga, a sense of ease settled in me like nothing I'd felt since coming here.

We parked in a crowded lot at Redondo Beach. In the sky was a patchwork of kites. "It's a festival," Paul said.

"How are they not getting tangled?" I asked.

"Festivals aren't for novices."

"But I'm a novice."

"I'll help you."

Once we'd positioned ourselves at the kite-launching area, Paul presented me with a creation I'd never seen before. "It's yours," he said. "A bird of paradise. I thought this would be a good place to debut it."

I studied the delicate fringes of vinyl, each a careful feather. The tail was made from red, blue, and green ribbons. "Thank you. But I don't think I should fly it, Paul. I might ruin it."

"If you do, I'll fix it."

He'd brought another kite for himself that he referred to as a sidewinder—a streamlined stunt kite in the shape of a boomerang. With a few efficient movements, the sidewinder was in the air, between an undulating dragon and a penguin.

"Hold this." He handed me his spool. I kept the sidewinder steady while he launched my kite.

"I'm going to get tangled," I said when he handed my spool back. My neck ached, but I couldn't take my eyes off the bird's rippling tail.

"You'll get in the groove, don't worry. You start to understand the air. Trust yourself."

We didn't talk for a while. Next to us, a family took turns flying a large box kite, which made unpredictable sweeps near mine. The box kite, bulky and graceless, looked like a gaping mouth, trying to seize my bird out of the sky.

"I always think of my brothers when I do this," Paul said, with his eyes on the sidewinder.

I was quiet for a moment before asking, "Did anyone else ever leave home?"

"I had a friend who did, but we all knew he'd come back. Sometimes the boys go for a little while, just to say they went. But I don't think anyone was surprised when I broke out for real. They expected it."

"Why?"

He smiled. "I was always a little different, the one reading secret books. Everything except the Bible. Jack London, Thoreau, Hawthorne. All that individualism, all that natural law."

The family beside us was laughing, the smallest boy falling to the sand. Paul didn't say anything else for a while. We flew our kites amid the music and laughter and the rumble of the Pacific Ocean. "I know it's weird, but these festivals remind me of church," he said. "All these different shapes and colors riding the same air currents. For some reason, it reminds me of the songs we used to sing, these slow German ones from the sixteenth century. It's that same feeling of connection, I guess."

A strong wind came, and I felt the pull of the animated fabric above me, fighting to be free. The tug at my hands was a solid force. As I pulled the spool, I remembered sitting with Shelby on the cold pier in the early morning, watching our father cast into Lake Michigan. A yellow perch had come out of the water, a flap of maddened muscle. I'd screamed at my father to put it back, but he held the pole steady, watching the creature thrash. "Take it off!" I shrieked. My sister had laughed at me, repeating mockingly: *Take it off, take it off!* Finally, with a chilling calm, my father reached to the end of the line. He'd gripped the fish's head so that its mouth sprang open and he could unthread the hook. Then, holding the perch by the tail, he swung it against the stone pier.

Paul and I stayed after everyone else had gone. The sun weakened until we could look right at it, a painted disc. At last, we pulled our kites in. Paul brought out sandwiches in aluminum foil, and bottles of beer, and we sat as the sun tugged out of sight.

He told me that he'd finally gained access to a shelter for unaccompanied refugee children. He'd met several kids already, and they'd grown comfortable with him. They'd begun to tell their stories. There was a boy named Armando who'd seen his brother shot to death in Guatemala. A Honduran girl named Yolanda had been raped by gang members and then again by the coyote who'd taken her over the border. There were two little brothers, aged three and four, separated from their mother while crossing Mexico. When they'd arrived at the facility, they'd been half-starved. As I listened, a valve in my heart slammed, familiar and painful.

"Hey, I want to ask you something," Paul said. "Remember how I said you need to learn how films work? I wonder if you'd like to help me with mine."

I didn't answer. I only looked at him.

"I think it would be good to have a woman on the project," he said. "The kids may open up more to you, especially the girls. I'd especially like to introduce you to Yolanda if I can arrange it."

I listened as he described the practical, tedious details—lighting, sound, editing—that went into making a film. Soon, the only light on the beach came from the parading headlamps on the road behind us. Paul's features became an impressionistic blur, his face a suggestion of lunar ash. In that shadowed moment, his face struck me as startlingly handsome in the way of old poets in etched portraits. The skin on my right arm, the one nearest him, felt abraded, the hairs stiff in their follicles. I was sharply aware of the air between us and a substance that seemed to be thickening it.

"What do you think?" he said.

"I have to wait until Elise is finished with the Didion film. But after that, I might be able to help."

"Ah, right. Elise comes first."

"Not forever," I said.

Paul stopped talking and lay back on the sand. The silence stretched, and I couldn't think of what to say. My experience with the opposite sex was grimly insubstantial. I'd had only a handful of kisses, each of which had been disheartening. The first time a boy's tongue had darted into my mouth, like a striking snake, I'd had to run to the bathroom to wipe my face. Now, in a kind of frenzy, I asked Paul, "What was it like to be a teenager? In the Amish world?"

He raised an eyebrow and lifted himself on an elbow. "In what way?"

"Were you allowed to date, or were your parents supposed to pick out who they wanted you to marry?"

"Oh, no, we dated," he said. "There were more opportunities than you'd think."

He shifted on the sand, closer to me. I felt weightless, the beer bottle an inadequate anchor in my hand. As he kissed me, a fishhook lowered through my body. I felt its barb pierce an interior membrane, which I visualized as a woven tapestry with something vast and unsafe on the other side. I pulled away.

"Are you okay?" Paul asked, his voice thickened and slow.

"I'm fine." My lips tingled. A damp chill had entered the air, and I shook. After a moment, Paul collected the empty bottles, and we walked over the sand to the parking lot, holding our limp kites.

When I returned to Malibu, your Mustang was back in the driveway, but when I walked into the house, you didn't greet me. Upstairs, the light was on in your bedroom, but I heard no voices. I paused but didn't call or knock. Instead I went to my room and closed the door. Sitting on the bed, I felt the chill from the beach deepen. My lips still buzzed, and I felt unmoored. Paul was out in the night now, in his cave-dark cabin, in possession of a memory of me. I couldn't stop thinking about the kiss. I berated myself for pulling away. If I'd only waited, there might have been something fluid on the other side of the tapestry. I'd felt the intimation of an approaching wave, which might have been warm and enveloping, which might have lifted me like a tide.

As I brooded over my failure, the silence in the house was sickening. My thoughts turned to you, Elise, and I feared that you hadn't greeted me because you were angry that I'd been out and hadn't awaited your return. You were unsatisfied with my companionship, my employment. Or you'd somehow discovered my secret life at the Rhizome. As I lay awake in the recriminating quiet, I was sure of it.

Finally I dipped into sleep, dreaming of kites in a night sky, like stingrays in murky water. I woke early to a pit of dread and went to the kitchen to make breakfast. When you finally came down, you were groggy and pale. Hungover, I assumed.

"Are you okay?" I asked in a thin voice.

"I'm just tired. Thanks for making coffee." You didn't meet my eyes. "Listen. That appointment I asked you to postpone with the gynecologist. Could you call and see if they can take me after all, as soon as possible?"

You were addressing me as an assistant, not a friend. I called right away, from the kitchen where you sat with your kombucha and yogurt. "They can take you this morning," I said.

"Tell Lorenzo I'll be there at eleven. Tell him something came up. You don't have to say what."

You left the table and went upstairs. Twenty minutes later you were in the Mustang, hair still wet from the shower, without having said good-bye. I paced the house and then sat with my drawings. I stared at them, tried to see them the way you would. In your eyes, they'd look like the doodles of a lunatic. You'd complimented them only out of charity. You hadn't meant anything you'd said. It was preposterous that I'd ever believed you'd help me, that you'd ever align yourself with me as anything but an employer. I was here in the service of your success, not the other way around.

I didn't dare go to the Rhizome that day, but stayed in the house like a butler. You returned late in the afternoon with no color in your face. I came to greet you, and when your eyes met mine, you sank to the floor in the entrance hall and began to cry. I slid down beside you, and all the bitterness I'd felt washed away. I rubbed your back and felt your spine beneath my fingers. I was the only one who could comfort you, whatever the problem may be.

"I'm not ready to be a mother," you sobbed. "I don't know if I want to be a mother."

My hand paused on your back.

"I have to get married now," you gasped. "I need to tell him that we have to get married."

"No, no," I heard myself say. "You don't have to do anything. You don't have to do anything."

For a moment, you couldn't speak. Your body shook, and I rubbed your back again, slowly and calmly, as a real mother would. Finally, you put your face in your hands. After a long moment, you took your hands away and looked at me, your eyes washed bright. "I talk a big game, Abby, but I'm still a traditional girl. I could never have a baby out of wedlock. I wouldn't do it to my parents, and I don't know, I just would never do it. I know it's normal in Hollywood, but I just can't. And I don't know if I want to marry Rafael. I mean, I love him, I really do, but I thought we had so much more time."

"You don't have to do anything," I repeated.

"He's wonderful, and so good to me. But, my God, he's such a flirt. You have no idea. I don't know if I can trust him, I mean long-term. Not as a husband. And I'm nowhere near ready to be a mother. Not now. It'd be suicide for my career. It'd be like stamping myself out for someone else."

A cold wave ran through me, and I lifted myself to standing. You looked up at me like a little girl. "You don't have to do anything," I said again. "You don't have to marry anyone."

You stared up at me in hope, or wonder.

"I'll raise the baby with you," I said. "I'll help you. One stupid mistake isn't going to ruin your life. I won't let it."

You smiled. With an effort of arms and legs, you gathered yourself and stood, then put your arms around me. "Oh, Abby. Thank you for being such a good friend. You are so kind, and so crazy."

I accepted your embrace. Despite myself, I felt a detonation of anger. You were stupid to let this happen, mind-numbingly stupid, no different from any naive young starlet, falling into the easiest pit of all. And now you'd be punished for it. This was a virulent place, contaminated by lust and materialism. You were already infected. You'd be a terrible mother, and you'd have a miserable child.

"Maybe I shouldn't have the baby," you said quietly.

I pulled away. In that moment, your face blotched and contorted from crying, you looked deformed. You turned from me and went into the living room, where you fell onto the couch. I followed and sat across from you. Your face was dry now, and you pulled your hair out of its elastic, letting it fall Madonna-like over your shoulders. I stared at you, but your gaze was caught on something in the middle distance.

"Have you told Rafael?" I asked quietly.

You didn't answer.

"Are you afraid to tell him?"

"No, of course not." You sighed and pulled your legs up. "Oh, Abby. I shouldn't complain about him. Raf's wonderful. I mean, he's the most romantic man I've ever met, without question. It's still like living in a dream, every day. But, how do I put this?" you breathed. "There's a kind of arrogance there. It's partly his culture, I know, but sometimes I feel like I'm expected to put up with his bad behavior just because he's a man. Like he has some special freedom that I don't." You looked at me for a cold moment. "Not much I can do about that, I guess."

Our eyes were mutually fixed now. "Are you sure?" I said.

"Sure of what?"

"Sure there's nothing you can do about it."

"What do you mean?" There was a shift in your voice, a hint of defensiveness.

"I mean you should leave him."

You stared. "No."

"What you're saying about him is true, Elise. Have you noticed how he acts around that French woman, Mireille Sauvage?"

"What are you saying?" You stared. "Don't you think I'd know if he were actually cheating on me? He's not perfect, but he wouldn't cheat on me. Ever." You unfolded your legs and stood. "Listen. I'm sorry. I shouldn't have broken down like that. Of course I want to have the baby," you said. "That's not a question. I'll figure it out. Raf and I will figure it out together."

You went out of the living room and into the entrance hall where you'd dropped your bag, a puckered leather backpack. You lifted it from the floor and put the straps over both shoulders like a papoose. Your eyes had dried and hardened again into jade.

Suddenly, I wanted to tell you about the bridge. For the first time, I wanted to tell you, to drop it all at your feet. I wanted to describe what had happened after I'd jumped. The hospital room, my parents' faces blinking in and out of focus. The hard, throbbing pain where the incision had been made for the nephrectomy. The television that was latched to the ceiling, displaying nature images, a butterfly folding and opening its wings. Wings up, wings down. The proboscis unfurling, dipping into a flower. A caterpillar creeping over a banyan leaf. Coming out of anesthesia, I'd asked the nurse to show me the destroyed kidney. It had been shredded by the ribs that broke upon my impact with the ice. The nurse had refused. I still dreamed about the kidney sometimes, like an aborted fetus, a horrific red lump. After the hospital, I'd gone home to my bedroom, the old rabbit wallpaper, the dim, sour light. I groped at my abdomen and found the layer of gauze, thick as a book. Inside my core was a deep ache, a tightening coil. The coil hardened and cramped, and when I pulled the gauze away from the wound, it exposed a deep red concavity, an open pool with no hope of healing.

XI.

WHAT I'D said must have stayed with you, because I heard Rafael shouting on the other side of your bedroom door: "This has nothing to do with Mireille."

I stood in the hallway and listened as your voice rose in indignation. I couldn't make out your words, but I heard Rafael say, "This! This is what I mean. You're like all American women. So jealous, always. I can't be free with you if you want to keep me like a pet. I'm a man, not a dog."

I smiled despite myself as I heard something smash. You were throwing things, as you should.

"And your friend, why is she always here? It's not normal. You want me to live here, but it's like you already have a wife. You need another wife? You need so many pets?"

You were screaming back at him now, incomprehensibly. I caught the words "friend" and "trust" and heard you say "more loyal than you." My smile spread, and I pressed my ear closer to the door.

"What baby?" Rafael was shouting. "There is no baby. There can't be a baby. Are you crazy?"

There was another crash, and then quiet. After a moment, I heard the sound of you crying, gasping for words. Your voice rose steadily as you repeated yourself. "I won't do it, Rafael. No. I won't. I won't do it."

"It's the baby, or me," Rafael said. Those last words were loud, unmistakable.

Later, after Rafael had gone, you came to me in my room. Your face was puffy and red like a little girl's. You told me what had happened, in a quaking voice, with your hands on your belly. When you finished—after you'd told me that it was all over, that Rafael was gone—violent sobs shook your body, tremors from your core.

I felt the need to calm you quickly. I thought nervously about the developing fetus drinking in the poisonous chemicals that were flowing through you. I wanted to protect the baby from any contact with sorrow, especially such unnecessary and misguided sadness. I was angry with you for bombarding your baby with it.

"Come here," I said, and you obeyed, coming to sit beside me on the bed. "You did the right thing," I told you, rubbing your back. "You did the best thing for you, and your baby. You did the right thing."

You collapsed, then, and laid your head on my lap. I felt the surprising solidity of your skull on my thighs, the rigid cranium. I stroked your hair, which slid over your face and unveiled the side of your neck. I was rarely in such close proximity to another person, and I was struck by the physicality of you, by the textures of skin and hair and by the visible pulse at your neck. No one had ever offered themselves to me this way. I felt what it must be like to be a mother. It was a warmth and wonder that I wanted to last forever.

"Everything will work out," I whispered to you. "Everything will be fine. It will be wonderful. We'll be like Joan and her family, here in Malibu. We'll work together, you and me, and raise our child together. Maybe it will be a little girl."

You didn't say anything, but I could tell you were listening. Your sobbing had stopped, and you were breathing steadily now, on my lap. I thought perhaps you could see what I was seeing: the two of us, sun-kissed and loose, invulnerable in our sealed paradise. We would live in harmony, like children, creating our own worlds together again. But this time they'd become movies, and the whole world would see them.

You didn't mention Rafael after that. You went back to filming, stoically, and I was surprised by your strength. I was proud of you for letting him go, for staying firm. He'd wanted you to end the pregnancy, you said, but you'd refused. You never mentioned what he'd said about me, but I knew that you'd come to my defense. You'd chosen me.

My own phone almost never rang. So, when my parents' phone number appeared on the screen one early June morning,

I was so blindsided that I answered almost without thinking. Perhaps the impulse was born of the new optimism I
was feeling, now that my course to happiness seemed fixed.
Michigan was no longer a threat; it no longer even seemed
real. I heard the brightness in my own voice as I said hello
to my mother, unafraid.

"I'm calling to tell you that you're an aunt," she said.
"Shelby gave birth to a daughter last night. I just thought I
should tell you." Her voice trembled slightly, as if she were
trying to contain some insurgent emotion. When she spoke
again, her voice was low. "She still asks for you, you know.
You should really visit her, Abby."

I didn't respond.

"Did you know she changed her last name? Obviously she
didn't marry the father of the baby. I don't know why she
changed it, to be honest, or where she got this name. She calls
herself Shelby Hightower now."

"Officially?"

"Apparently, yes, though I don't know why."

The farcical image came to mind of my sister cross-legged
atop a water tower, refusing to come down.

"You should try to have a good relationship with her,
Abby. She really doesn't have much. And when your father
and I are gone, you'll only have each other."

I swallowed against an eddy of bile and waited a beat before
asking, "How are you and Dad?"

"Not good," she said. "Your father's health hasn't been great. He's been worried about you, Abby, and it's affecting his blood pressure."

I hung up the phone.

A few days later, you surprised me with a gift. "I found it at a vintage boutique on Melrose," you said. "They had a whole costume section. It was hard to choose, but this seemed right for you." You took a bundle of black fabric from a shopping bag and handed it to me. I held it up, and a velvet robe unfolded, with a hood and flared sleeves.

"It comes with an eye mask, too," you said. "I thought it looked kind of powerful."

Standing in the living room, I put the robe on over my clothes and let it drape to the floor. It was like a longer version of the witch shawl you'd bought me on Abbot Kinney. You gave me the mask, and I pulled it over my eyes. I looked at you questioningly through the oblong holes.

"It's for the Rhizome's solstice party," you said. "It's a giant masked ball, really glamorous and wild. It's the biggest event of the year, always on the night of the summer solstice. They encourage everyone to go and to bring a guest, because it's a chance to bring dream imagery into the waking world, to inhabit our dream roles. People get really creative. I think you'll love it."

I wanted to shake my head. The robe felt too heavy on me—it was making me light-headed—and I wanted to take it off. The thrilling prospect of attending a party with you was subsumed by dread. I reminded myself that only Tello and the daycare workers knew me at the Rhizome. Only those few people would possibly recognize me, would possibly approach me. And, it was a costume party. How would they find me in my mask and cloak? Still, I was afraid that the moment we entered the building you'd somehow sense that I'd been going there, that I had a life beyond your orbit.

You cheerfully drew a zebra-striped bodysuit out of the shopping bag, and a half mask with attached ears.

"It's from this dream I keep having, that I'm in a herd of zebras running from danger. I don't know what we're running from, but it's a feeling of being pursued, a life-and-death situation, and I always have to wake myself up from it. It's a nightmare, I guess. I'm hoping that dressing up like a zebra in real life might help."

I was having trouble taking full breaths but managed to say, "Maybe it's about the media. Symbolically."

"Huh," you said. "Interesting theory." You stood for another moment in your zebra skin, then brought me with you to the powder room, where we looked at ourselves in the mirror. "You look spooky," you said.

"What am I?" I asked thinly.

"I'm not sure. You're a dream sorcerer or something. A dream magician."

So that was how you saw me. I let it sink in. As I looked at the two of us in the mirror, there was no question who was dominant. I was reminded of our childhood games, our animal imitations, and remembered my original role as your leader and director. My anxiety abated.

"Will Rafael be there?" I asked.

"No." You frowned beneath the mask. "It's members and their guests only, and as you know, he always refused to join."

The night of the party, tiki torches lined the entrance path to the Rhizome, and a large man in a jester's costume stood to the side of the door, surveying the guests as they approached. You presented your membership card, and the jester waved us inside. The marble lobby was decorated with flowered garlands and candle sconces, and a bar was set up near the reception desk. Voices roared to the ceiling. People spilled into the garden courtyard, where lights sequined the trees and torches studded the periphery. There was a woman in a powdered wig and bustle, holding a fan. There was a Carnival dancer in a lamé bustier. A geisha and a mime, a lion and a lion tamer. The music was percussive, ritualistic, without any discernible melody. I lost you in the crowd immediately, and felt both distressed and relieved. I didn't want to be exposed, but I also didn't want to be alone. Throughout the next few hours I caught an occasional glimpse of your zebra stripes in some knot of laughing people, but I resisted going to you.

On my own, I could find no social entry point. I stood in the courtyard, near the tiered fountain, apart from the jostling crowd. It was disorienting to be surrounded by masked figures. I riled myself with the thought that Perren might be among them. A tall, thin person dressed as the Tin Man appeared in my field of vision from time to time, leaning over this woman or that. Each time I saw him, my chest clutched. If there were ever a time to approach, to take a chance, it was now. With just a few words, I'd know if it was him. All I had to do was walk over.

The Tin Man withdrew and disappeared behind a wall of people. Some were dancing, rotating bare shoulders, shuffling platform shoes. Lipsticked mouths pouted beneath eye masks. I saw you scamper through the courtyard, nimble game animal, and enter the building with a Renaissance king. A group of men in capes swept past, intent on something. A mummy lurked in the shadow of a jacaranda. A red-eyed gorilla sprang upon a Greek goddess. As the evening deepened, I stayed in place and watched the movements of the crowd intensify. My breathing turned shallow, and the drumfire began in my skull. This hadn't happened in a long time, not since I'd come to California. For these past months, I'd been balanced, content, complacent. Now, the old feeling of emergency powered through me. One of these horrifying creatures would, at any moment, pull out a gun and turn the bacchanalia into a bloodbath. It was at times just like this that it happened. Everything was safe, until it wasn't.

I felt that I needed to find you right away. I pushed through the people, their puppet mouths and drink cups. I went into the building and flew up the staircase to search for you.

The door to the actors' lounge was open. I saw a sheikh and a mermaid sitting on the floor with a hookah. And there, sprawled on a royal-blue daybed, I found your striped carcass.

At first glance, I thought you were dead. I was too late, and you'd overdosed on something. For one expanding moment, time stopped. You looked so small in your costume that in a confused flash I saw you as a child again. I remembered the hair-braiding trains, the dark chants. *Concentrate, concentrate.* After pummeling each girl's back—after cracking the egg and stabbing the knife—we'd give her a shove, make her lose her balance. She was being pushed off a high ledge, we'd tell her, and whatever color she saw when she fell predicted the manner of her future death. There were so many colors: blue for drowning, yellow for poison, orange for fire. There was one for everything. Whatever color you'd report to me, I'd always tell you it meant you would die of old age and go to heaven.

I went to the daybed and dropped to your side. Like a penitent, I put my hand to your cheek, bracing for the feel of chilled marble. But your skin was warm. Your eyelids fluttered. The relief I felt was undercut by white fury. I prodded you and pulled you to your feet, perhaps more roughly than necessary. Brusquely, I took you down the stairs, through the parking lot, and into the Mustang. Your head lolled to the side as I drove, and you murmured something unintelligible.

Several unfamiliar cars were parked outside your gate when we arrived. Their windows were rolled down, and camera lenses jutted out. The shutters clicked as I reached out to enter the code for the gate. "Get down," I commanded, but you were asleep. The telephoto lenses could probably capture something. It was amazing what they were able to hustle. The zebra mask had been displaced, and I could already see the photographs that would run: the blurred but unmistakable profile of your stupefied face.

I hadn't told you about all the other times photographers had staked out the property. It would have only upset you. I hadn't told you, either, about the phone calls from reporters and how often I'd hung up on them. Some of the most brazen ones had even approached me in person while I was on my errands and ambushed me with questions about you and Rafael. You didn't know how I deflected them, how I stared daggers at them and threatened to call the police. You had no idea how much I did for you.

XII.

I HARDLY saw you the next few days. You were in and out all weekend, carrying your thermos travel mug, which I now suspected contained something other than kombucha. As stupid as it was, I knew you were avoiding me. You were embarrassed about the solstice party and probably thought I'd lecture you about drinking during pregnancy. You were right about this. You had every reason to be humiliated.

Finally, I left the house in disgust. I wasn't in the mood for the Rhizome, for the babies. Instead, I traveled up and down PCH. I descended the stairs to El Matador beach and huddled in a rock cave, listening to the soft cursing of the waves.

Then, on Monday morning, you were awake before me, waiting downstairs. You smiled warmly as I descended.

"I'm so glad to see you this morning," you said. "I want to show you something."

You held out your left hand, and I saw the ring. My eyes registered harlequin colors: blue, red, green, in a bright gold setting. A small Saturnalia. It took a moment for my brain to transcend the visual delight and grasp the darker message.

"Sapphire, ruby, emerald, diamond." You indicated each stone with a fingernail.

I said nothing. It wasn't necessarily an engagement ring, I told myself. It could be a high-end bauble you'd bought at the Rhizome gift shop.

You replaced the ring and your eyes flashed. "Raf changed his mind about the baby. He said that he tried, but he couldn't live without me. He's going to commit completely and be a good husband and father. He's finally ready."

"What?" I couldn't blunt the blade in my voice.

You pulled back your hand. "I'm sorry I didn't tell you right away. It happened so fast, I didn't have a chance."

"I can't believe this."

"Abby, I'm sorry. I know it's unexpected." Beneath your whine was something thorny I didn't want to touch. "It's as much as a surprise to me as it is to you, believe me."

"Right. Of course," I said and felt a pain like a branding iron in my chest.

"But it's such a relief. I'm so happy. I hope you'll be happy for me."

I wanted to rush out of the room. It was torture to stand there in your kitchen, in the onslaught of what was happening. It was like a bad scene in a movie. I forced myself to stay in place, to remain upright, and I felt as if I were reading a scripted line as I answered, "I'm happy if you want me to be."

"Well, I hope so." You stared uncertainly at me. "Anyway, please don't tell anyone about it. Raf and I are planning to keep it secret from the press, so it's just between you and me for now, okay? Some people announce these things right away, but Polly says that's a mistake. It's better to sit on this kind of news until the timing is optimal."

I snorted. "Who would I tell?"

You stared and blinked at me, your long foolish eyelashes like a horse's. "Well, just don't say anything."

The last thing I wanted to do was give you an engagement gift, but I knew that I had no choice. I wouldn't have wanted to purchase anything, even if I'd had the money to do so. Instead, I pasted together a collage of old photographs that I'd brought from Michigan, pictures of the two of us as children. It was more a tribute to our friendship than a celebration of your betrothal. I wanted to put it in front of you and make you consider what you were rejecting.

I found you outside by the pool on a wooden lounge chair. "Go get your bathing suit and come back," you instructed. I'd become accustomed to commands like this, delivered nonchalantly. Of course I'd do what you asked, like a dutiful assistant. You had no reason to think that I wouldn't.

I changed into the nautical two-piece from the Rhizome and tied a sarong high around my waist to cover the scar. I dragged another chaise next to yours, and we were quiet for a while beside the pool. It was a pristine day, windless. On the water's surface, I saw a flickering apparition of two little girls playing "shark," splashing and flipping like snappers. Those girls were beached now, their grown bodies the size of marlins.

I stole glances at you in your crocheted bikini. Your midriff was a milky slab with a tidy divot of navel, no sign of the intruder inside. You wore the big black sunglasses, and wooden hoops in your ears. Your toes were capped with opaline nails like seashells, and your hair was swept up in a loose twist. My own hair lay like a skunk pelt on my neck as I weighed down the chaise beside you. It should have been the most natural thing in the world, to lie beside an old friend, to stare together at the bare blue sky. The rest of the world was shut out, denied access to this confidential moment.

On the little table beside you was the thermos. I considered asking for a sip of whatever was inside, just to make you squirm. I knew you were drinking. There were wine bottles missing from the last case I'd brought home. But I wasn't here for a confrontation.

I waited a long time before breaking the silence. "I brought a little something for you."

You rose up from your chaise and took the package. "What is it?"

"Just a memento."

You pushed the sunglasses onto your head and ripped the wrapping paper, fashioned from aluminum foil I'd taken from your kitchen.

"Oh my God, this is so great." You ran your finger over the photo collage and laughed. There were pictures of us at your house, dressed as kittens, with eyeliner whiskers and cat-ear headbands. There were pictures of each of us jumping into your pool, suspended in midair. "Look at this! I can't believe that was us," you said.

"There's a card, too. But you don't have to open it now."

You tore open the envelope and pulled out the generically baroque card that said "On Your Engagement" in gold cursive text. I'd chosen it for its elegance, but it now struck me as grandmotherly. I watched your eyes scan the stanzas I'd written inside, a poem by Emily Brontë:

> Love is like the wild rose-briar,
> Friendship like the holly-tree—
> The holly is dark when the rose-briar blooms
> But which will bloom most constantly?
>
> The wild rose-briar is sweet in spring,
> Its summer blossoms scent the air;
> Yet wait till winter comes again
> And who will call the wild-briar fair?
>
> Then scorn the silly rose-wreath now
> And deck thee with the holly's sheen,
> That when December blights thy brow
> He still may leave thy garland green.

After struggling with the appropriate degree of endearment for the sign-off, I'd settled for: *Your constant friend, Abby.* Now you closed the card and looked at the watercolor roses on the front.

"This is really sweet. Thank you." The tone of your voice had dropped a register, gone strangely dull. You held the card and collage a moment longer, then rested them on the stone patio beside your chair. You pulled your sunglasses down.

Of all the moments you disappointed me, I return to this one most often. For some reason, it stings the most. The truth is that I'd nurtured the hope that Brontë's words, like an incantation, might finally jolt you from your trance, that you'd awaken and look at me in appreciation, take my hand, and revert to the old Elise. This was my last chance to rescue you, to bring us both back to our childhood garden. But, as you dropped my gift to the ground and pulled your sunglasses down, I understood that you were gone. I saw that you'd never return to me fully, that we'd forever remain on parallel tracks, never to mesh again, no matter how I twisted and swerved. At that moment, the cold fact began to penetrate.

"So, I still haven't told you about Raf's proposal," you said quietly and took a sip from the thermos.

"No, you haven't." I said after a moment.

"Well," you sighed, adjusting yourself in the chair. "He surprised me while I was in the bath, under the stingrays. You were out that day, I guess. He came in without knocking, like he does, and sat down on the toilet in his clothes. He just sat there for a minute, and then he gave this whole speech about not being able to live without me, all the stuff I told you. Then he pulled the ring out of his pocket and handed it to me in the bathtub." You stopped talking. After a long moment, you said, "I didn't really think about it until later. I was too distracted by the ring, you know? Those incredible colors. And I was so relieved that Raf had come back. When I looked at him he was just beautiful. And all these prenatal hormones were flooding through me, I guess, and I was a little delirious. He said, 'Is that a yes?' And I got out of the bath, dripping wet, and kissed him. I didn't even really think about it until later. It took a while for the glow to wear off and to realize he proposed to me on the toilet."

I couldn't tell if your eyes, beneath the sunglasses, were open or closed. You put a forearm over your face, showing the pale bowl of your underarm.

"Anyway, the wedding's going to be soon. Probably in just a few weeks. Raf wants it to be very small, intimate. *Intimo*, as he says."

"How small?"

You turned to me, and I saw my warped reflection in your sunglasses. "Just family, basically. It's going to be in Buenos Aires, at the church he went to as a kid, which is really tiny. It'll be at the end of August, which is good because it's still winter there and not so hot."

You lifted your sunglasses and looked at me for a long moment. "Listen," you said. "You're coming, of course. I don't know about the ceremony itself, but you're coming to Argentina."

"It's okay. I don't need to be there," I began.

"No, you're coming." You replaced your sunglasses, turned back to the sky.

We were silent for a few minutes among the gossiping birds. I closed my eyes and conjured Michigan, your backyard pool. I remembered your mother, how she took pride in nice things, like the hand-painted tray with peacock feathers that she'd set on the poolside table. I remembered how she'd ask me to make sure you put on sunscreen. You were so fair; you'd burn quickly.

"The timing's actually pretty good," you were saying. "Filming will be done in two weeks, and then after the honeymoon Raf will move in."

A pause, a breath. I didn't speak.

"It's obvious, I know, but I thought I should give you some official notice."

How casually you struck me with brass knuckles. I don't know where I found the strength to prop myself on an elbow to look at you. As I did, the fat on my stomach folded inward, rolling over the top of the sarong. You lay flat on the chaise. The photo collage rested on the patio stone where you'd put it with the ripped aluminum foil. The sunlight volleyed off the surface of the pool in glittering pixels. All at once, I had a vision of the Rhizome, the grand staircase leading to the second story, the tight interlocking pattern of the carpet. In the vision, I saw myself traversing the carpet, ascending the staircase.

"I'll need your help planning the wedding, of course."

"*Intimo.*"

"Right."

You turned away from me so that your sunglasses reflected the sky again. Your exposed abdomen rose and fell with each breath. You hadn't used sunscreen and were already beginning to burn.

I felt no guilt about skipping the laundry on Tuesday and going with Paul to the children's shelter. I no longer felt any deep obligation to you. You could do your own laundry.

The shelter wasn't the bleak penitentiary I'd pictured, but a yellow building with a Spanish tile roof and flowering courtyard. We waited in a conference room, cool and spare but for a vase of gerbera daisies on the table. A woman came into the room with a girl trailing behind her. The girl was broad faced with a tight slot for a mouth. She wouldn't meet our eyes.

"This is Yolanda," the woman said in a loud, slow voice, touching the girl's shoulder. "She has agreed to talk to you. You may ask questions, and I will translate."

The girl's hair was long and dark, parted in the middle, and she wore a sleeveless pink shirt with ruffles at the shoulders. There was a crater in her upper arm where she must have received some vaccination. I couldn't remember how old Paul had said Yolanda was, and it was impossible to tell—she seemed both child and adult—but I knew she was the one who'd been raped. She sat stiffly, eyes fixed on the vase of red daisies.

This was the moment, I understood, to ask the compassionate questions that would earn her trust and draw her out. This was the moment to form a feminine bond that would prompt this girl to divulge the details of her ordeal, to itemize the exact methodology of her violation. As I looked at her, a film played in my imagination—the knives and guns, the rotten teeth and pubic hair—and my body went cold.

Paul looked at me, raised an eyebrow. "Go ahead," he whispered.

"Hello," I said quickly. "My name is Abby."

The translator echoed this in melodious Spanish, lending a false grace to my words. "Buenos días, me llamo Abby."

"Thank you for agreeing to talk with us," I said.

"Gracias por aceptar conversar nosotros."

"We are interested—we hope you will share with us, your journey to this place."

"Esperamos que nos cuente su viaje aquí."

The girl raised her eyes from the flower vase, then, and looked at me. My face turned to rubber in her gaze. I couldn't bring myself to smile. The air-conditioning in the room was suddenly intolerable, and I began to quake uncontrollably.

I turned to Paul. "I can't do this."

The children swarmed my dreams that night. I found them in the white house on the hill, in a cold dark room, huddled beneath a blanket. Yolanda was among them, naked, trying to cover herself. In the dream, I tried to join them beneath the blanket, but they pushed me away. A little boy hissed and said, "Vete, bruja." Through the loose curtain between sleep and waking, I saw the Perren photograph on the wall, but it was different, three-dimensional. As I stared at it, black insects, hard-bodied beetles or cockroaches, emerged from the gash in the woman's face and skittered over the print and onto the wall. I pulled away, slammed against the headboard. The insects swarmed onto the bed, and I screamed.

I didn't answer Paul's phone calls. He left a dozen messages that I failed to acknowledge, but he was undeterred and left a dozen more. Finally, I sent him a short note that said simply: *I'm sorry, I need to figure some things out right now.* He replied: *I'll be here when you're ready.*

I lay in bed and thought about Paul. I thought of the polyester shirts, the saggy black trousers, the stiff belt. I remembered the layered, greasy hair, the stained teeth and untrimmed fingernails. He was savagely valiant. Any ounce of him was better than me. When I'd turned to him at the conference table in fear and pleading, he'd understood, and taken me gently away. He hadn't scolded or shamed me. He'd simply returned to the room and questioned the poor girl himself.

XIII.

I DREAMED about you and Shelby. In the dreams, you were together in a swamp, dipping your babies in the muck. I was in the forest watching, my feet heavy, unable to move. The babies were purple-faced, screaming, as you let them go. You sat down together on the wet ground as your babies sank. I lunged forward from the trees, just in time to clutch the nearer child from the quagmire. I felt her chest palpitate against mine. Then the scene shifted and I was in a shabby room with baby bottles on the floor. There was a snarling animal somewhere in the room, and I had the sense of racing against time as I searched for a bag that contained supplies I needed, something for the baby. The snarling grew closer as I found the bag next to the door, a soiled white purse with drooping fringes like a pony's mane. In the dream, I lifted the purse and sprinted through the door as the animal pounced behind me.

My first alarm rang at dawn. I slipped back into sleep, and again I was in Ann Arbor, walking barefoot in the snow. I saw the movie theater and restaurants, shuttered and darkened. On the bridge, the car headlights were narrowed tiger eyes. A force hit me like a wave, and I catapulted forward. My arms shot to the sides. Swan dives from the pier into Lake Michigan. August sunshine. The warning sign posted there, with photographs of the boys who'd died from jumping. In the dream, I hung in the air for a moment. I saw the picture of an open eye spray-painted on the concrete abutment. I saw the surface of the Huron River, glassed with ice. Then I was in the water, plunging to the bottom of the river, where the green darkened to black. No color, light, or shape. A blockage in my ears, a terrifying solidity inside my skull. Utter silence, darkness. This was death. I jolted upright in bed.

When my second alarm rang, I turned it off. I was exhausted, as if I hadn't slept at all. I didn't want to leave the bed. I didn't want to see you. I lay under the satin duvet, staring at the woman in the Perren photograph, reading a global truth in the nature of her lesion. A condition of permeability. I came to believe it was a portrait of me.

You finally knocked. Through the door, you asked if I was okay. I put false vigor into my voice from my tangle of bedsheets. "I'm okay, just overslept." I waited for you to ask if you could come in, but you didn't. Instead, you spoke through the door again. "Are you sick?" I detected a note of impatience in your voice, a note of authority. I still worked for you, after all. "No," I piped back. "I'll be out soon." I heard your footsteps retreat and closed my eyes.

Once I'd spilled out of bed, I had only enough energy to rinse myself in the shower. After that, I trudged down the stairs, one step at a time, and sat in the kitchen. There, on the table in front of me, lay the new issue of *GQ*. Rafael was on the cover, in a fitted white T-shirt and jeans, astride a polo pony. I picked up the magazine and ran my fingers over the glossy surface, to be sure it was real, that I was awake. Rafael stared back from atop the pony. He was naturally regal, his bloodline refined over centuries. This brazen beauty was unfair, this chiseled face the product of generations of plundering. I felt queasy as I opened the magazine to read the interview. He spoke about his acting work, his hopes of becoming a director, and the screenplay he'd allegedly been writing. There was only one question about his relationship with you, and his response was disingenuously self-deprecating. *I don't know what I've done to deserve her. I'm incredibly lucky to have found a woman saintly, or crazy, enough to put up with me.*

I slapped the magazine closed, only to be confronted with the cover again: that pony, that vanity. His eyes bore into me in mocking challenge. I turned the magazine facedown on the table where you'd left it.

We almost never talked about the media. It was better to pretend the media didn't exist, you said, in order to stay sane. My own addiction to the magazines had waned, of course, since I came here. I saw only the sanctioned profiles that made it into the house, forwarded by Polly, your publicist, with laudatory sticky notes. You were dismissive of these.

"Ugh. I always hate how I sound in interviews," you said later that week, throwing a copy of *InStyle* onto the kitchen table. Your own face beamed from the cover, burnished with bronzer, a feathery pink collar at the neck. "And I look like a powder puff."

After you left for the day, I took *InStyle* in my hands and studied the cover, your airbrushed metallic skin, the outré saffron sweep at your eyelids, the horrid pink plumage. I'd been present at the photo shoot when they'd done all this, had watched you submit to the foolery. Now, I sat and read the interview alone, as in the old days.

Tell us about your typical day. What's life like with Rafael Solar?

Oh, it's pretty ordinary, actually. I mean, we're just as busy and crazed as any other working couple and have to carve out special time for each other. On most days we're both so tired we just crash in our pajamas and watch TV. I'm also incredibly lucky to have my best friend living with me. She came to visit four months ago, and I wouldn't let her leave! I have a publicist and a stylist who make my world go round, but I couldn't do a single thing without Abby. We've known each other since kindergarten. She knows things about me no one else does, not even my parents.

How are things going with Rafael? Are we hearing wedding bells?

We're very happy. He's a wonderful man. We're taking it one day at a time.

What about children? Do you hope to be a mother someday? What's your philosophy about parenthood in Hollywood?

To be honest, I'm horrified by the way mothers are expected to sacrifice themselves for their children. I have no intention of forfeiting my own career goals and life purpose. Ideally, I'd want to raise children in a secluded place, away from Los Angeles and all the pressures of celebrity, though I don't know how realistic that is. I'm lucky to have grown up in the Midwest, but there'd be no chance for my own children to have a normal childhood here.

Wow, sounds like you've really thought this through.

Yeah, I guess I have. [Laughs.]

I was nauseated when I finished reading. The way you'd referred to me as your best friend—as if you had any concept of friendship—was a farce. I impulsively brought the magazine to the kitchen trash can. As I was about to drop it in, I saw a collection of cigarette butts mixed in with a pile of fruit rinds.

"Where did these come from?" I asked when you came home, my voice trembling with anger.

"Oh, I don't know." Your voice was silvery, girlish. "Maybe Flora dumped them there."

"Flora was here on Monday. Today's Thursday. And I don't think she smokes."

You looked at me and blinked, an infuriating little smile beginning at your mouth. "Oh, so what," you said, turning away. "Our mothers did it. Lots of people do it, even if they say they don't. If it's not a lot, it doesn't matter."

I dropped the butt I was holding back into the trash and let the lid close. Looking back, I realize I couldn't have been cognizant of what I was doing, at that moment. As the words came to me, I was blindly heeding some instinctual cue. I spoke in a new, bright voice. "I saw your *InStyle* interview," I said. "I liked what you said about raising children. Have you actually started to think about child care, for when the baby comes?"

You were quiet for a moment. "Honestly, no. I've been too preoccupied with the wedding. I can't even get my head around the rest of it yet."

"I meant to tell you something a while back," I said evenly. "That time you took me to the Rhizome for my birthday, I had a tour of the daycare center. Did I ever mention that? I don't think I did. While you were in the actors' lounge after your session, I had a tour of the campus, and the woman who took me around happened to work in the daycare, so she showed it to me. It looked pretty great, actually."

"I'm sure it is," you said.

"Did you know that you can even leave a baby overnight? There's always at least one person on hand for the night shift, so you don't have to worry about babysitters. The baby can stay where it's comfortable, with familiar people. Some people leave their children for weeks at a time. They think of it as enrichment."

"Yeah, I've heard about that," you said in your vacant, buttery way. "There's a lot of flexibility."

"The woman who gave me the tour, though, she was so into the babies. I mean, I guess that's the kind of enthusiasm you want, but still, it was kind of unnerving. She kept talking about how she couldn't wait to have a baby of her own."

You shook your head. "So many women are like that, don't you think? They can't *wait* to have babies. It's like they equate motherhood with some kind of feminine achievement. Any other ambition just goes out the window."

I leaned on the counter and nodded thoughtfully. "That's especially true for the women back home, I think. When I saw Christy Peters at the reunion, she seemed so self-satisfied with being a mother. It's too bad. She was so interesting when we were younger." I paused. "But this woman at the Rhizome was different. The baby-wanting thing seemed kind of disturbing."

You looked at me, a fish circling bait. "Who was she? Did you get her name?"

"Tasha."

"I don't think I know her," you said.

I launched away from the counter, feeling the buzz an actress must feel when she knows she's nailing her lines. I paused, considering what should come next. "I don't understand it, myself," I said with a little shrug. "Then again, I'm not good with babies. They kind of freak me out, to be honest."

You gave me a strange look. Maybe you were remembering my offer to help raise your child—but you'd never believed I was serious, of course.

"Oh, Abby," you gushed theatrically. "I'm sure you'd be great with your own baby, if you had one. It's different when it's yours. At least that's what they say." You came up behind me and put your hands on my shoulders. You squeezed them once, firmly, and I felt the pressure of your fingers on my muscles well after you'd taken them away.

You'd been struck with morning sickness but still dragged yourself to lunch at trendy restaurants where you'd be available to the cameras. I tagged along in modest but presentable clothing, your homely but loyal companion, the best friend without whom you couldn't do a single thing.

"Polly says it's important to stay on the radar during filming," you said. "I don't like it, though. I'm working all day on set, and I'd much rather go somewhere private. Publicity is so much easier when the movie's finished. I wish I could just avoid everything now."

"Why can't you?"

"It's just not how it works. You have to feed the machine, or it'll eat someone else."

I rolled my eyes. I didn't care who saw. "But you don't *have* to, do you? Does everyone do it?"

"The men don't have to, at least not as much. You notice Raf hardly ever goes out to lunch." There was a note of contempt in your voice.

I paused, thinking of the yellow Jaguar. "I've wondered what he does while we're out."

"I don't know what the hell he does," you spat.

We were in a spacious restaurant with high ceilings and white faux-leather booth seating—too vast for our dining neighbors to hear us. Sputnik-style light fixtures hung above, like sea urchins, each arm ending in a blinding bulb. You were in a striped cotton top that hung off one shoulder, exposing a bra strap. With your loose hair, you were a picture of easy style, the tension visible only at close range, as you pushed a kale and chicken salad around in its bowl.

At the other side of the restaurant was an actress whose name I didn't know. She sat enthroned at the head of a table filled with handmaidens. When I commented on the arrangement, you scoffed. "So many actresses are like that. They love being worshipped and manipulating their worshipers. It's like middle school. One girl comes into favor, and another gets rebuffed."

"You're not like that," I said sweetly. You didn't need a group of subservients. Only one.

"No, I think entourages are gross. And you know I don't trust the women here. They all *want* something." You blinked and simpered at me. "I'm so lucky I have you, Abby. I know I've been distracted lately, but I just want to tell you again how glad I am you came out here and stayed with me. I don't know how I could cope with everything alone. I know we haven't talked about it yet, but I'm hoping we can find someplace new for you to live, near the house, so you can pop over easily. Expenses paid, of course."

I stared. What you were saying was ridiculous. But you must have believed I was pathetic enough to shuttle between your house and my kennel like a little pet. You didn't see that there was no place I could occupy with dignity anymore. I finished chewing my food. "I'm sure we'll work something out," I said. "I'll look for an apartment while you're on your honeymoon."

You shifted in the booth toward me and gave me an awkward hug. There was no bulge yet at your abdomen, but I thought I could feel the vibrating life inside.

"I'm sick to my stomach again," you said as you pulled away.

We sat in silence after that. I kept my eyes on my plate, carefully cutting my crepe and glancing up furtively. You didn't look sick. The turquoise earrings against your hair were bewitching. You knew this. You'd been using color to your advantage since childhood. I remembered the ribbons you'd threaded through your braids in fourth grade, turning yourself into a May Queen, and how all the girls had gone home after school to find ribbons for themselves. I was the only one who hadn't, the only one who'd never tried to imitate you.

You paid the bill, and we came out into the blaring sun. The cameras were waiting. They snapped and swarmed, and I felt the physical effort it took for you to turn around to face them before getting into the car, to dig deep and pull out a heart-stopping smile.

That night, I dreamed of waking in my bed. I heard voices. I got out of bed, quietly opened the door of my room, and listened. The voices were coming from down the hall, from your dream room with the hanging orbs. I stepped silently into the corridor and heard a murmur and laughter. The door to the orb room was ajar, pushed inward. Rafael's voice came from inside, saying, "Yes, like that." I pushed the door in.

It took a moment to interpret the scene. The orbs were gone, and there were several figures on the floor. I looked at the one nearest the door, and understood before my mind could fill in the details. The nude woman turned her head to me from where she knelt on all fours. There was a saddle on her back, strapped and buckled. It would have been an almost comical sight, were it not for the bridle fastened to her face. There was a horse bit, tight as a ball gag, pulling at the sides of her mouth. My eyes darted around the room, found several other nude women in horse tack. I looked back to the first woman, and her eyes met mine with a look of pained endurance. I recognized her, then, as the French actress Mireille Sauvage. A necklace of yellow gemstones hung incongruously at her clavicle.

Finally, I spotted Rafael against the far wall, the only one fully dressed, in his black shirt and jeans. "Hello," he said. "I was hoping you'd come. Would you like to join?"

I stood still in the doorway as he came nearer, holding a small bucket.

"This is the last touch," he said, raising the bucket. "You can just watch, if you like, but I'd love it if you joined us." He dipped a hand into the bucket. "Look," he said, pulling something out. He looked straight into my eyes and—again—there was the sharp voltage. I knew that it was really him. He was really there, sharing the dream. "It reminds me a little bit of your other dream," he said. "The one you wouldn't tell me. The oozing and sliding."

He went to the French actress, and I watched him place a small dark object on her haunch. It adhered, then began to creep along her skin, leaving a wet trail. "Oh God, so slow," he said in a low, raspy voice. The woman's hip twitched, jostling the saddle. She closed her eyes. "Perfect," Rafael told her. "Keep still, just like that."

I stood watching as the slug moved over the woman's body, from hip to torso, sliding under her rib cage, disappearing beneath a hanging breast. Her eyes remained closed, as if she were forcefully meditating. Rafael moved to the next woman and placed a slug on each cheek of her buttocks. He turned to me and said, "I'm getting so hard." He moved his hand to the front of his jeans and rubbed himself slowly. "Are you sure you don't want to try?"

I took a step toward him in the dream, and he laughed.

"No, Abby, not you. It was only a joke."

The woman laughed, too, through the horse bit. I fell backward through the door and swept through the hallway into my room. When I looked down at my feet, I saw that they were a few inches above the floor. I went into the bathroom, fastened the lock, and sat on the toilet seat. The room was black, with only a thin line of light in the mirror from the crack beneath the door.

Filming ended, at last. I opted to stay in the house rather than attend the wrap party with you and Rafael. I didn't even want to look at him. Every time his eyes met mine, it was in an intolerably viscid, furtive way that stroked at our secret. I didn't want to be near either of you.

You came home alone from the party before midnight, your skin pallid, and went right to sleep. The next day we had lunch in Topanga. You said that you were sick of the hot spots, that you wanted to get away for a minute, just be in a different place. The wedding was in a week, and your mind was already in Argentina—the dress was finished, the guest rooms booked, the honeymoon scheduled—but for now, Topanga was the closest thing to leaving. Climbing up the canyon road, slowing around the curves, we passed the public art wall with its masks and relief sculptures. It was darker here, secretive. The road narrowed and snaked, and at one point you were forced to brake hard to avoid a head-on collision. This mountain was a reckless place, for reckless people. The houses were built on slopes prone to mudslides, in a game of chicken with nature. I didn't know where Paul's cabin was in this network of harebrained roads, but I knew it was close. I could sense it like a mountain lion breathing in the woods.

At the restaurant, we took an outdoor table beside a stream. The chairs were wooden and rickety, and there was a mason jar of white and purple larkspur on the table. A bearded waiter came to our table and took our orders. You asked for herbal tea; I ordered champagne.

You looked better today, as if you'd slept well. Your hair was tied back and your face was fresh without makeup. You wore no jewelry, not even earrings, and your natural radiance—the beauty of an adored child—shone through. You picked up the paper menu, then put it down. "I honestly don't think I can eat," you said. "I'm just too upset."

"What is it?" I asked, though I'd felt an instant spark of knowledge, as if I'd touched a socket. It had to be Rafael. Your engagement was over, or beginning its terminal throes. You'd discovered his infidelities. My dream had been accurate.

"Perren invited me to audition." You gazed darkly at me. "And Abby, his new film sounds incredible. It all takes place in the ocean, and he wants me to audition as a siren. Not a beautiful one, but a feathery bird-woman with wings and scaly legs, like how the Greeks first imagined them."

My chair rocked and threatened to tip. I held the edge of the table to steady myself.

"I don't know if it's a big part or not," you said. "But it doesn't matter. I can't do it. How can I do it? I'd have to tell him I'm pregnant. It'll be obvious soon. And then he can't use me."

Our drinks arrived, and I gripped my champagne flute. "You should do it anyway," I heard myself say. "If he wants to cast you, maybe you can work something out."

You smiled faintly and closed your eyes. When you opened them again, they locked on mine, bright and vapid. There was nothing in them. You hadn't been filled, over all these years, but had been left carefully hollow. This, I imagined, was why actresses cracked so easily with age, like glass vases—why they were so swiftly and thoroughly ruined.

I drank the champagne fast, and as you sipped your tea, I ordered another glass. You glanced disapprovingly, but I said nothing. The sound of Perren's name had lit something in me. You weren't the one who mattered. I was. I was the one who was filled to bursting, the one who deserved feathered wings.

"You're right," you said finally. "I should do it."

There were, ludicrously, tears in your eyes.

XIV.

THE SOUTH American sky was inverted. The day was
blue and clear, but through my sunglasses, everything
was dimmed as through a tinted window. I drank
sangria and restlessly ate olives from a little bowl on the café
table as I observed the church across the street. It was a stone
chapel with an arched door and ruffled steeple, one of the
oldest in Buenos Aires. I'd already been watching the church
for over an hour, feeling the adrenaline swirl inside me. The
photographers had been staked out since morning, resting
their equipment on the ground, taking desultory pictures of
the facade. I'd had vague instructions to divert them, but it
was useless. They knew the location was correct.

It was my first time outside the country. My expedited
passport had arrived forty-eight hours before, and I'd boarded
a jet with you and Rafael and a few select companions. Now,
sitting on la calle Bolívar on this Wednesday in January, I
thought of Meijer, thousands of miles away, where I would
have been in that other life. At this very moment, the magazine

distributors would be rotating the weeklies, refreshing the racks at the checkout aisles. The customers would be pausing with their carts to drink in the new scandals and spectacles. I would have been one of them, in that other life, searching for you like a lovesick girl.

I'd pictured Buenos Aires as a dusty city of slums and was surprised as our car took us from the airport over elegant boulevards with designer shops. An obscene obelisk marked the end of one avenue, which was as wide and loud as the 405 freeway in California. The side streets were calmer, with faded verandas and old, twisting trees. The hotel was a white-washed inn with tall windows and wrought-iron railings. You'd generously reserved a single room for me, with a bed as spacious and deep as a cumulus cloud. Still I'd hoped, irrationally, that you and I might have shared a room, that we might have had that last intimacy.

My presence here seemed a formality only. Bianca, your stylist, had co-opted the role of maid of honor, nitpicking your dress and makeup, gossiping about the wedding guests. When I heard her say Mireille Sauvage's name, I felt it as a strike in the gut. The guest list wasn't just family, I understood now. You'd lied. But I betrayed nothing and smiled at you in your spotlight of attention. The qualms about Rafael that you'd confessed to me seemed to have evaporated. Perhaps this was the real reason I was not to enter the church. The bride had used me as a repository for her doubt, and now I was tainted. In order for the ceremony to remain pure, for the marriage to knit together cleanly, I was to stay outside.

I'd slept badly in the beautiful hotel. Since leaving California, I'd felt the approach of a surge, the familiar beginnings of an updraft at my feet. For two nights I'd lain awake on the cumulus bed, powerless against the accelerating cyclone. My heart revved. The scraps of sleep that touched me were embroidered with bright, erratic dreams. These were often lucid, and I felt I could pull them toward me and push them away when I wanted. A hummingbird flew at me and morphed into a small human, with wings on either side of its head where the ears should be. I slapped it away, and it came back. When I thought I was awake, it reemerged from the white window curtains, flapping at my face.

I sat at the café table and rippled with impotent energy, just as I had on the airplane, coming to California. I knew from experience that when this feeling came, this tidal power, I had to direct it wisely. Pulling an olive pit from my mouth, I watched as one of the photographers left the paparazzi throng. He came striding across the street toward the café and flashed a smile as he sat at an adjacent table. His face had a pleasant golden bristle, and he wore a baby-blue linen shirt. He struck me as familiar. Perhaps all photographers resembled one another, with that same aloof, immoral gleam in the eye. After he set his camera down, this one could have passed for an ordinary patron as he gestured to the waiter.

He ordered coffee in Spanish, and when the waiter withdrew, he turned to me and smiled.

"So, what brings you here?" he asked in plain American English. "Are you a reporter?"

I looked sharply at him. "No hablo inglés."

He smilingly held up a hand and apologized in a river of Spanish. I returned to my sangria and hoped the interaction would end there. The alcohol had already soaked into my veins, but I was dressed too lightly for the weather and still shivered. The white-diamond sunlight didn't warm me. I drew a long breath and bit into another olive, adding its pit to the wet pile on the table.

The man leaned toward me. "Me puedo unir a ustedes?" he said. When I didn't reply, he tried again in English. "May I join you?"

His eyes were the same placid blue as his shirt. It seemed unlikely that anything bad could come from talking with the owner of these eyes. I nodded, and he smiled and dragged his chair to my table, tugging his camera by the strap. "Thanks," he said. "It gets lonely in the crowd." He gestured to my glass. "What are you drinking there?" Before I could answer, he called to the waiter and requested a *jarra de sangria*. "Too good not to share," he said. "I'm Lucas." He held out a hand. The linen shirtsleeves were rolled up, revealing the fine gold hairs of his forearms.

The name was somehow ready on my lips. "Jessica."

"Hello, Jessica. Where are you visiting from?"

We were interrupted by the waiter, who lay down a giant pitcher of sangria, orange slices layered like lily pads over a lower stratum of darker clumped fruit. Lucas topped off my glass, filled his own, and lifted his drink. "To the newlyweds."

For a moment, I considered whether to pretend not to understand. But my hand lifted and our glasses clinked.

"I'm so glad to be here," Lucas said. "It's a nice change from L.A."

"I'm surprised you came all this way."

He raised his eyebrows. "Are you kidding? This is a great assignment. I love this city."

"Isn't it risky to leave your post, though? I haven't seen anyone else budge since I've been sitting here."

He shrugged. "The action won't start till afternoon, that's definite. No one in this country does anything early." He smiled. "I already have my position, and a couple of guys will hold it for me. We trade favors like that. Plus, I believe in taking sanity breaks. A drink helps keep you mellow. Celebs don't like it when paps are agitated. Think about it. Would you turn and give your best smile to someone who's practically cursing at you? You convey a lot by the tone of your voice. They can hear it. You need to modulate yourself when you call to them. Make it so *you're* the one they want to look at." He pushed his chair back and crossed his legs. "You look familiar. Are you from L.A.?"

I gave a small smile.

"I knew it." He winked and raised his glass. "Another toast, then. To the City of Angels."

We drank again, and Lucas refilled my glass. Somehow the pitcher was already half-empty. I hadn't had anything to eat besides olives all day. I hadn't felt hunger.

"You still haven't told me what brings you here. I don't think you just happen to be on vacation, staking out this church."

The day was relentlessly bright, turning the metal café tables into reflective discs. I felt cloistered inside my sunglasses—trapped, but safe. My body had finally warmed from the sangria, and my heartbeat was still in overdrive. I wanted to talk. It wouldn't make a difference, I decided, if I confided in this one friendly photographer. I paused a moment, taking a long sip of my drink before answering.

"I'm a friend of the couple's," I said.

As soon as the words were out, I felt that I'd stepped outside a barrier. Lucas's face transformed, brightening. He uncrossed his legs, sat straighter in his chair. "Really! I can't believe my luck."

My body grew warmer, and I smirked.

"You think I'm kidding? Do you know how many people over there"—he gestured toward the crowd at the church—"would love to talk to a friend of the couple's?"

I raised my eyebrows and took another drink. He gave a wicked smile, and I felt my face heat. My hand brought the glass to my lips, and I took a long, deep drink.

Another pitcher arrived. I began to talk. Lucas moved his chair closer. He ordered food in a jumble of Spanish. The minutes blurred and looped, one into the next, and I never saw the waiter, though I was aware of plates being cleared and replaced. I was conscious only of Lucas's face, the pleasing geometry of his eyes and lips, the smooth slope from nose to brow. I felt as if I'd been looking at his face forever, that it had been planted in my memory long ago.

I realized that I'd been talking at length, delivering a monologue, but I couldn't stop, and he didn't interrupt. He only listened, with a nod or tilt of the head at pivotal moments, in a way that invited more. I felt I was divining a soft profundity in him that deepened as I spoke and that echoed an equivalent depth in me. The history of Michigan and college and the bridge poured out of me, across the café table, into this twin hollow. And now, as I spoke your name, as I approached the doom of Malibu, of Rafael, a plug formed in my throat. I swallowed against it. I'd forgotten the church, forgotten where I was. This felt like a private confession, occurring in limbo. I sipped the sangria and put my hand on the tabletop, palm down, to keep the table from spinning.

"They fight all the time. They had such a bad fight at Cecconi's that Elise ran into the ladies' room crying. She was a mess."

Lucas gave a sympathetic look.

"It got so bad that the maître d' had to ask them to leave."

"Oh my God, how humiliating."

"The truth is that Rafael's a terrible person," I said loudly, spray coming from my mouth. "Elise is making a huge mistake. She knows, but she's in denial. And there are even worse things about him she has no idea about."

I lifted my glass and drained the rest of its contents, the swollen wedges of orange colliding with my lips. The mass of fruit dropped back to the bottom of the glass, wilted and bloody.

"Oh, that can't be right," Lucas said with a frown. His face was tense, his eyelids blinking. "What could possibly be so bad? You said you're a friend of the couple's, so he's your friend, too, right?"

On some level I knew what he was doing. I heard my inner voice warning me of it, in an amusing, untranslatable language. "I can tell you exactly what's so bad," I said.

As I continued, in detail, I felt an unburdening that I imagined was what they called catharsis. I became lighter with each grain of elaborated perversion and depravity I swept out of my dreams and into the light. The bridle, and the slugs. As I spoke, I knew that what I was doing was absolutely correct, the only way to save you from your hideous error. It was something only a true friend would do. My final gift to you.

Afterward, I was spent. I leaned back in my chair and felt a sudden need to sleep. A new plate of food had arrived, some quiche or tortilla. I lifted a wedge of the food onto my plate, and at the moment I took my first bite, a buzz rose up from across the street. A white Rolls-Royce rumbled into view, and the camera shutters exploded. Lucas sprang from his seat, thrusting a handful of pesos onto the table.

"You'd better hurry, if you don't want to miss the ceremony," he said. Then he leaned down to me, took my face in his dry golden hands, and placed his mouth on mine. The kiss was long and full, and I had the sensation of sinking in water, circling down. "Adios," he said as he jogged away, then turned and called back: "Muchas gracias."

The Rolls-Royce had released its occupants and driven away. A matching car appeared and disappeared, swallowed and disgorged by the crowd. Then another. I sat alone and watched the motorcade. The sun had lowered, casting my side of the street into shadow and fixing the far side in a nostalgic sepia bath. The heat of the sangria and of Lucas had left me, and I shivered. For a long time, the waiter didn't return. I ate my wedge of tortilla and let the rest go cold. The money was still on the table.

At last, a white limousine slid into view, presumably the bridal carriage. The photographers swarmed the vehicle. My first instinct was to hide, to run into the café behind me, shut myself in the ladies' room. For some reason, now that you were just paces away, it felt crucial that you didn't see me here watching. Still, I forced myself to stay seated. The truth was that you couldn't see me if you tried, you were so tightly surrounded by the photographers who ascended the church steps until the heavy doors finally shut in their faces.

You'd be entering the dark vestibule now, wearing the dress I helped choose: the antique beaded sheath that draped on you like a negligée. Your hair, swept back, would show the diamond teardrops at your ears, equal to four years' worth of food in Honduras. I saw you closing your eyes for a moment. I closed my own eyes, and in my mind I heard the first notes of the organ, saw the inner doors swing wide, your first steps down the aisle. The intricate beading on your gown straps reflecting the light like fire. Your father at your side, clutching your slim arm. And your mother in the front pew, her face distorted in joy and loss.

You left for your honeymoon in the Pacific, and I flew back with the other personnel. Owing to some administrative oversight, my seat was in coach for the return trip. The others gave me pitying looks as I dragged my suitcase past them through first class to the back of the plane. Truthfully, I was more comfortable there. The seven hours to Panama City— and the following seven to L.A.—were mine. I could spin in my personal whirlwind. My eyes closed, and I flew to the firmament. The wedding was over; my job was done. I had no fear of falling to earth.

By the time the plane landed at LAX, the tabloids were afire. In the arrivals hall, your team jabbed at smartphones, barked into Bluetooths. I strayed to a newsstand and picked up the fresh copy of *Star*. Through some metaphysical transfer, you were already on the cover of this magazine in your wedding gown. Your eyes were cast aslant as if in suspicion of something outside the frame.

BETRAYED! screamed the headline over your head. HOW RAFAEL CHEATED HIS PREGNANT BRIDE! PERVERSIONS AND KINKY ROLE PLAY! THE SORDID TRUTH SHE NEVER SUSPECTED!

I carefully replaced the magazine in its stand and returned to the team. In the flurry, no one looked at me. No one appreciated the expression of shock I'd designed for my face. I'd already been forgotten.

The tabloids rolled it out sweetly and thoroughly. They'd gone deep into the archives for photographs to match the occasion: tormented expressions on your face, a yawn that could be mistaken for outrage, a hand over the eyes that telegraphed shame. There was a photograph from our trendy lunch, angled to show swelling at your belly. BETRAYED! the headlines screamed. BETRAYED!

I thought of you on a remote island, obliviously resting beside your fraudulent new husband. No one would tell you about the tabloids now, I reasoned. Not on your honeymoon. What good would it do? The print couldn't be unprinted. For your sake, I hoped there were no magazines on your island. The fallout, when it came, would be painful, even if it was for the best. I didn't begrudge you a few days of ignorant joy.

Meanwhile, I was still flying. The blood flamed through my veins as I wrenched my best things from their closet hangers in Malibu and threw them into my suitcase. I scrunched underwear into the mesh pocket and forced the zipper closed. I spun, leaving your house, as I'd done when I'd left mine. My reflection mimed me in the vanity mirror, and I knew, as if I were reading a sentence in a story, that this would be the last time my face would appear there.

In my final hour, I walked through your house, opening all the doors. I went into the orb room and swept my hand over the childish globes, making them sway and collide. They clanged as I went down the hall to the library and plucked at the spines of the books. I took down Jung's colossal *Red Book*. I hauled it to the floor and flipped through the pages until I found one that arrested my attention: an illustration of a hooded figure on a boat, a gnashing sea monster beneath. A German paragraph ran in calligraphic text, its translation at the side, and I left the book open on the floor, for you to see when you returned.

> *The part that you take over from the devil—joy, that is—leads you into adventure. In this way you will find your lower as well as your upper limits. It is necessary for you to know your limits. If you do not know them, you run into the artificial barriers of your imagination and the expectations of your fellow men. . . . These barriers are not your real limits, but artificial limitations that do unnecessary violence to you.*

I sat on the brown velvet chair and wrote my letter. When I finished, I spread it over the open pages of the book.

I'm sorry to be writing this in a letter instead of telling you in person, but I didn't want to spoil your happiness. I'm sure you'll understand why I can't be your assistant anymore. It's better if I leave, so that your new marriage can grow and flourish. Our friendship is too close, too intimate, to coexist with a marital bond. As much as it hurts me, I know it's the right thing to pull back and untangle myself from your life. You'll be better off with a professional assistant who can keep a healthier distance. It will be better for me, too. I'm going home to Michigan, where I belong. But you and I will meet again soon enough and celebrate the arrival of your baby.

Beneath the body of the letter, I signed off the same way you'd done in my yearbook, echoed that same lie: *I hope we'll be close again someday. My love always, Abby.*

Last, I went to the master bathroom and watched the captive stingrays pass over me. I sat on the toilet seat where Rafael would have sat when he'd proposed, and stared at the tub where you would have lain. It was like visiting the scene of a crime. I was reminded of the painting of Marat, the dead revolutionary, his arm hanging from the bath, feather pen still in hand. I thought of the dreamy smile on his face, the closed eyes that could be mistaken for rapture. The stingrays passed overhead, traveling their infinite causeway.

XV.

In Grand Rapids, I rented a tiny Hyundai and drove north. I was startled by the austere surroundings I'd forgotten, the houses that looked incomplete somehow, as if they'd been pushed out in public half-dressed. The ground was muddy from some recent rain, and the overcast sky was like a stained white sheet. I'd become so accustomed to color in California, lush saturation with no expense spared.

But coming out of the city onto wide, traffic-free Route 96, I felt a lift of clear purpose. The surge was as strong as ever, a motor propelling me forward. I felt that I was the car's engine, delivering fuel through my foot on the accelerator. It was hard not to speed, to stay behind traffic in the fast lane. As I blew past my parents' exit, I thought of their house and its contents. Instead of the box of magazine clippings under my bed, all those treasured pictures of you, I thought of my Perren collection neatly stored in its cherrywood DVD case on top of my bedroom dresser. I thought of the satisfying snap the case made when I closed it. All of the films were there, minor and major—*Eureka Valley, Land of the Beings, Nyx/Nox, Horn and Ivory*—a whole world sealed safely away for me, and inaccessible to you. You wouldn't audition now that your pregnancy was public. It was gratifying to know that Perren's world remained mine. And as I drove, it was gratifying to know that my collection was just half a mile away, if I wanted it. But I had no desire to stop and retrieve it, to subject myself to my parents' bloodless faces, their excoriation, the crusty old scabs of the past. I had no wish to see the black patch in the yard where the bonfire once burned, or the garage where the gas can was kept.

When I reached Fremont, I turned east. Not an extreme detour but a slightly different route. I slowed as I passed the cornfields and silos of Paul's hometown, the neat houses with shutters, clotheslines strung with black and white garments. I came upon a boy in a hat and suspenders pedaling a bicycle, like an apparition. After I passed him, I looked in the rearview mirror and thought of Paul as a boy, cycling toward his future. It was possible that one of these houses was his, that his mother had hung its clothesline. The boy on the bike could have been his real-life nephew. I closed my eyes for a moment as I drove, and Paul's face flickered in my mind. I hadn't told him anything of what had happened these past few weeks, or what I was doing. I realized that I missed him, his uncomplicated company, and that the feeling of our kiss still lingered in me, a persistent abrasion.

I continued over the plains, closing the windows against the fetid smell of turkey barns, until I finally crossed into Hesperia. I pushed onward, past a Family Dollar and a Jiffy Lube, full of my own power. All these years I'd resisted coming here. I'd been afraid that once I entered this town's borders, I'd never get back out. Now, I felt no such threat.

It wasn't difficult to find the trailer, which sat just off the main stretch of town. I felt a touch of disquiet as I approached it, the same distress that came in nightmares about pets I'd forgotten to care for. In the dreams, I was afraid to discover that the animal had died, just as now I was afraid to discover what squalor might have swallowed my sister.

The trailer was blue and rusted at the edges, but had been fixed to resemble a house, with a peaked roof, modest satellite dish, handrail up the steps. There was plastic sheeting in the window frames. At the base of the trailer was a pinwheel garden spinner. I stood at the top of the steps for a long moment, waiting for my racing pulse to steady, studying a set of rusted wind chimes and a wreath of dried flowers. I drew a breath and knocked. Immediately, a dog barked and blitzed the inside of the door. Then, my sister's voice, loose and loud over the scratching. I suddenly wanted to rewind, go back down the steps, and run for the car. She'd hear me reversing into the road and assume it was someone at the wrong address.

The door opened slightly, and I saw the dog's black snout before it was yanked back and my sister's face appeared. In that first instant, when she hadn't yet recognized me, I saw her the way she appeared to others. A coarse woman with bad skin and hard blue eyes. Then she saw me. Still bent over, holding the dog's collar, she said, "Holy shit." The door closed again. "Just a minute, I need to crate Ozzy." I heard the scrambling of toenails inside. When the door opened again, all the way, my sister was there in full form, big-chested in a blue Lions shirt with a deep-scissored V-neck. "Holy shit," she said again. In this first full view of her, I could feel the years that had passed, the seesaw that was always between us, rising and falling. I could see my sister's metamorphosis from girl to woman. The dangerous thing she'd walked into years ago had been much bigger than her, and now she'd filled it.

"Oh, my little sister," Shelby cried and hugged me. The embrace was hard, nearly violent. "I thought you hated me."

Over her shoulder, I saw a baby in a bouncer seat on the floor. The dog barked from its crate. Shelby went to the bouncer, picked up the baby, and brought her to the door. Her voice turned lispy and thin. "Bree, this is your aunt Abby."

I stepped into the trailer and breathed a blend of sour milk and cigarette smoke. Shelby busied herself as she talked, scraping something from a couch cushion, picking a blanket off the floor. I learned that she was a waitress and worked part-time in a medical office. The baby's father was long gone. The only evidence of his existence was the bar of metal that jutted from the trunk of the maple outside the trailer. He'd impaled the bar there and tied a rope to it, she said, with the idea of hanging a tree swing for Briella. He hadn't even lasted to the birth, and now the maple was dying. She'd never seen him again. He was unemployable, useless for child support, not even listed on the birth certificate. She didn't need his help, though. She and Briella were fine. Her friend Judith was lonely and was going to take care of Briella for free.

"I'm off today, so we're going to town for the Labor Day fair. We were just getting ready to leave, so it's a good thing you came when you did." She half turned her head. "Ha. I can't believe you're here. Come, let's go."

I followed my sister outside to her car and sat in the passenger seat, crushing snack wrappers beneath me. I watched Shelby lift her daughter into the car seat without pausing to brush the crumbs from the fabric. The baby was so small that the straps and buckle covered her whole torso. Shelby dropped into the driver's seat, and with a cursory glance into the rearview mirror pulled backward out of the driveway. It occurred to me that I'd never ridden in a car she was driving.

On the way to town, we passed yard sales, people sorting through rubber bins. We parked and walked along the main street. Among the meaty midwesterners ran a strain of young men in sleeveless shirts with tattoos and hollow faces, jittery women beside them. Whether they knew Shelby or not, they didn't raise their eyes. No one seemed to see me at all. Shelby had clipped Briella's car seat to the top of a stroller, which she wheeled past the booths of a craft fair. From time to time a matronly woman hunched down to the baby and made a kissy face. "What a sweetie pie," the woman would say, and Shelby would say, "Thanks," as if the sweetness were her doing.

"Oh, look at those," Shelby said at a craft tent, pointing to a row of soft headbands with red, white, and blue fabric flowers.

"I'll buy one for her," I said impulsively.

"No, don't do that."

"It's what an aunt does." I wasn't accustomed to being an aunt, and the word flapped on my tongue. I was a stranger to this girl, no more familiar than the women blowing kisses. As I put the headband on Briella, pulling the fabric over her little ears, she gazed at me with her glossy eyes, and I felt a jet shoot up from a hidden well inside me.

We watched the tractor-pull contest and ate hot dogs. Sitting beside Shelby, I was able to study her. Her dark hair angled down sharply: longer in the front and chopped shorter in the back. She wore no makeup that I could see, and her skin was pebbled with whiteheads. Her face maintained its heart shape—the tapered chin and widow's peak—but carved crescents parenthesized her mouth now, as if she were permanently displeased.

"What last name does Briella have?" I asked, perhaps too suddenly.

Shelby shifted her eyes to me. "Hightower. I changed my last name a few years ago."

I nodded. "Mom told me about that. Why Hightower?"

"I got it from the Hightower Saloon." She shrugged. "I just always liked that word. Makes me think of being above it all. Unreachable."

An empty pause stretched between us as I turned over this irony.

"So, what have you been doing with yourself?" Shelby finally asked me. There was a tightness in her voice, and her cobalt eyes were distant.

"Well, weirdly enough, I'm in L.A. now," I said.

She glanced at me and I saw the pure surprise before she said, "Oh, huh. That sounds great. Good for you."

I waited for her to ask more, but she didn't. Instead, she rummaged in her purse and brought out a round plastic compact. She opened it and pinched something out, which she put on her tongue.

"What's that?" I asked.

She shot me a look. "Just something for my pain. I had a C-section."

It was hard to sit quietly, not to ask more questions, but I controlled myself. When the tractor pull was over, Shelby asked if I wouldn't mind staying with Briella while she stopped in the beer tent for a few minutes. "She'll fall asleep soon, anyway. When she does, just put her in her stroller and she'll be fine." As she walked away, I saw her reach into her purse and bring out the pill case again.

I waited on the bottom rung of the tractor-pull bleachers. Hard music came from the beer tent, and below that the jangle of voices and laughter. The sky darkened, and I thought of Malibu, a fabled city twinkling far beyond the horizon. From this vantage, it seemed as unreal as Atlantis. The night unrolled swiftly here, full and profound, a familiar black afghan of stars. I felt a curious calm beneath this arrangement of constellations that had covered me since childhood. There was comfort in the land that stretched flat forever, simple and fertile and constant, its huddled trees alive with crickets and owls. I had a sense of rightness, sitting here, of gathering certainty. Briella was curled in the stroller, her face clear and untroubled in sleep. I imagined that she was my child, and tried to feel what it would be like to be a mother. I touched the velvet head, warm with dreams.

A memory came to me of playing hide-and-seek when we were small. I remembered hiding with Shelby in the tub, behind the shower curtain, and watching our mother's shadow approach. I remembered that moment of apprehension, the tingling possibility that it wasn't our mother at all, but a monster. The clank of the rings on the rod. How our mother had jumped, too, although she must have known we were there. How we'd all looked at each other, our faces rough mirror images, and laughed.

When an hour had passed, I wheeled the stroller to the beer tent and found my sister leaning into a man in a leather vest. Other men stood around her like projections of the grinding music. She smiled when she saw me and took me into a clumsy headlock. "My little sister," she drawled, and

I stiffened. "You're sleeping over tonight, right? You have to! I have a couch!"

The man beside my sister rubbed his face against hers. I stood still, gripping the stroller handle. Finally Shelby remembered Briella, her gaze shifting downward to her sleeping daughter's face. With a fluid movement, she pulled away from the man and seized the stroller. I followed her out of the tent. At the car, I lifted her purse off her shoulder and took the car keys. Shelby slid into the passenger seat and closed her eyes.

When I pulled into her driveway, she didn't move. I shook her until her head bobbed. Finally her eyes opened halfway and blinked. I went around and opened the passenger door, and she staggered out toward the trailer. I watched her fumble with the door key, nearly losing her balance on the step, then disappear inside. The dog barked, but Briella slept as I unbuckled her and lifted her out of the car seat. I carried the girl against my chest, feeling her hot cheek at my shoulder.

Inside, I was hit again with the smell of smoke and old milk. Ozzy ran up to me, a stained yellow beast, and circled my legs sniffing. Shelby was already laid out on the sagging couch. I stood for a long moment, holding Briella against me, imagining what would happen if I turned around and carried her back out the door. I could find a small place for us to live. I could make drawings and invent stories just for her. Whatever she dreamed in her sleep I'd try to bring to life.

The couch springs groaned as Shelby turned on her back and threw an arm over her face. "Just put her in her crib," she murmured. "She can keep her clothes on, it's fine."

The animal followed at my heels as I stepped over toys and found the crib in a room with vinyl princess decals. I laid the child down gingerly on the blotched mattress. I straightened myself and watched her for a moment, her arms splayed and lips parted. It would be so easy to pick her up again and walk out the door. From inside my ears came a low drone, like a trapped insect. I reached my arms into the crib. Carefully, I took the headband off the baby's head, for fear it might strangle her in her sleep, then leaned down and kissed her forehead. It felt like a subversive act, the casting of a spell. As I withdrew from the crib, my heart juddered, and the drone in my ears intensified.

I scanned the trailer's living room. It was the same room I'd dreamed about, I saw now. And just as I'd known where to find the meteorite in the desert, I knew where the bag would be. I knew from the dream that there was something in it I needed, and so I didn't hesitate the way I might have. There beside the front door I found Shelby's purse—fat and slovenly, the fake white leather and pony fringe—and took it with me.

XVI.

P AUL'S CABIN was nearly black in the evening light. As the taxi withdrew, I noticed the places where the wooden siding had been chewed away and saw the rusted trash can that slumped outside. He opened the door, and for a silent moment he stared at me with my suitcase, his face stern, the skin raw and patchy. I noticed flecks of white in his sideburns.

The cabin's interior seemed smaller than before, gloomier. Paul switched on the floor lamp, and I saw black punctuation marks where dead insects were stuck to the inside of the shade. The kites hung from the wall like sleeping bats.

"Would you like some tea?"

From the kitchen area came the sound of a cabinet creaking open, the clunk of a kettle on the stovetop.

"Thank you," I said. "I know this is a surprise."

"It's all right." He stood in his brown shirt and chinos, blending with the kitchen cabinets, part of the woodwork, a bas-relief. He turned away from me, toward the stove.

"I've been thinking about your project," I said quietly. "I'd like to try helping again in some way."

There was a stretch of silence before the kettle began to clatter. Paul turned the burner off just as the steam started to rise, but before the whistle screamed. He turned to look at me. He didn't say anything for a long moment, and I began to think I was too late, that he'd already shut me out. I'd have to take my suitcase someplace else.

Finally, he said, "Are you sure?" He poured the hot water into two mugs. "I was actually planning to go to the shelter tomorrow. Yolanda's warmed up a lot since you met her that time, and I think it would go much smoother now. She's ready to talk, if you are."

I remembered Yolanda's face, the searing ray of her gaze. "I'll come."

Paul looked appraisingly at me. "You don't have to interview her if you don't want to. You can just stay in the room. Just having you there will help, I think."

I nodded. "Okay."

He brought the tea to the table, and we sat together, the checkered oilcloth between us. As he sipped from his steaming mug, I tried to imagine living here with him. I imagined a simple life, sewing kites. I'd see him every day, absorb his shifting moods, watch him in every angle of sunlight and moonlight. We'd talk through the night, the only people in Topanga Canyon, or we'd lie quietly with no need to talk. In daylight, we'd be soldiers. It shouldn't have been difficult to see, but I couldn't see it.

To my relief, he didn't ask about me, or Elise. He didn't mention the tabloid reports, although I was sure he knew what had happened. He didn't even ask why I'd come. Instead, he talked about the refugee children. Armando had been sent back to Guatemala, but new children had arrived at the shelter. There were teenage brothers who'd ridden atop a freight train through Mexico, along with hundreds of others. The migrants called it El Tren de la Muerte, he said. The brothers had seen a man fall between the train cars and be decapitated. Most of the other migrants on the train had been detained, but the boys had escaped. They'd arrived at the shelter with bleeding cuts on their soles of their feet. They were likely to be deported after their cases were reviewed, Paul said. In the meantime, he wanted to get more of their story on film. He wanted to document their pursuit of asylum in the United States. Also, he was beginning to think he needed to go to Central America himself.

"I want to structure the film as a dual narrative, if I can," he said, "following one child trying to emigrate to the United States and another child who's already here, going through the system. The footage would alternate between their stories. But I'd have to go down there in person to follow the journey, to show what they're escaping from. It might be impossible to do it without endangering them or risking my own life. But I can't make a responsible film without actually being there."

"But that's crazy. You'll be killed."

He shrugged and lifted his tea mug. "Not necessarily. Other people have done it. Plenty of journalists have gone down there to report. The BBC has footage of kids sniffing glue in San Pedro Sula, kids working in the dumps, bodies lying in the street. It's already been filmed. It's already out there, but people aren't seeing it. That's because no one's bothered to make a commercial, full-length film yet, something people will actually go watch. If I want to do it right, I have to go myself and get my own footage. I have to ride the Train of Death, so to speak."

He smiled through the steam of his tea, and I felt a mix of aversion and awe, along with a flash of regret that I'd never introduced him to you, Elise. I was sure you'd never met anyone like him and probably never would.

You called me at eight the next morning. I shouldn't have been surprised that you'd seen the tabloid hysteria by now. There was no safe place anywhere, not even in your island paradise. It must have been the middle of the night for you when you called. You must have been suffering, waiting until the hour I'd be awake to answer the phone. I let the call go to voicemail and listened to the message later, while Paul was in the shower. I could barely make out your words, you were sobbing so noisily.

"I know it was Jessica Starck who did it," you gasped. "It's obvious, because she talked about Cecconi's. She doesn't even care that I know. I'm going to talk to my lawyer about suing her. It's libel or slander or one of those. That evil, malicious bitch." There was a jumbled pause, in which you might have wiped your nose, collected yourself. "Call me back, Abby. I really need to talk to you."

My pulse responded to the sound of your voice. Its inflections were so familiar and sweet, like sugar in my ear, so that my first instinct was to call you back, to say the words that would soothe and reassure you. It was difficult, as I knew it would be, to listen to the message and do nothing. But I'd closed that door, for your good and my own, and it had to stay closed.

At the shelter, Paul led the interview while I assisted with the camera. Yolanda wore a fuchsia sundress that brightened her face, and although she spoke in a clipped, halting way—attempting to pepper her Spanish with a few English words—it was clear that she wanted to tell her story as well as she could. Paul nodded when she paused, gently encouraging her. His voice was soft and reassuring. Ronald, the gruff middle-aged cameraman, demonstrated the camera's operation. I hovered, watching his movements while listening to the translator's clinical rendition of Yolanda's saga. For a thousand dollars, her parents had hired the coyote who raped her in transit. It was part of the deal, he told her. Her parents had known that, he said. He paid off the gang that approached them, but not before allowing one of the members to assault her on the side of the road near Tenosique. He told her afterward that they'd wanted to do worse, but he'd saved her life.

While she was detailing the next stage of her journey, I felt my phone vibrate in the back pocket of my jeans.

I listened to the message later, while riding in the car with Paul. Your voice in my ear again: "We're coming home early. It's terrible, Abby. Raf isn't even defending himself. He's just shrugging it off, like it's no big deal, like my career isn't going to be totally ruined by this. Abby, call me back. I need to talk to you."

I turned the phone off without comment, and Paul didn't ask who'd called. Your drama seemed so small now compared with the plight of the children. You seemed more self-absorbed, shallower than ever. Paul and I went to a diner and ordered pancakes for lunch. I still heard your words as I listened to him talk about the film. *Abby, call me back. I need to talk to you.*

"It's just about collecting raw footage now," Paul said. "The more the better. I don't know yet which strands we're going to follow." As he poured syrup, he said, matter-of-factly, "I'm thinking we should go to Yolanda's hometown in Honduras to film, because she's told me so much about it already."

I chewed my pancake quietly. It didn't seem right to interrupt him, to tell him I had no intention of going to Honduras. I said nothing as he complained that we couldn't leave sooner. First, he had to crew the next studio project he'd signed on for—a dumb comedy in Atlanta. "You're welcome to stay in my house while I'm gone, if you want," he said, and those were the words I wanted to hear.

Back in the cabin, I unpacked the rest of my things. When I took the drawings out of my backpack, Paul said, "What are those?" and I showed them to him. He looked at my pictures silently, his eyes traveling across each page.

"There are more of them back in Michigan," I offered. I waited for words of admiration but reminded myself that he wasn't the effusive type. Still, I was stung when he nodded and said nothing. I pulled the drawings away from him and slid them into a drawer.

Later, we lay down on the futon together, and he helped me undress in his slow, deliberate manner. I said nothing about my inexperience. I was unable to speak. I thought of you and Rafael together, remembered the rising sounds from your bedroom. Paul's body was pale, spiked with coarse hair, and muscled in a way that put me in mind of an archangel warrior. I let him put my limbs where he wanted. As we folded together, naked, I tried to turn off my scrabbling mind, to simply feel the sensations as they came, to let my unconscious and conscious selves merge in harmony. But as we moved on the futon, I couldn't override the feeling of being dangerously exposed. I imagined the two of us in Honduras, the drug gangs executing us both, a bullet to each of our heads. I imagined our bare bodies left in the road to be scavenged by buzzards.

* * *

The next message you left was distraught. "Abby, I found your letter. Please come home. You can't leave me now." You were crying, shouting on the phone. "I understand you want to break out on your own. I get that, I really do. But you have to just come back for a little bit. I can't get through this by myself. Raf and I had a huge fight and we aren't speaking. I need you, Abby."

The desperation in your voice was like a riptide. I took the phone away from my ear and put it in my pocket. I breathed deeply. It wouldn't be easy to stay the course, but I'd come this far already. I had to be strong, because you weren't. Only alone could you possibly recognize the mistakes you'd made, with Rafael and with me. Only alone could you learn.

The phone continued to vibrate in my pocket until I finally turned it off and buried it in my suitcase, deep under my clothes.

When Paul went to Atlanta, he left me the keys to his car, and I drove to the Rhizome. In my session, I told Tello about my recurring dreams.

"I knew you'd be an extraordinary student," he told me. "Yes, any returning scenario is worth incubating through lucid dreaming."

I balked. This hadn't been a topic in Perren's book. "I don't have lucid dreams."

"You'll learn to create them," he said. "First of all, while you're awake, get into the habit of asking yourself if you are, in fact, dreaming. The cliché is to pinch yourself, and there's some use in that. You don't actually need to pinch, per se, but you could tug your hair or bite a finger. You can also try jumping. If you're dreaming, you'll float down lightly. If you build the habit of questioning your waking life, the habit will bleed into your sleep, and you'll begin questioning your dreaming life, too. That's what brings about lucidity, when you recognize the dream as a dream and can become an active participant."

Once I'd grasped the steering wheel of lucidity, Tello said, I should move about in my dream and explore the terrain. It was a balancing act, he warned, to remain both within the dream and without—at a slight remove—both participant and observer.

"Keep a small object with you during the day as a reminder to do reality checks. You'll see that the object will follow you into your dreams and help erode the barrier between day and night. In fact, you may even have a lucid dream tonight," he added as I was going to the door. "It's not unusual to experience lucidity the same night you first learn about it."

I thanked him for the guidance. As I was preparing to leave, he spoke again.

"Abby, I've noticed that you seem to have a special gift for this work." I turned back toward him and studied the puzzle of his face—its oval shape, the obsidian eyes, the features that never quite harmonized. "Do you agree?"

"I don't know." My face heated. "I've always had vivid dreams."

"I suspect that you may be having premonitory or veridical dreams."

I paused. "Yes."

Tello leaned forward. "It's very important that you listen to those dreams. Their messages can be truer than life."

"Truer than life," I repeated.

I began using the meteorite to incubate lucid dreams. If the meteorite changed shape when I squeezed it, I knew I was dreaming. I became omnipotent then, able to string the dream to the next scene and the next. When I dreamed of the white house on the hill now, I could follow the children into its hidden rooms. They took me to a room of clocks and showed me how the clocks were manipulated to run backward. Upon waking, I drew the gears of the clocks and the worried eyes of the children.

When Paul returned from Atlanta, I helped him with the documentary. Eventually, I learned to operate the camera on my own when Ronald was unavailable. I stood silently in the room while Paul interviewed the children, some as young as five.

"I never want to have children," I told him one day, after shooting. The words were corrosive on my tongue, but I made myself say them, to mask this one truth.

Paul blinked and looked thoughtful. "I understand that," he said. "If anything, I'd want to adopt. Or be a foster parent.

There are so many kids who need us already, without bringing any more in."

I was touched, despite myself, to hear him use the word "us," and felt sorry for my lie.

"You know, it would actually be great to talk with foster families who've taken in migrant children," he said. "But not yet. First, I have to convince ICE to let me do a ride-along. That might take a while to accomplish. They won't even talk to me."

I was quiet for a moment. "But I have to ask, if they ever did let you film a ride-along, do you really think it would help?"

"What do you mean? Of course it would help."

"No, I mean, more generally." I stopped, trying to stanch the flow of my words, but they were leaking out of me. "I mean, do you really think that making this film will help? Even if you get the funding, even if it's a wonderful film and millions of people see it, will it change anything?"

Paul sat across from me at the card table, his posture rigid. "You're doubting the purpose of making the film at all?"

"I'm not doubting the purpose, just the assumption that anything will come of it." I wasn't sure why I was saying these things to him.

A shadow passed through his eyes, a prowling hawk. "It's about awareness, Abby. People don't even know what's happening. Or they do know, but they think of these kids as aliens, not worth their concern. Our job is to show that these are human beings who are suffering."

"But the people who'll actually go to see the film already know that. I just keep thinking of the children, putting their pain on camera. There's something wrong about it. And there's something wrong about putting all those anguished kids in people's faces, making their hearts bleed, when there's nothing they can do to help."

Paul's mouth was a taut line. "They can demand policy change."

I was quiet. It would be unkind to continue.

For weeks, you continued to call and leave overwrought messages, even though I never called back. Instead, I wrote a letter with pen and paper. In the letter, I asked you to stop trying to reach me. It was interfering with the distance we both needed and sabotaging any hope you might have of saving your marriage. It hurt me to write the words, but I wrote them well, in a tone that was kind but detached. I sent the letter without a return address.

You stopped calling after that, and over the next months, I went back to following you through the tabloids. When Paul was away on a shoot, I sat alone paging through them, witnessing the course of your crisis. The cover of *Us Weekly* featured a photograph of you and Rafael with a jagged rip down the middle. Divorce proceedings were under way. As much as I welcomed this news, I failed to feel gladdened by it. Anonymous sources claimed to be privy to your state of mind; you were devastated but stoic, they said. You were a

strong woman, and this challenge would make you even stronger. Someone used the word "empowered." The photographs,
however, told another story. You looked terrible. I gasped
when I saw a picture of you outside the natural food store,
with bony shoulders and a distorted abdomen, heavy makeup
overpowering your features. Your expression in the pictures
was contemptuous. You were drifting around Hollywood.
You'd been spotted in nightclubs on Sunset Boulevard, and
there was a link to a seedy musician that made me cringe,
but that I didn't believe. I had the sense that you were utterly
alone. It was a necessary education, I knew, but the process
was painful to see. The pictures grew steadily darker, the cap-
tions uglier. Rafael, in the meantime, had been photographed
with Mireille Sauvage, who stood of equal height beside
him in a necklace of yellow jewels, identical to the one she'd
worn in my dream.

I wondered if, at any moment during your downfall, you'd
remembered my engagement card. I wondered if you'd ever
reflected on the verse I'd inscribed inside. The wild-briar
had finally withered, as it had been destined to do, but the
holly would have remained green and true. It had been your
mistake to scorn it.

The bridge dream always began the same way, but this time
I was aware of its beginning, as if I'd chosen to play the reel.
I gripped my meteorite and watched it flatten in my hand,
betraying the dream. I walked toward the bridge, the fresh

snow beneath my feet, the darkened apartment blocks, the enchanted descent of a million snow crystals. The air seemed to harden and become brittle as I pushed onward. There was no feeling in my feet. When I looked down, they were no longer touching the sidewalk, but hovering a few inches above. And then: the bridge, the headlights.

I tipped over the railing. But this time, I was a camera, able to zoom in on details at will. There was no fear but instead a sense of wonder as I plummeted, twisting my body in midair to look at the sky, the glittered confetti falling alongside me. I had time to study the graffiti on the bridge abutments, the pink interlaced letters spelling "Mom," the blue cartoon mouse with a wedge of cheese. The open eye, staring. I was able to slow my velocity, to feel the impact on the icy water—and what I expected to be hard, neck-breaking, was not. Instead, it was a soft invitation, a pleasant sucking, and I relaxed into it. The interior of the river was dark-veined emerald. A welcome return to a forest, a slow cradle.

XVII.

I n April, just after Paul left for Honduras, the tabloids
reported the birth of your child. When I saw the picture
of you with the baby, my heart stopped. It was a vetted
photograph, clearly preapproved by you or your publicist,
if you still had one. You were in a hospital room, with full
makeup and hair brushed over one shoulder in that virgin-
mother way. The child was bundled in your arms—*Amara*
was her name—just a pink face and dark eyes. A new feeling
came through me. It wasn't joy or jealousy, or any popular
emotion, but a peculiar, discordant feeling of foreboding—a
kind of instinctual awakening. A vibration began inside me,
disturbing my blood. Again, as in Shelby's trailer, a low drone
came into my ears.

For a long time, I stared at the picture of you and your
daughter. I looked hard at your eyes, past the reflection of
the photographers, and tried to read the message in them.
The smile you gave the cameras was tightly artificial. But in
your gaze I saw the truth, the proof of my suspicion. You

were suffocating, silently screaming for help. You were unable` to be a mother, unable to give yourself to someone else. You didn't have enough inside you to share.

Over the next few weeks, you appeared regularly in the magazines. Drunk in public with your baby. The sources said you were "experiencing some of the bumps of new motherhood," but your drunkenness was plain to see from the languid eyelids, the lazy lopsided smile, the ubiquitous thermos of booze. The eye makeup was worse than before, and the clothing you wore—once carefully earthy and offbeat—now seemed sloppy. The earlier sympathy I'd felt for you barely broke through my antipathy now. You were even weaker than I'd thought. Carrying your child in some sort of woven wrap, you looked like a slattern.

I saw the pleading in your eyes, but I knew enough to wait. I stayed in Paul's cabin while he was gone and worked on my drawings. I drew at the card table at first, then spread the paper out on the floor. It was emancipating, a thrilling release after all the pent-up months. It felt almost adulterous to kneel in Paul's cabin and draw. I drew the children huddled in the white house, surrounded by clocks. I colored the stripes on their blanket, and when I filled in their faces, I shamelessly borrowed the features of the young refugees.

Paul had given in and bought a smartphone for his journey, and he kept in irregular contact. I skimmed his emails, skipping over the harrowing details of child prostitutes and bullet-riddled bus drivers. Between the lines, I gathered that he was in a town near the capital with Yolanda's mother and younger sister. He'd seen the *maras* in person, the gangs with horrific face tattoos. His purity of hope was beautiful and sad—his mission the mission of a child. He'd surely be killed in Honduras. I'd written him a one-line email that said, "Come home while you still can," which he didn't acknowledge.

While he was gone, I put in a request for more shifts at the Rhizome and spent almost every day there, sitting for sessions with Tello and tending the babies. There seemed to be a radiant new aura surrounding my charges now. They were imbued with deeper identity and purpose, each of them; they held more value than ordinary infants. The pale-eyed among them were ethereal saints, while the dark-eyed were oracles. I cherished each of their singular, exceptional faces. There were Marco and Dante, elvish twins who never cried. There was plump, golden Harper. There was serious, colicky Helen—a recent addition, adopted from China—whose mother had just begun breastfeeding her. Apparently, there were ways to do everything if the desire was strong enough.

As much as I wanted to be in the nursery continually, I continued to avoid Wednesdays. I didn't really think you'd return to your schedule, but I couldn't risk seeing you. It was best to remain hidden in just two places: room seven with Tello, and the confines of the daycare. Going to the restaurant or into the gardens was too dangerous, as much as I hated the possibility of missing Perren. Of course, the chances of encountering him during the course of my narrow routine were minimal. But I was certain this would change, that this was a temporary limbo. I was certain we'd find each other soon.

I was intimate with all the daycare occupants now, and so on a Thursday in June, I noticed the new arrival at once. I'd known, of course, that this day would eventually come, and yet it was an epiphany, like lightning from the gods. I went to the crib where the tiny infant lay. She had a shock of black hair and wide, elliptical eyes. She was neither you nor Rafael. She was something else completely. I stood staring. The women in the room seemed to be watching me, even as they hovered over other cribs or worked at the changing tables.

There was a fog to the girl, as if she were still affixed to the tendrils of creation. Her skin appeared silted, still coated by loam from the source, and the big black eyes had knowledge in them that came from Before, that flowed straight from the Spring. She was beautiful, an exquisite dark jewel. The moment I saw her, the iron cuff at my ankle was cut. All my dreams had been advancing toward this, preparing me. I believe that on some deep level you knew what you were doing, Elise, when you brought her to me. Rationally, there was no way you could have known I was here, that I was waiting, and yet I felt that you knew.

XVIII.

I T WAS harder to leave Paul's house than it had been to leave yours. I'd grown accustomed to the junipers and pines of Topanga, the shadowed, sheltered feeling of the canyon. There was a sense of withdrawal away from the city's studded sheets of light, a comforting echo of Michigan. I liked the way time seemed to pass more slowly. And, of course, I'd grown attached to Paul. I thought of him coming home to an empty house, registering my absence. I thought, achingly, of him sitting with a cup of tea at the card table and sleeping alone beneath his kites. And yet the scene seemed distant to me, inaccessible, like a movie still.

It was possible that I'd return someday, I told myself, although I knew that it wasn't. It wasn't possible to live simultaneous lives, at least in this world. I closed the low door of the cabin behind me and lifted my suitcases into Paul's Cavalier. Perhaps I'd regret my decision someday. Perhaps it would become a thorn I'd never dislodge. Some errors were irreparable, I knew. They could only be lived with, incorporated into the body like a foreign object.

Who can tell what breath entered into me, after that, and told me what movements to make? I have as much grasp of it as you do, Elise.

Perhaps I knew what I was doing. It's hard to be honest about something I don't fully understand. For so long I'd attended to the winds of suggestion, relied on the subtle cues of the universe and my own subliminal moods. It's difficult, impossible really, for any of us to know all the ways we're tethered to unknown forces, or to gauge the true reasons for our actions. We're open-pored beings, after all. We're lotus roots suspended in the Spring and haired with tentacles, instinctual creatures wearing halos of consciousness.

What happened is that I left all the phones—Shelby's, yours, and mine—at a gas station in Topanga, where I bought a map of Southern California. I sat in the Cavalier, breathing its ghost smell of cigarette smoke, and unfolded the map over the steering wheel. I took the meteorite in my hand and closed my eyes for a moment. Like that, I achieved Unity Gain. Sparks leaped between planes of consciousness. I don't know if you ever experienced this. My sense is that you never did. I believe you were doing it wrong the whole time. And so maybe you'd say it was just my imagination, or a retroactive application of pattern and meaning, but I swear to you it happened just this way. I opened the map, and right there was a dot with the word "Hesperia." Not the town in Michigan, but a place in Southern California, about two hours' drive from Topanga. A sister city. Its flip side. How did my eyes find it so quickly if it hadn't been placed there for me?

The Econo Lodge had a room for forty-five dollars a night. I still had what remained of the petty cash you'd given me, almost three thousand dollars. I rented a post office box, and sent away for the birth certificate. It was scandalously easy to do. Only my sister would be lazy or ignorant enough to keep Social Security cards in her wallet. Both hers and Briella's were there, crisp and new.

My hair had grown out since the long-ago day we'd gone to Abbot Kinney, so I went to Supercuts in a strip mall and came out with a short, angled style like Shelby's that curtained the sides of my face. I ran my hand up through the layers as I settled into my room, which was nice for the money. There was faux mahogany furniture, and a gray sateen dust ruffle on the bed. The black carpet was patterned with ovals running on the bias with dots in the middle, like repeating eyes. There was the flat black portal of the television. Crucially, there was a mini fridge. Like a rodent preparing for hibernation, I went to the supermarket and gathered cans of chili and green beans, cartons of mini muffins, and tabloid magazines. Handing the magazines to the checkout clerk, I glimpsed the register screen, the color-coded buttons darkened with grime. I'd never press buttons like that again, never wear a navy polo shirt, never go back to that life. The boy dropped the magazines into a plastic bag, and I grabbed the bag away from him.

I looked through all the magazines. You weren't there. Other actresses peacocked for the camera. The pages—all of them—were jammed with newly minted faces. Each issue was fresh and amnesiac, toasting whatever starlet was next, the latest bijou to bob atop the cultural tide. It was tragic, I suppose, to think that each new arrival was duped into thinking she was unique, that she possessed some unusual flair, or even her own personality. You'd find this tragic, I was sure. Its truth would already be descending upon you.

I rolled up the magazines and put them in the wastebasket. I sat at the little motel desk and, on a scrap of drawing paper, wrote a letter to Paul, who deserved an explanation. I considered for a few moments, then wrote that I needed to go back to Michigan to see my new niece. I'd most likely stay there for a while, to help take care of my father. I'd be in touch when I had a sense of when I might return.

I folded the letter and left it on the desk. I turned off the lights and closed the blackout curtains against the sun and asphalt. With the bed linens nested around me on the carpet, I sank into the Spring. In my dream, I opened the door of the room where the orbs hung and found that the room had been paved black. In the middle of the floor was a cement trough, an industrial bathtub filled with water—warm when I dipped a finger in, salty when I licked it. In the dream, I climbed into the trough and lay submerged in water the temperature of blood. You were somewhere in the house, but you didn't know I was there. The room itself was stygian, and I was afraid the door would lock, that you'd never find me. I was afraid I'd be trapped in this tank, that I'd drink the salt water and die.

I sprang upright in bed and clutched at air. By slow degrees, I recognized my surroundings, the glossy dresser, the textured blanket over my legs. I wanted to fling away the blanket and break through the window to the parking lot, but my brain came awake in time to calm itself. This room was a cell of my own choosing, I remembered, and I was not captive but freer than ever.

I mobilized myself only to use the bathroom, eat, and take the fenugreek capsules I'd bought at CVS. Lying back in my blankets, I touched my breasts with my fingertips and circled my nipples until they stiffened. At first, I was aroused by this and couldn't resist sliding my hands down my own body and imagining myself with a man. I began by thinking about Paul, but he transformed into Rafael. Eventually, though, the nipple massages became more procedural. I did them eight times a day for twenty minutes as I fell into sleep or trance, and again when I awoke. The visions flickered like film stills. I saw the interior of Shelby's trailer, the caged dog snarling. I saw a zebra running with her colt, and the burning savanna behind them.

After six days, when I felt a surge beginning, I drew myself up from the blankets and sat on the toilet. On the evening of the summer solstice, I packed my things, threw away the remaining food, and checked out of the Econo Lodge. I'd showered and washed my hair before leaving the room, but the receptionist's gaze still lingered as I handed back the key card. When I asked, she told me that Party City and Babies "R" Us were located in the same strip mall in Victorville, so I loaded my suitcases into the Cavalier and drove there.

I wore my sunglasses as I drove, and pulled down the visor. My eyes were still dry from the arid motel room, the air conditioner, and the dust motes. My hands massaged the steering wheel. The freedom of a car was familiar, welcome—this simple American thing, a steel shell and gas tank, a pedal to press with one foot. It was an extension of me, a conductor of my horsepower.

Tinny music played as I walked through the store aisles. I did my shopping quickly. At Party City, I didn't know what I was looking for until I saw it. A hairy cloak, furred mask and gloves, ram horns. I brought it all to the checkout counter. Behind the counter, Mylar balloons were pinned to the wall, and I thought distantly of Paul's kites. In front of the counter were bins of glow rings, and in a flash of inspiration I scooped them up and paid for those, too.

I coasted all the way to Calabasas. Turning off the 101, I stopped at the post office to mail my letter, then followed the map into the mountains. Las Virgenes Road past Mulholland Drive, past the Hindu temple, past the entrance to the Rhizome. About a mile farther down, I turned off the main road and followed an unnamed lane that doubled back up, winding through the mountains. It was easy to drive off the lane into the trees, to hide the car among the oaks and chaparral. From here, it was only a few hundred yards on foot to the edge of the Rhizome's property. I could see the twin protuberances of the Goat Buttes, the same view I'd seen through the windows of the nursery.

As I sat on the ground to wait for nightfall, my senses were sharpened. A slight breeze stirred the air, and I caught the burnt-wood smell of creosote, the faint marijuana lift of sagebrush. The rattling call of a towhee, the squawk of a jay. I put a fenugreek capsule on my tongue. I reached beneath my shirt and touched my breasts as I watched the light retreat over the hills, its copper glow like flame in the trees, until at last the fire was extinguished and the trees blackened. For a moment, in the gloaming's indigo confusion, I imagined a zebra and her colt galloping past. I blinked, and the vision evaporated.

This being the longest day of the year, it wouldn't be fully dark until ten o'clock. As the last blue light in the sky clung to the horizon, I put on my fur cloak and mask so that I was completely covered, and I adjusted the cord that held the horns to the sides of my head. I wanted to run but made myself go slowly. With calm focus, I tramped a path to the Rhizome. I heard the sound of my own breath and the crunching of dry grass underfoot. Every few yards, I drew a glow-in-the-dark ring from the Party City bag inside my purse and dropped it to the ground. I traced a wide circle around the side of the property in order to approach from the front. Finally, I came out into the parking lot, where costumed figures were emerging from Porsches and BMWs. I walked with purpose alongside them to the entrance path lined with tiki torches. I was fully costumed, my disguise impenetrable, my confidence total. I was safe within my own waking dream. With my furred hand, I showed my membership card to the brunette leopard at the door and went in behind a couple dressed as a magician and a rabbit.

I didn't recognize any costumes from the previous year. Naturally, these weren't people who recycled ensembles for an annual event. These were all new spirits, freshly quarried from recent night visions. There was a Green Man, with eyes peering through a mask of leaves. There was a macaw wearing its own gilded cage. There was a woman in a nude bodysuit with a trompe l'oeil painted upon her chest, a cavity containing a glistening heart.

There was an open bar in the lobby again. I requested a glass of water, just to have something to hold, to fit in with the ritual. Outdoors was the ring of fire, the garden courtyard in its periphery of torchlight. I went deeper into the garden. As I came toward the outer band of torchlight, where it met the leafy shadows, I saw a dancer in a midnight-blue leotard. Her red hair was tied back, and she wore a sequined eye mask with a headdress of feathers. Horn bulbs protruded from her temples. Of course it was you. I spun away and edged behind a fountain where I could watch you without being seen. Even from this distance, I could see that the tabloid reports were true, that you were a shadow of yourself. You were drinking, and in deep conversation with a tall Jesus in a crown of thorns. There was no evidence of your recent pregnancy. Your arms were bony, your abdomen was flat as a girl's, and your breasts were still the size of dumplings. A thought drove through me like a spike, that you'd somehow failed to give birth, that the baby in the photos was a prop, that the child in the nursery crib was a different Amara, who belonged to someone else. You might have lost your nerve and sought a late-term abortion. Looking at you there in the licking torchlight, I could have convinced myself of it.

You laughed at something Jesus said, and my vision clouded. It was the same laugh that had rung in my ears since I was a child, awake and asleep. The bright sound of a plucked harpsichord, golden and reverberating. It was part of what had made you dear to me and what had made you famous, what made you envied and hated. But further than that—and this is the truth that dug its way into me at that moment—it was the sound of your utter vacancy and hopelessness. Only something empty could ring that way.

There was no point in waiting. I left you and went back through the garden toward the building. I remembered the ugly sound of Shelby's laugh that night in the beer tent. I remembered the leather vest of the man who'd held her, the unfixed wheels of her eyes. I remembered the pills—I knew they'd be oxycodone before I took them from her stolen purse and flushed them down the toilet—and I remembered the tender wrinkled lids of Briella's eyes as she'd slept. The plastic handle had jutted from her car seat. It would have been so easy to grip and lift it, to take her away. Why hadn't I done it? I'd balked at the act, at a punishment too severe for any sister, any mother. And so I'd left the baby in the rotting cave of that trailer—and saw now that I'd punished her, instead. I'd thought of the child every day since. I'd imagined the mice that would eventually come, and the maggots. I'd imagined the bedbugs and lice, my sister unconscious on the couch as the baby screamed.

Inside the building, I took the stairs steadily, feeling the reserves of strength in my thigh muscles, unexercised for these sedentary weeks. At the top of the stairs I stood for a moment, a beast of potential, before moving down the hallway. I reached the nursery window and saw the daycare workers: Tasha, Marlene, and all the others, disguised in eye masks with rabbit ears. And there was Amara, in her crib, just beside the door. I withdrew to the end of the corridor, to the fire alarm on the wall near the emergency stairs. It was a simple red handle, part of the environment, long ignored. With my fur-gloved hand, I gripped the handle and felt the thrill of a consummated fate. I pulled the handle down. As the first light pulsed on and the first alarm blast sounded, I was already striding back to the nursery. My lungs felt larger, each breath pulling in a surfeit of oxygen. One of the daycare women slammed the door open and ran past with two babies bundled in her arms. A deep power coiled inside me as I caught the door and entered the room. A mother in search of her child. The alarm bleated. The women were fast, scooping two babies at a time. "Just take one," someone yelled to me. "We have to get them all out."

Amara was swaddled in a white blanket like a cocoon. Her fox-kit eyes met mine as I lifted her to my chest and ran out of the room.

In the hallway, the alarm was louder, a blaring admonition. A commotion rose from below, shouts carrying over the music that was still playing. I heard the pounding steps of people on the main staircase as I fled through the hallway to the emergency exit. You would be on your way up, I knew. Any woman would rush upstairs for her child when she understood what was happening. Even you. I was faster, though, and I'd had a head start. I knew that the emergency stairs led down to the back door of the building, to the gardens and spa, and this is where I went.

The courtyard that had been pulsing with life just minutes before was barren now; only torches stood guard. The stampede would have herded out the front door to the parking lot. The baby was a tight package in her swaddling blanket, and I cradled her like a football as I rushed through the courtyard and into the hedge maze. The alarm was still audible, and I heard the distant sound of sirens as I navigated the path, shielded by boxwood ramparts. Once out of the hedge maze, we were safely hidden from view. With raw power, my legs carried me to the edge of the property, to the first glowing ring on the ground. I bent to retrieve the phosphorescent objects as I went, secreting them away in my purse. The sounds of the Rhizome were muffled by the time I reached the car, which was dimly visible in the grayscale dark, a fairy-tale carriage.

XIX.

You know more than I do, of course, about what happened at the Rhizome later that night, but I think I can imagine it. By the time you got to the nursery, most of the cribs would already have been empty. Assuming that a daycare worker had taken Amara outside, you would turn and go back down the stairs, among the last to evacuate, pushing through the bottleneck at the door. The fire trucks would just be arriving, spinning their lights over the parking lot, turning the costumed crowd into demons. You would find the daycare workers huddled on the ground, holding all the babies, and you'd lift your sequined mask and go to them. You'd look at each baby until their faces blurred and you began to doubt your own memory. The firefighters would bustle past the ridiculous party guests and their luxury cars and push into the frilly, defenseless building. Some of the guests would get into their cars and leave; others would savor the excitement, the primordial atmosphere of fire and disguise. There would be animated talk and gesturing, everyone linked together in this dream-memory, so thoroughly Per-renian. The firefighters would emerge at last and irascibly announce the false alarm. It would be safe to reenter the building, to continue the party, but you'd be suddenly sober as you followed the daycare workers upstairs to the nursery again, asking, "Where is my child?"

Then, panic and recrimination. Which one of them had brought her out? Had someone put her down somewhere in the parking lot or the weeds and forgotten her? A frantic search around the nursery, the building, the premises. At some point—when?—the police would be called. The wider search would begin. Eventually, suddenly, you'd remember something specific I'd once told you, and Tasha would be summoned for questioning.

"My friend told me that she seemed unusually attached to the babies," you'd tell the police through tears and mucus.

"And which friend is this?"

"Abby, my friend Abby."

And where is Abby? the police would ask. They'd call the number you gave them, and somewhere in Topanga my phone, out of batteries, would go straight to voicemail.

Back in Hesperia, I checked into a different motel under the name Shelby Hightower, just as I'd done at the Econo Lodge. The new place encircled a pool and had iron rail-ings to prevent guests from falling into the water. Our room was small and dank with a mud-colored carpet and scratchy orange bedspread. Although it was late at night, Amara was awake and beginning to cry. The sound was an alarm in itself. Holding her, I clambered onto the bed and propped myself up. When I took off my shirt, she stopped crying, and my nipples hardened with anticipation. She put her tiny hand to the side of my breast and began to suck, sure of belonging. The tide in my blood crested. I knew that even with my preparations, it would take several days of suckling before the aqueduct finally opened and my breasts grew heavy, before my body convinced itself that your baby was mine.

That night, curled in the motel bed with Amara, I had the bridge dream for the last time. Bare feet, snow crystals, headlights. The shock of the ice, the shock of my speed through the water. But this time, it was ecstatic. This time, I was a torpedo. Instead of sinking, I kept going. I shot through the river, navigated its delta, and broke out into the open sea. This time, I could breathe underwater. I soared over reefs and caves, through darting schools of herring and bluefish, a pod of humpback whales. At last, I surfaced in a sapphire lake. Another place, another continent. Around me was an alpine village. Trees, white mountains.

Once the birth certificate arrived from Michigan, we went to the post office to apply for passports. I presented the whole collection: Shelby's driver's license, her medical office ID, the Social Security cards, the birth certificate. The postal clerk with a lazy eye xeroxed everything crooked, dropped it all back onto the counter. I stood in front of the white backdrop for my photograph, then held Amara up for hers. In the picture, you can see my fingers encircling her waist.

We rarely left our room in the weeks while we waited. Amara is fair skinned, like you, so it was better that we stayed indoors. If we'd gone out into the desert sun, she would have burned. Instead, we spent the days curled on the bed. I gave her just enough formula, but not too much, and eventually, incredibly, lactation began. It was a miracle. The baby nursed herself to sleep.

With Amara against my chest, I felt the tender swell that must come to women postpartum. I stroked her head, and she melted into my body. Had my own mother held me like this? Had she felt the kind of ardor for me, or for Shelby, that I felt for this child? It was impossible. The feeling I had was incapable of ever lessening, ever souring. I could never be disappointed by Amara the way our mother had been disappointed in us. And yet it made a kind of sense. Perhaps it was biology that poisoned maternal love. Holding expectations for one's genetic heir was natural but ruinous, a product of eugenic narcissism, inimical to love. What I felt for Amara was superior. My love was undiluted by pride, and stronger in that it wasn't required but freely given.

At last the passports arrived in the post office box. With the Cavalier loaded, we drove south past San Diego, to San Ysidro. The border agent smiled when he saw the diaper box in the backseat, the rear-facing car seat. "Buen vieje," he said.

You should know that I never endangered her. We didn't spend the night in Tijuana but flew to Mexico City the same day and to Amsterdam that night. Amara slept through most of it, and within twenty-four hours we'd cleared the mountains and entered a new world.

Epilogue

I'VE STOPPED reading the news. I know the innocent still roam the world helplessly. The girls are still raped; the guns are still drawn. But here in Küsnacht, we're safe. Above the lake is the white house on the hill. I'd found it in the first hour of our arrival. It was impossible to miss, visible from all parts of town. The door was the door from my dreams—the thick blue paint, the knocker in the shape of a winged head: Hypnos, the god of sleep—and when I rapped the knocker on the brass plate, there'd been a brief moment of suspension, a dizzy reel, before the sound of footsteps came through the hall and the madman opened the door to me.

He wore a wrinkled seersucker suit. When his clear eyes struck mine, I saw a change in them, an advancing movement of recognition, as if he'd stepped forward to meet me. "Je peux vous aider, mademoiselle?" he said, in a voice that came from deep in the sea.

I hesitated. My own voice was thin, birdlike. "I hope I'm not intruding."

Amara wriggled in my grip and arched her back like a cat. Up close, Perren's white skin was like softly crinkled paper. He looked down at me, and I squinted up into that bright light.

"Have we met?" he asked.

For a suspended moment I felt that we were surrounded by liquid, warm and dense, and were both weightless inside it. There was a low thrum of kinship, a reverberating tremolo that confirmed my long-held conviction. He opened the door, and I walked in as I'd rehearsed so many times in my sleep. I went into the house and sat on the gilded sofa, which was where I knew it would be. He sat across from me on the pink damask wing chair. I looked up at the familiar ceiling, the plaster medallion, the crystal chandelier, the crown molding like wedding cake.

"You've traveled a long way I think," he said. "Why have you come?" There was expectancy in his eyes. I sensed that he knew the answer already.

I took the drawings from my backpack and gave them to him. We sat in the room that I knew, and he looked at my drawings of the satyrs, the bridge, the loveseat. He looked at my detailed drawings of the sofa where I now sat, the wing chair, the plaster medallion, the chandelier. He looked at my pictures of the children and the clocks. He slowly examined each page.

On my lap, Amara tucked her face inward and whimpered, and I lifted my blouse to nurse her. I did this without hesitation, with a movement that was instinctive and sure. There was no need for shame here. This was an ease so complete and utter, this certainty that I was understood, that nothing I did or said could be shocking, offensive, or even new—like falling into the arms of a saint.

When he finished, he looked up at me and asked if I was planning to stay.

"Yes," I answered.

"Good," he said.

That was all. The rest is money, and you know there's no absence of that.

In the back of the white house is a room full of clocks. Some of the clocks run backward and some don't run at all. It's in this room that Auguste keeps his flat files—dozens of them, stacked one upon another—containing children's drawings. Some are by his own children, others by those at the Rhizome. The youngest children's drawings are particularly evocative for him. The native imagery of their nightmares, their frequent dreams of animals. Evolutionary, elemental. He doesn't mention any of this in interviews. Using the dream images of others could be misinterpreted as stealing or cheating. But he knows—and I know—that there's no crime in it. A true artist is never a thief. He's a borrower, an inventor, a magician. You know this too, Elise. No artist is a thief the way an actor is.

He's adopted children from all over the world and lavished them with freedom. The house contains a multitude of little studios for them to draw and paint in. It's a creative daycare of its own. The children are beautiful—eccentrically dressed in their own designs, or naked—and always making something. There are twelve of them, all different colors and ages. He likes to have at least one very small child at all times, and so is in a continuous process of adoption.

Now he has Amara, and me. He doesn't ask questions, doesn't want to know. Our understanding is implicit. We're of the same breed, haunted, unfit for human society. But in the deep-folded caverns of imagination, we survive. We protrude, and disseminate. I harvest images, and Auguste applies his wizardry. He's making my swimming pool film now. He's built a set with a suburban yard and an aboveground pool, and he's finding actors to play the woman who refuses to come out of the water and the man she's left behind. My name won't be on the movie—either my old name or my new one—but still, the movie is mine.

Auguste is reclusive, soft-spoken, volatile, as I am. He stays in the house on the hill. I stay in the cottage near the lake, which he purchased for me and furnished himself. It resembles a Swiss stage set, with traditional woodworking. To close the shutters against the dazzling lake, to dwell inside with Amara—or Briella, as she's called now—is to receive a secret communion. Her hair is growing into heartbreaking ringlets. It's remained black as ink, as dark as mine. Her skin is so fair that the emotions are visible upon it, the blood vessels painting cherries of pleasure, scarlet patches of frustration. Other than that, she's nothing like you.

When she wakes, there's a liminal look in her eyes, as if she's rising from undersea forests and cities. At these moments, I remember myself as a child. I remember the dirty snow of Michigan, the mayonnaise pot roasts, the lonely hours in my bedroom, the bleak future that seemed written for me. I think of Shelby and Briella languishing in their trailer. They'll never think of leaving. They'll never need passports, never apply and learn that they have them already, that they're living in Switzerland.

We cherish our island out of time, here in Küsnacht, the erstwhile home of Jung himself. Amara and I are learning French and German together. I'm giving her what you wanted her to have: a childhood out of the lights, away from the cameras and tabloid hacks, the suppurating crudeness of Hollywood, of America. We wander the curving Swiss alleys, and I teach her the names of things. Together, we examine the mountain flora. When I come across an interesting stone, I pause to pick it up and put it in her hand. Who knows what meaning it might hold? These early moments are sacred, I know, the basis of all her future dreams. I hold my own stone, too. I check my meteorite often, even now, to confirm that this dream is real.

After Amara's disappearance, you vanished from public view. There were articles about you, guesswork, speculation that you went mad. There was speculation that you spiraled out of control, drank yourself to oblivion. There was speculation that you drowned yourself quietly in the Pacific or in the frigid depths of Lake Michigan.

I don't pretend to know. To wonder isn't useful, can only pollute my mind. Regardless of the details, your disappearance proves that I was right. Even rid of your burden, you couldn't save yourself. My decision had been a sound one. The execution of the plan had been inspired, miraculous in the way of ordained things. Every moment had clicked firmly into place, revolving into the next like the gear of a clock. When I finally came down from my elevation, a few weeks after my arrival in Switzerland, when I finally landed from that long, divine flight that had begun in Topanga, it was like awakening at home.

I do hope you've found your way to some sort of peace. I still harbor a habitual kind of concern for you, Elise, a nostalgic affection, although it doesn't really matter. Ultimately we're all part of the same vast organism, drifting and bubbling through history, this eternal Spring. We're the same being, only temporarily fragmented into bodies. Throughout our lifetimes, we busily observe each other, bewitched by our varied incarnations.

Whether you're alive or dead, happy or miserable, your role in this life is over, the stage set has changed. You've danced, and the satyrs have ravished you.

Curiously, our cottage in the woods is not so different from Paul's. I imagine, sometimes, that we're in the woods of Topanga. I've learned to sew by hand and have begun making kites. Auguste is tickled by this; he orders the fabric and hardware for me. The hills of Küsnacht are ideal for flying, and Amara loves to hold the spool, toddling and falling, laughing as the kite tries to pull her aloft.

Sometimes I think I see Paul—just an impression, a dark flash in a crowd. But he wouldn't know to look for me here, if he looked for me at all. I've heard nothing of his film, read no rhapsodic review. He's still looking for funding, most likely: studio backing, distribution. But he'll find none. There will be no interest. Things have changed these past years. Now people know about the crisis, which has only worsened. They know about the fractured families, the lost children. They're all too aware of the detention centers; the fiendishly named "tender age shelters" like prison barracks, like something from a war; the proposed border wall of concrete and razor wire. They know too much already. What good would a movie do? No one would see it. Only a few theaters would even screen it. What Paul is learning, I'm sure—what I would have told him if I'd known how—is that no one wants the truth. We don't want to live with it; we don't want to bathe in it. We want to supplant it. We want the dream, not the real. We long for fabrication, hallucination, false catastrophe. We hunger—all of us—for the distorted mirages that Auguste and I can provide.

The girls are still raped, the guns are still drawn. The world still burns.

Paul and I nearly meet in dreams sometimes. It's always the same dream, walking in the desert toward a campground of tents where I know him to be. In the dream, I walk through deep sand toward the tents, but they recede from reach. Sometimes the dream turns lucid, and I fly over the desert and enter a tent where he sits, surrounded by bruised, dirty children. He holds out a hand, but my grasp goes through.

Not everything that's found can be claimed. I know this now. Choices must be made, one firmly embraced, the others rejected. I've learned to release the things I've refused. Whatever I lack, I can pull up through the Spring, through that infinite well of *yes*. And, really, there's so little lacking.

We look at the lake. The sun snaps off its surface, blinding like the light of the afterlife. The water is silken and clear, far from the gelid murk of the Huron River, the jagged teeth that once pulled me down. This water is gentle, pellucid, reflective. Another kind of death, much closer to the one we want.

ACKNOWLEDGMENTS

DEEP THANKS to the wise and wonderful Elisabeth Schmitz and Katie Raissian and to all at Grove: Morgan Entrekin, Judy Hottensen, Deb Seager, Justina Batchelor, Paula Cooper Hughes, and Julia Berner-Tobin. My gratitude always to Bill Clegg. For special insight and guidance, thanks to Michelle Caplan, Melissa Hile, Sara Shepard, Sana Krasikov, Sandra Bark, Kate Fujimoto, and Markus Mentzer—and to Emily Fromm, who lit the first spark. Love and thanks always to my mother, Mary Ann Acampora; to Tom and Linda Doyle; and forever to Thomas and Amity.

Help us make the next generation of readers

We – both author and publisher – hope you enjoyed this book.
We believe that you can become a reader at any time in your life,
but we'd love your help to give the next generation a head start.

Did you know that 9% of children don't have a book of their
own in their home, rising to 13% in disadvantaged families*?
We'd like to try to change that by asking you to consider the role
you could play in helping to build readers of the future.

We'd love you to think of sharing, borrowing, reading, buying or talking
about a book with a child in your life and spreading the love of reading.
We want to make sure the next generation continue to have access
to books, wherever they come from.

And if you would like to consider donating to charities that help
fund literacy projects, find out more at www.literacytrust.org.uk
and www.booktrust.org.uk.

Thank you.

hachette
CHILDREN'S GROUP

*As reported by the National Literacy Trust